# DEEP, DEEP

## IN THE

# ROUGH, ROUGH

*Lory Smith*

For Dorothy,
It was a joy
seeing your area.
Enjoy my silly little
book.

iUniverse, Inc.
Bloomington

Athens
10/31/15

Lory
Smith

Deep, Deep in the Rough, Rough

Copyright © 2011 Lory Smith

This is a work of fiction. All of the characters, names, incidents, organizations, and dialogue in this novel are either the products of the author's imagination or are used fictitiously.

iUniverse books may be ordered through booksellers or by contacting:

iUniverse
1663 Liberty Drive
Bloomington, IN 47403
www.iuniverse.com
1-800-Authors (1-800-288-4677)

Because of the dynamic nature of the Internet, any Web addresses or links contained in this book may have changed since publication and may no longer be valid. The views expressed in this work are solely those of the author and do not necessarily reflect the views of the publisher, and the publisher hereby disclaims any responsibility for them.

ISBN: 978-1-4502-7603-0 (pbk)
ISBN: 978-1-4502-7604-7 (ebk)

Printed in the United States of America

iUniverse rev. date: 2/8/2011

More by Lory Smith

Non-Fiction
PARTY IN A BOX: THE STORY OF THE
SUNDANCE FILM FESTIVAL (1999, Gibbs Smith)

Fiction
SOMETHING FOR NOTHING (2005, iUniverse)
GO FAST, GO CRAZY (2007, iUniverse)

*"Man against nature,*
*Woman against all."*
Anonymous


*"The legacy of modern man*
*is the asphalt road and*
*a thousand lost golf balls."*
T. S. Eliot


*"I could never belong to a club*
*that would have me as a member."*
Groucho Marx

## Dedication

To fathers and sons and all the games we play. And to my two fathers. I've been lucky enough to have two "Dads" in my life, Stanley W. Smith and Dr. Reed L. Holt. Both sporting guys, one loved and taught me golf, the other tennis. To this day I love both sports and both guys. Thank goodness, they both loved my Mom. They are two great guys, just playing with different sets of balls.

*Lory Smith*
*Cold Spring, New York*
*2011*

We can hear the sounds of the mighty surf pounding the shoreline. We are in some kind of primordial landscape, fog enshrouded, mystical, beyond time. The beach grasses sway in a gentle breeze. The laughing seagulls hover and swoop overhead. The ancient and ever moving dunes make their march inland one grain of sand at a time. And then we see it, through the fog. A magnificent green manicured lawn stretches out ahead, as far as the eye can see. If there is a golf course in heaven, this must be the place. Suddenly a very old man's voice is heard almost whispering, almost praying. The accent is strong but somehow indistinct, like you can't quite put your finger on it. Perhaps it is the voice of God.

"This was the path of our fathers. This too will be the path of our sons. It came to me in a powerful vision. I always chew Juicy Fruit gum when I'm having visions. You wouldn't happen to have any would you? Juicy Fruit gum I mean, not visions. Visions aren't for everybody. The average person has got to be very careful with having visions. You could end up in the loony bin."

# CHAPTER 1

## "THE GAME IS SET IN STONE"

THE ANCIENT AND HISTORIC Burning Bridges Country Club sits magnificently on the top of a bluff, overlooking vast tracts of manicured grass, a bastion to Old World clubbiness. This golf mecca was founded during the birth of golf in the New World, near the pounding surf, fashioned out of the extant potato fields of the time, and built over an area where during the Revolution the British had burned several bridges, thus giving it its unique moniker. Built during the Empire, and meant to convey power, exclusivity, absolute wealth and status. The Burning Bridges Country Club, like all country clubs, practically screams out, "Do Not Enter Here."

Architecturally, it resembles a massive stone monastery or a gothic turn of the century insane asylum. Fittingly, to play golf on its course, requires either a strong belief in a higher power or an obsession bordering on utter madness. It also helps to have a lot of money. And be white. And be a man. But, especially in the old days, not a Catholic or Jewish one. Unless, of course, you're applying for a job, as a grounds man, waiter, caddy or office manager. Or you happen to be lucky enough to be on friendly terms with a member in good standing who would invite you to be a guest. In other words, not bloody likely.

The mahogany walls inside the ancient and historic Burning Bridges clubhouse are lined with old black and white photos from the birth of golf. Ancient Scots in kilts, playing through the tall grass, undulating fairways and windswept greens. The seaside mists convey a mystical magic to the photos, an ethereal wonderland of transformed nature, meant to tame the wild lands into something more controllable and conducive to attack a little white ball with a large wooden club until it rolls into a little black hole.

All the golf gods are pictured here too. The good-looking rail of a man in Bobby Jones, dressed in knickers, a crisp white shirt, tie and jacket, as he executes one of the most perfect swings ever to grace the earth; the centrifugal power of the ferocious man in the porkpie hat, Slammin' Sammy Snead, and, of course, the most famous rivals in golf, Arnold Palmer, Gary Player and the one and only Golden Bear, Jack Nicklaus. Frozen in time, like the memories of their greatest moments, fading around the edges, like the burnished trophies sitting on their mantels, but still vivid in the minds of golfers all around the globe.

A globe, by the way, which watches the moon rise and fall each day. A moon which looks remarkably like a golf ball. It is as though the entire universe was set up just for the purpose of chasing a little white ball. It was no accident that when men landed on the moon, the first thing they did was to pull out a 9-iron and hit golf balls. That picture is on the wall as well, signed by none other than astronaut Neil Armstrong himself. Scrawled in permanent black ink, it says, "One small step for man, one giant leap for a Titleist 2."

On the 18th tee box of Burning Bridge's championship golf course, a set of ancient hands grip the shaft of a golf club, the Mighty Driver. The wrinkled hands grip and reform on the leather handle over and over. There is something tender, almost reverential, about the hands as they caress the shaft. Over and over, until they are just right. Then they set and it is as though the entire world stops for one brief moment. The old man takes the club head back in slow motion, displaying pace, rhythm, experience and timing all melded together in one confident and fluid motion. The masterful swing reaches its apex and now the old man drives the club head down like a hammer towards the tiny white ball. Physics at its finest. All torque and radius. Mass and energy. Mind and body. It really is poetry in motion. The old guy's going to cream it.

On impact, the ball shudders from the force. It explodes off the tee like a rocket as blades of grass fall back to earth. The ball screams into the sky, cutting through the molecules like a jet at full throttle climbing into the wild blue yonder.

On the 18<sup>th</sup> tee box stands an ancient and historic foursome, mouths agape, jowls trembling and misty-eyed as they watch in awe at this wondrous golf shot. As the golf ball enters the clouds, nearly on its way to heaven, the ball hits the upper branches of a large and rather rude tree. The sound of the ball hitting the tall timber echoes over the course. It is a sickening sound. The kind of sound that can reduce grown, mature men into blithering babies, stamping their little feet up and down in two-toned leather wingtips with wildly bouncing little tassels, until they become a pool of sobbing blubber with their heads buried in their hands, kicking and screaming in the Kentucky bluegrass.

The old man who hit the shot, Riley J. Hancock, winces at the sound. What was nearly perfection is now the shits.

"Welcome to the game of golf," Riley's twin brother, Wiley J. Hancock mutters. They make quite a pair. Both old, old money. Their family was involved in oil, gas and mining and cashing big fat checks. They both sport handlebar mustaches, throwbacks to another era, when decency and honor were paramount. Tanned, fit and trim and still wearing golfing knickers and plaid stockings, Wiley and Riley are the patriarchs of the club. The old timers who still believe in the old fashioned values of cashing big fat checks from investments made long ago by people they barely remember.

Their nemesis on this day, and on most days, are the nouveau riche of 50 years ago, Sal Gravani and Monty Delillo. They are dressed in those gaudy pastel golf clothes, they look more like Pez dispensers with big heads than actual people. They are shifty and shady. Made their money in dry cleaning and funeral parlors, respectively. When it comes to golf, especially if there is some wagering going on, which there always is, these guys can clean you out and bury you. Just don't look at them too long. Their outfits could make you dizzy. In fact, that may be part of their strategy.

"That shot is going to kill you," Sal chortles as he steps up to the tee box.

"Yeah, my first wife wasn't even that ugly." Monty cracks up.

"Don't let them snooker you. That's playable out there." Wiley almost believes it.

Sal places his ball on the tee. He's a little spark plug of a guy. Cocky, even with a bad toupee.

"Grip it and rip it," Monty practically growls.

Sal steps up and with no practice swing hits a nice old-man shot down the middle of the fairway. He matter-of-factly retrieves his tee and looks up to see his ball land, just where he wanted it to. Just another day at the office.

"That's my partner. Mr. Consistent," Monty says as he takes the tee box. He sets his ball on the tee, moves into position and begins his series of twitches and tweaks, weight shifts and half-starts, golfing rituals that border on epileptic seizures. When he finally settles, he hits it dead solid perfect.

"Tubular!" Sal says as he high fives Monty coming off the tee box.

Finally it is Wiley's turn. He has a limp from the War, that being WWII, and as a result has an awkward stance. But he's a crusty old dude and proud as a pit-bull, which he actually resembles. He digs into it. The ball sails up, up and away. On to the 16th green. The ball rolls between a twosome standing over their putts. They look back towards the 18th tee box.

"Fore!" Wiley shouts way too late to make a difference. He

slams the driver back in his golf bag, and pulls one of those funny knit socks over the club head, almost as though the club is embarrassed and doesn't want to be seen by the other clubs in the bag.

Sal and Monty step on the gas peddle of the golf cart. As they pass Wiley and Riley, they can hardly contain their glee at their playing partners' misfortune.

"I hope you guys brought your checkbooks, cause we don't take MasterCard or Visa." Sal and Monty's laughter can be heard all the way down the 18th fairway. Golf, like life, can be so unfair sometimes it makes your teeth hurt. It probably doesn't help to follow behind Sal and Monty's cart, breathing gas fumes, cigar smoke and all that hot air.

---

On a grainy black and white television we are in outer space. The canopy of stars are everywhere. Or maybe that's just bad reception. We recognize the opening strains to *Star Trek*. Captain Kirk and Mr. Spock are on an alien planet. For all we know, they could be looking for a lost golf ball. We hear some strange sounds in the background. A can tips over and we can hear golf balls scatter on the concrete floor. There is the distinct sound of heavy breathing.

*"These are the voyages of the Starship Enterprise,"* Captain Kirk intones.

The heavy breathing has turned to heavy groaning. The tempo is picking up. We are in the back of the golf repair shack. On the workbench, we see where all the heavy groaning is coming from. There is a naked man's rear end, his pants dropped at his ankles, and a woman's long red fingernails digging into his back. This is the image of Blaze Jones, gifted golfer, major screw up, we will always remember.

*"To boldly go where no man has gone before."*

"Don't stop," the woman with the fingernails implores breathlessly. Her nails gouge deeper into his flesh. He jumps.

"Ow, that tickles."

Just then an errant golf ball comes smashing through the window. The goofy *Star Trek* music kicks in as Blaze and the woman uncouple. Call it coitus interruptus with a pitching wedge. At least a two stroke penalty. The woman gathers herself quickly and departs.

As he pulls his pants up, Blaze shouts out after her. "Aw, thanks Mrs. Rogers. I'll get this driver fixed for you and call you next week. I'll even regrip it for you at no extra charge!" He reaches down for the errant golf ball and mutters under his breath, "Women!"

Back on the 18th fairway, we can see that the errant ball belonged to Monty Delillo. "Shit!" He buries his pitching wedge into the soft grass.

Now it is Wiley and Riley's turn to be smiling.

Sal steps up to his ball and as is his custom, takes no practice swing. This time he tops the ball badly and it advances only a few feet.

"Tough break Sal." Riley is beside himself.

"Yeah, Sal. I don't think Monty's second wife was even that ugly."

Wiley gives as good as he gets.

On the practice fairway next to the pro shop, a long line of rather large women are taking a group lesson from Gyll Harbinger, the sleazy, slim, mustached, double-knit club pro. Each prospective golfer stands inside a little fenced-in section, as though their practice shots could be so errant that they might actually kill the golfer next to them. Of course this rarely happens. Most deaths on golf courses are heart attack related. Otherwise death on a golf course is through a hundred tiny slices.

Gyll Harbinger holds a 5-iron, like a teacher with a pointer. He addresses a striped ball teed up on a little AstroTurf mat.

"Remember ladies, it's all in the hips. Keep your arms stiff and your chins down." He cocks his eye toward the ball, takes back the club and smacks a beauty right to the bull's-eye sign marked as 175 yards. As the ladies watch, mouths agape in admiration, for the shot and for the man, his ball hits the bull's-eye. "That's all there is to it. It's all in the hips."

A particularly heavy woman, in peddle-pushers and saddle-oxford golf shoes, with several chins to keep down, attempts to take a swing at her little red-striped ball on her little green mat. She misses the ball completely. Several times. Total whiffs. Everyone can see the blood rushing to her face. She takes one more swing and misses again by a mile. She swings the club so hard in her follow-through, it hits her in the derriere. She is so embarrassed, without a hesitation, she takes the club and breaks it over her rather ample knee.

Gyll tries to intervene. "Now, now Mrs. Swayze, remember golf is supposed to be fun. Let's try again with a 7-iron."

Whereupon, she takes the 7-iron out of her bag and breaks it over her rather ample and now slightly sore knee.

"Have you ever thought about playing tennis, Mrs. Swayze? The balls are bigger and the equipment is harder to break."

She storms off the practice area in utter humiliation. Gyll turns to the other women left in their cages. "Golf is not for everyone. And even the best golfers in the world can have a bad day. Now let's work on those swings. Remember it's <u>all</u> in the hips."

———

Back on the 18th fairway, Riley finds his ball in the deep rough. It is buried in tall grass, a tough lie if there ever was one. He has his club in hand, twists the ends of his handlebar mustache, eyes the flag on the green, sizes up the breeze and approaches the ball as if it were a bird about to take flight. He grinds his feet into the turf, eyeballs the flag one last time, gets set and swings for all he is worth. He catches the ball just right and it explodes out of the rough, only to hit four trees in a row, like a pinball bouncing off the rubber bumpers. The ball rolls out of the woods and on to the green. A miracle shot if there ever was one. If you didn't believe in miracles before, this shot would make you a believer. Sal and Monty can't believe their eyes. Wiley turns to them, with a sly grin.

"Don't you just love this game?" Wiley snickers as he pulls his putter out of his bag. He waves to his brother Riley just exiting the forest. "Nice shot, little brother!"

Wiley turns back to Sal and Monty. "Gentlemen, I believe this is the part where we press the bet." Meaning the brothers are doubling down. Sal's and Monty's jaws tighten. They know the drill all too well. Golf is largely a psychological game and a lucky break can turn a miserable round into a memorable one. And vice versa, a bad break can turn a great round into a nightmare. And with each shot you have all the possibilities in the universe, for perfection and for failure, for heaven and for hell, and everything that comes in between.

Inside the clubhouse lounge, things move along at a more leisurely pace. Drinking strong liquor and playing golf kind of go hand in hand. After 18 holes at Burning Bridges, you do need a little something to take the edge off. It is from the frontal lobotomy versus the bottle in front of me school of philosophy. Whatever it takes to kill the pain.

Inside the mahogany walls, behind the Old World bar that has seen more than its share of triumph and misery, a jolly, rotund, bear of a guy, Hub Hogle, puts a series of miniature golf club swizzle sticks into the tall cocktail glasses in front of him. He's the cocktail waiter and bartender at this venerable watering hole. He delivers the exotic looking drinks on a silver platter to a group of beautiful women and rich-looking men, all suntanned and dressed in assorted shades of pastels. They look like a chiseled set of Starburst candies.

"Let's see, who had the screwdriver?"

A provocative women in lime green raises her hand. She eyes Hub seductively, with her husband glaring at her. We recognize her from her rather hasty retreat at the repair shop.

"Don't worry Mr. Rogers, women just find me terribly attractive. I'm a big, fat slob on the outside, but I'm a tiger in bed. I guess they just sense it. Who had the Mai Tai?"

Back at the bar, a wiry little Japanese guy, Ben Ichi, part golf philosopher and part sponger of free drinks, has engaged an avid follower of the game in an endless harangue on the inner game of golf. At least as long as the free drinks keep flowing.

"Golf has a way of making a man naked," Ben says reverently. The avid follower of the game is all ears.

"It brings out every aspect of a man. Power and subtlety. Anger and pleasure. Camaraderie and loneliness."

Hub returns to the bar.

"Has he gotten to the part about golf being just like marriage? It starts out full of promise and then ends in miserable failure and costs a lot of money in between. Another round gents?"

---

The four old timers are nearing the green on 18. Monty steps up to hit his approach. He bounces, adjusts, settles. Then he does it again. He's got a nervous tick, especially with a wedge shot. Wiley and Riley give each other a knowing look. Monty finally settles, gathers his concentration in earnest and takes his shot. He tops the ball badly and it advances only a couple of feet.

"Your third wife wasn't even that ugly," mumbles his disappointed partner Sal.

"Would you guys stop it already about my wives. Who can play golf while they're thinking of alimony payments?" Monty tries to explain in his defense, as he shoves the embarrassed pitching wedge deep into his bag.

---

The inside of the golf shop at Burning Bridges is just like any other golf shop in any other golf club in any other golf-loving nation. Golf paraphernalia abounds. Rows of ridiculous looking sweaters and foul weather rain gear capable of surviving a tsunami. An endless array of putters and wedges for all occasions, golf hats, golf gloves, golf balls in fluorescent colors, gaily colored oversized umbrellas meant to withstand a hurricane, should you find yourself playing golf through weather named after someone.

All manner of golf aids meant to hold out the illusion, that with just a slight change in equipment, you might somehow alter the inevitable outcome of the game. And yet somehow the score always remains the same. Or gets worse.

The most menacing object in the entire golf shop, the one that most dictates, predicts and records the highs and lows of the game like nothing else, is found in the little box next to the cash register, the boxes of identical miniature number 2 pencils. These tiny pinnacles of graphite lead are the foundation on which the game of golf rests. Without the little pencils, golf as we know it would not exist.

Standing at the cash register is E.Z. Harbinger, the club pro Gyll's asshole-in-the-making younger brother. He's a slightly sleazier, younger version of Gyll, all polyester and polish, with Robert Goulet's looks, but Bella Lugosi's heart. He's trim and clean cut on the outside, all Brillcream and Burma Shave, but when he opens his mouth, his inner Don Rickles is finally released. He can't help himself. He's an insult waiting to happen.

The phone rings. And in golf shops all around the world, the phone rings a lot.

E.Z. clears his throat as he answers. "Burning Bridges Country Club. Oh, hi Giselle. No, he's not here. He's got a group lesson with Eater's Anonymous until 3:00. I'll tell him you called. That's right, the minute he walks in. Okay, goodbye." He hangs up and rolls his eyes. "Women. Can't live with 'em and you can't live with 'em."

Just then a beautiful woman walks into the golf shop.

"A large bucket of balls please."

E.Z. tries to turn on the charm. "This must be my lucky day."

"Mine too. I just shot a 69. But I still need to work on my take back a little. Figured I'd hit a large bucket."

"Actually, take back is one of my personal specialties. You thinking of taking a lesson? I'm available after 3:00. I do think I could teach you a thing or two." E.Z. smiles leeringly.

"Have you ever shot a 69?"

"Well, I've come close a couple of times. I'm great off the tee, but my short game kills me."

"Why don't you just get me the bucket of balls?" She doesn't really like his tone. No one does.

"Large bucket of balls. Yes ma'am. Coming right up."

He retrieves the large bucket of balls and places them on the counter.

"A large bucket of balls. That's 10 bucks."

She hands him the 10 and takes the balls. As she reaches the door, E.Z. just can't resist taking one more shot.

"Now don't you strain nothin' honey."

She turns back his direction. "Hey screw you pal."

"No, screw..." Before he can finish, Gyll walks in the door and catches E.Z. before he can do any more damage.

"Loose! That's what he meant to say. He's got a SCREW LOOSE! That brother of mine. He's such a kidder this one."

The beautiful woman exits in disgust, with all her balls intact.

Gyll turns on E.Z. with a vengeance known mostly between warring mobsters and nearly all siblings.

"How many times I gotta tell you little brother? This is it E.Z. You don't make it at this job, I can't keep bailing you out forever."

"Speaking of forever, Giselle called. You're supposed to call her the minute you walk in. I think your minute is up big brother."

"What is it with women? They don't talk to you every couple of hours, they think you're up to no good. I'll tell you, you want to get good at golf? Don't ever get married." Gyll picks up the phone and dials home.

---

The foursome is now on the 18<sup>th</sup> green. Monty sizes up his long putt. Just as he strokes it, an errant golf shot comes screaming into their circle. Needless to say, he misses his putt. The hacker, on the ninth tee, yells lamely "Fore," but to no avail. The damage is done. It turns out, that the hacker is none other than Willie Nelson. He waves sheepishly and takes a mulligan, without bothering to retrieve his misfire.

"I call interference." Sal stands up for his partner.

"Oh, come on," Wiley groans. "With his hearing he didn't even know it happened!"

"No, you're right Sal." Riley says. "Absolutely right. Monty, re-rack it and take it over. We insist, don't we Wiley?"

"Only if we can double press the bet," Wiley answers. He and his brother Riley are shrewd gamblers.

"You're on! Come on Monty. Put this one to bed."

Monty replaces his ball. Now the pressure is on. He lines up the putt. Settles. Then shifts. And settles. Then shifts. And settles. Just as he is about to hit it, a bee starts to swarm around his head. He swats at it, which just gets the bee mad. It attacks him like a kamikaze. The others stand in shock as Monty dances around the green waving his putter at what appears to be an invisible force. He looks like a mad man having a bad cane day.

"Sal, are you just going to stand there? Help me out here!" Monty shrieks.

Sal reaches into his golf bag and pulls out a large can of bug spray. He sprays a cloud around a dancing and thrusting Monty, whereupon the bee sputters, falls to the green and rolls over on its back, wings still vibrating, spins in spasmodic circles and eventually succumbs.

"I hate nature," Sal says as he puts the can back in his bag.

"I guess that's the way the bee bumbles," Wiley says wistfully.

"Take your time Monty. I don't need to remind you, you've got a shit load riding on this shot." Riley knows whereof he speaks and is only too happy to try to psyche out his nemesis.

Monty sizes up the putt again. He settles and shifts. And shifts and settles. Just as he hits the putt, a large laughing seagull flies over his head and drops a load of excrement on his shoulder. The gull shrieks in glorious relief. The putt miraculously rolls in, and Monty and Sal high-five each other.

"Looks like the eagle has landed," Riley sighs.

"Make that seagull has landed," Wiley says in disgust looking at Monty's shoulder.

"Like I told you, I hate nature," Sal says as he wipes the bird do-do off Monty's sweater. "But I love my partner." He plants a big wet kiss on Monty's cheek.

"Gentlemen, I say we retire to the bar, settle our outstanding bets and concoct as many wild tales as they will allow us to tell," Riley says as he pats Monty on the shoulder. "Too bad about the sweater, Monty. Sometimes, I guess, shit just happens."

One of those funny plastic sombrero-topped bottles of tequila is retrieved from behind the bar by Hub Hogle, who deftly dispenses the golden liquid into four shot glasses. He quarters a lime with a large black knife and grabs a salt shaker. He delivers the exquisite ingredients for dulling the memory to the table of our four old duffers. They immediately salt their hands, grab their limes and take their shots with nary a wince.

"Another round!" The four old guys shout in unison as they slam the glasses down hard on the table. Hub knows the drill well and grabs the bottle with the sombrero from the top of the bar.

"I'll just leave this with you. It'll save me going back and forth. You guys must have had a tough day."

Riley and Wiley pull out their checkbooks.

"I don't have my glasses," Wiley complains squinting. "How many zeros in 10,000?"

"Four," Sal volunteers.

"Wrong as usual. There are six. You've got to count the pennies past the decimal," Wiley retorts indignantly.

"You count the pennies. I'll just take the dollars," Sal smiles.

"This should buy you a lot of bug spray Sal," Riley says as he signs his check.

"Yeah, there won't be a bug left standing for a hundred miles." Wiley hands over his check.

"Leave him alone will ya?" Monty folds his check and puts it in his shirt pocket.

"I've just never seen anyone who was so neurotic about bugs that they had to carry around a can of bug spray with them on the golf course. To each his own." Wiley pours another round.

"Personally, I think golf would be better if it was played indoors. You wouldn't have all the distractions." Sal knocks his shot back.

"Like the sun and the sky." Riley raises his glass.

"And the wind and the rain." Wiley clinks his glass with his brother and they down their shots.

"And the birds," Monty adds, daubing at his sweater.

"And the bees," Sal says as he pours another round.

"Good grief man!" Riley laments. "That would be contrary to the very game itself. To be out of doors, to take it all in, to watch the long shadows across the greens, or the golden glow at twilight. That's what the game is all about, man!"

"Think what the game must have been like back in the day, when the Scots were smacking an animal sack with a wooden mashee along the dunes. Now that was really something!" Wiley chimes in. "Nowadays, we drive around in an electric cart on a manicured lawn, have imported pure white sand, with clubs and balls designed by scientists for maximum efficiency, and we still complain about how damned hard the game is to master. We're just a big, bunch of crybabies."

Several of the patrons in the bar have picked up on the conversation, including Blaze, sitting at the bar with Ben Ichi and the avid follower of the game. Gyll and E.Z. are also seated at the bar, nursing scotch and sodas. As I mentioned before, strong drink and golf are natural partners.

"The fundamentals of golf would apply no matter where or when the game is played. Past, present or future." Riley pours more salt between his thumb and forefinger, licks it and polishes off another shot. He squeezes another lime wedge into his mouth.

"As long as it is played out of doors." Wiley reloads too.

"You know what my proudest moment was?" Sal gets misty eyed. "When the astronauts played golf on the moon. I was proud to be a golfer then."

"You know, they could have chosen any sport, but they chose golf," Monty says reverentially.

"Really, I got choked up. The lump in the throat and everything." A tear wells up in Sal's eye.

"You think people could play golf like they used to? You know, out in the wilds?" Wiley wonders out loud.

"No way. Who'd want to? What for?" Monty has never been accused of being a romantic, despite his numerous marriages.

"For money. Maybe to prove something about the game. To prove that golf isn't just a game played out on a velvety surface.

It's a game that is about life." Wiley is getting himself all worked up.

"Whatever it is, I don't like it. Your crazy ideas usually cost us all a lot of money." Monty really doesn't like what he is hearing.

"Hear me out. How about a game of golf out in the wilds?" Wiley looks absolutely bug-eyed.

"I told you I hate nature," Sal says flatly.

"Surely, you're not thinking of the four of us playing?" Riley is at least realistic.

"No, each of us would have to hire a player," Wiley explains.

"I tell you, this is going to cost us some money." Monty is holding his head in his hand.

"What are you chicken?" Wiley knows this strategy always works with Sal and Monty.

"How many zeros in $100,000 wise guy?" Sal loves to gamble. He's going all in on a sucker's bet. He downs another shot but skips the salt and lime formalities. If these guys have learned anything in life, they do know how to party hardy.

Seated at the bar, Blaze sits next to Ben Ichi. He mumbles under his breath to the golf mystic, as he drowns his sorrows, which are plentiful beyond belief, in the healing waters of Dr. Smirnov.

"What are the old farts up to?" Blaze asks under his breath.

"Some crazy idea of a golf game played out in the wilds," Hub answers as he tops off Blaze's tumbler.

"Any money to be made at it?"

"I doubt it. Probably just a pissing contest." Hub scrubs the wine glasses with a towel, blowing on a lipstick spot on the rim.

At the other end of the bar, Gyll and E.Z. sit eating peanuts by the handful from the communal bar bowl.

"Probably just a pissing contest," Gyll says as he tosses back a shot of salted peanuts. "They'll all sober up in the morning and forget all about it."

"Yeah, forget all about it," E.Z. says as he drains the bottom of his scotch and soda. "What was it we were forgetting about? I forgot already."

"I mean, the game is tough enough on a golf course," Gyll says as he signals for another round. "Imagine playing through Yosemite or something."

"You know what I've always wanted to see? I've always wanted to see the Grand Canyon!" E.Z. enthuses with a slight Scottish slur.

Riley overhears E.Z.'s comment, as he is approaching the bar with the empty sombrero bottle.

"That's it! We'll set it up through the Grand Canyon!" Riley slams the bottle down on the bar.

"Set up what exactly?" Ben Ichi perceptively asks, turning on his seat to face Riley.

"The Greatest Golf Game Ever Played!" Riley raises the sombrero cap to the heavens.

"Through The Wilds!" Wiley joins him at the bar. "It'll be 400 miles!"

"In 40 days!" Riley and Wiley high-five each other.

"All right, no more tequila shots!" Hub shouts out.

"FOR AN EVEN MILLION DOLLARS!" Riley and Wiley shout in unison. Apparently the tequila has been quite effective at easing the pain of the previous round. "What do you fellows say? That's just a half a million each. Winner take all." Riley smiles like a Cheshire cat inside the birdcage.

"Come on, Monty. Your ex-wives got more than that in plastic surgery!" Wiley drives the dare home.

Monty is holding his head in his hands.

"I knew this was going to cost us a lot of money."

Sal swaggers to the bar like the floor was floating on the high seas. He thrusts his right hand forward to shake on the deal and knocks over a glass of beer belonging to the avid follower. The four old duffers, snockered as four old guys can get with the sun still shining, all shake hands on the deal. As they do, a strange and peculiar bright beam of light comes streaming through the window as the sun sinks low in the sky. It gives a solemnity to the occasion, an eerie holiness settles over the room, almost as though they were all witnessing a miracle. A woman in the corner of the bar is playing a golden harp that wasn't there a minute ago.

"Wait a minute!" Sal shouts momentarily coming to his senses. "Who are we going to get to go out into the wilderness and play golf for 40 days and 400 miles?"

The four old duffers all turn and begin to look around the room. There standing in the emerging, magical light is Blaze Jones, Ben Ichi, the brothers Gyll and E.Z. Harbinger, Hub Hogle, the avid follower, now wiping beer off his pants, and the lady in the corner still working out on the golden harp. Some might call it fate. Some might call it destiny. Some might call it mighty slim pickin's.

"We'll pick Gyll," Sal and Monty shout in unison. Gyll steps forward into the light like an astronaut ready for launch.

Riley and Wiley look over the group of contenders, like the last kids picked for kick soccer. Only the dregs remain.

"We'll take Blaze."

"I think you guys are totally out of your gourds. But hey, you buy, I'll fly." Blaze isn't sure what he is getting into, but what else is new? He's never been sure of anything except that he is a royal fuck up.

"We'll pick E.Z." Sal and Monty beam.

"Wait a minute. That's not fair," Wiley protests.

"Why not?" Sal asks.

"Because they're brothers. That gives them an unfair advantage." Wiley says, knowing whereof he speaks.

"Well, you guys are brothers! It hasn't exactly helped your game," Sal answers with some authority.

"Gyll is a professional. And who'd hold down the club? Besides, his wife would never let him go. You've got to pick someone else," Riley says convincingly.

Sal and Monty look at what is left. Let's just call it a rather limited gene pool.

"This really isn't fair," Sal insists.

"Who you gonna pick?" Riley puts the pressure on.

"I guess we'll take Ben Ichi, the golf mystic." Ben gets down off his bar stool proudly, only to reveal his slight stature. He's all of five foot two with his shoes on. He shakes hands with E.Z., who rolls his eyes at his partner's diminutive size, and Ben Ichi notices his reaction.

"Remember, ancient Chinese saying, 'Good things come in small packages,'" Ben says as he smiles wide.

"I thought you were Japanese not Chinese," Blaze whispers.

"Ancient saying is ancient saying. Doesn't matter where your ancestors came from. The meaning is the same for everybody." Ben really is kind of mystical, even if most of his tidbits of ancient wisdom are actually derived from Hallmark greeting cards and stale fortune cookies.

The only others left unpicked are Hub Hogle, the avid follower, and the lady in the corner still playing the harp. Hub steps forward, anxious, hoping, waiting. He's been in this position all his life. The last one picked for everything.

Wiley and Riley have little choice. "I guess we'll take the fat guy."

Hub smiles broadly and high-fives Blaze.

"Yes! And I wasn't even picked last!" Hub enthuses as he pans the leftovers, the avid follower of the game and the lady in the corner whaling on the harp. "Sorry about that. Nobody wants to be last. I know that more than anybody."

The avid follower drains his beer and lets out a mighty belch.

"Then it's a done deal," Riley says with only a hint of a slurred word.

"I'll have our lawyers call your lawyers in the morning." Saying the word 'lawyer' with six tequilas under your belt can be harder than you think.

"Who knows, this might even catch on," Wiley suggests. "Give the old club some notoriety. Home of the Greatest Golf Game

Ever Played." His eyes mist up and we can see these guys are really serious.

You can't tell by looking at the players gathered at the end of the bar. They're not exactly the legends of the game. These guys look more like a police line-up, disheveled and more than a little uncomfortable in the harsh glare of the spotlight. What on earth are they getting themselves in for?

"We gotta have rules. We gotta keep score!" Sal says loudly overstating the obvious.

"I've got friends at the Royal and Ancient Golf Union" Riley announces. "They are the arbiters of the rules of the game. They'll have to be involved if it is to have any meaning at all."

"And they've got to have greens. I mean, who could putt without a green?" Monty offers.

"Who can putt with a green?" Wiley says ironically.

"Absolutely! We'll lay down AstroTurf for the greens," Riley says.

"We'll have surveyors plot the course. 18 holes, 400 miles, 40 days!" Wiley is getting all fired up, when the vision hits him. "Through FOUR STATES!"

"I told you this was going to cost us a lot of money," Monty bemoans.

"Hear me out. We'll play the first hole here at Burning Bridges, then play through New Mexico to Colorado, Colorado over to Utah, then on to Arizona, and finish the last hole on 18 back here at the club!"

"Brilliant! This is going to be big! Bigger than big!" Riley is like a kid again. Gambling is like that. The rush of adrenaline for having so much at risk at such slim odds makes us feel just like when we were kids and the world was full of possibilities.

"This could be huge. It'll get covered by all the networks. CNN. I'll call Ted Turner." Wiley is excited.

"We could be on ESPN!" Even Monty sounds excited.

"More like *Unsolved Mysteries*," Blaze says under his breath.

"Or *America's Funniest Home Videos*," Hub retorts.

"More like *Rescue 911*," E.Z. adds without a hint of irony.

The four old duffers step back into the eerie white light and all look to the heavens as they all say in unison, as if some kind of special reverence is being observed, "THE WIDE WORLD OF SPORTS!" It is as if there is a chill in the air.

"More like the Weird World of Sports," Ben Ichi says. "Old Chinese saying, 'You pay peanuts, you get monkeys.'"

"Yeah," Blaze says, his brain finally engaging with what is being proposed. "What do we get out of this? I mean, golfing through 400 miles isn't exactly going to be a walk in the park."

"Yeah," Hub weighs in. "How am I going to pay my rent if I'm out playing golf for 40 days?"

"Don't worry fellows. We'll pay your normal wages and add, let's say $100 a day, for each of you," Riley says without hesitation.

"Couldn't we make it $50 a day?" Monty asks, ever the cheapskate.

"That's $4,000 for each of you, plus your normal wages, and all expenses paid." Wiley is good at math.

"You mean you'll pay us $100 a day just to play golf?" Blaze is catching on.

"That's right. Who knows, you might even get famous," Riley beams.

"This must be our lucky day! To get paid to play golf, and all expenses paid!" Hub is ecstatic.

"Gentlemen, I propose a toast." Riley starts pouring tequila shots. "To all the crazy golfers all around the world. This may just be the craziest game ever conceived. To all the dreamers and schemers and screamers!" They all hoist their glasses and knock them back with a vengeance.

The woman on the golden harp finally stops playing and says to no one in particular, "What is it with men and sports and alcohol? It's like their I.Q. drops 50 points whenever they get together. My first husband wasn't even that stupid! God rest his soul and theirs too." She hoists her martini glass skyward, as though her husband were looking down at her, and drains the gin lovingly referred to by old timers as mother's milk.

"I don't think they've got any idea what it is they are getting into. Men are so stupid that way. Who else could come up with such a harebrained idea as a golf game out in the wild? Why the next thing you know, they'll all be dancing naked around a bonfire, swinging their clubs around howling at the moon. Between the bunch of them, they don't have enough sense to come in out of a lightning storm. And don't even get me started about playing in metal cleats on wet grass, holding a steel shaft at the top of the backswing as the lightning starts crackling. These boys are cruising for a bruising, plain and simple."

# CHAPTER 2

## "PARTING IS SUCH SWEET SORROW, UNLESS YOU REALLY NEED TO GET OUT OF DODGE"

THE NEXT DAY ARRIVES like a lightning burst of clarity for the four old duffers and their minions. Each one, though uniquely individualized, nurses a hangover of similar magnitude, severity and general fogginess. And yet, sadly, they remember all too clearly the height of their folly from the previous day's escapades and brandishments. With each throbbing of the brain, tens of thousands of dollars are being spent and the deadline for departure draws nearer. Though the night before was full of reverie, the daylight hours bring a seriousness of purpose and a backing up of all the swagger and grandiosity. These guys certainly are willing to put their money where their mouths are, even if they can barely remember what they said or where they said it. The wheels are in motion and with these guys, the wheels are substantial. They are capable of moving heaven and earth to accomplish their goals, which is fortunate, because in the case of the players hired to play the Greatest Game of Golf Ever Played in the Wild, they'll need more than a song and a prayer to get it done.

---

Blaze wakes with a start, drowning in a sea of disheveled

grayish sheets. The bed, like its inhabitant, looks like it hasn't been made, or changed, in years. In fact, the whole apartment, a third floor walk-up, with the entrance in the back, up the old rickety staircase, where the garbage cans are kept, leaves a lot to be desired. But the rent is cheap, the beers in the fridge cold and the ambitions long gone. Blaze's hey day, which actually was only a single day, was way back when he nearly won the state amateur golf tournament. Down three strokes with two holes to go, he birdied 17, then miraculously eagled 18 to tie, only to choke in the sudden death playoff, when he three-putted 16. The story of Blaze Jones' life, glimmers of promise only to be overwhelmed by the inertia of mediocrity. Bad luck meets bad timing. Blaze had long ago resigned himself to his reduced expectations. Like so many other talented players, who can only go so far with their God-given gifts, the finer points of the game, and all the success that comes with it, had eluded and deluded him. He'd stopped caring about it long ago. That's why there's beer in the fridge. In fact, that's about all there is in the fridge, and he's lucky to have that.

Blaze rolls out of bed, goes to the fridge, pulls out a cold one, it never really mattered what flavor, pops the top and takes the first guzzle of what will through the day become a torrent. He lights a cigarette, a Marlboro, one of the few things in his life he has a loyalty to, and reaches for the phone. He dials a number, takes a drag on the cig, repositions his balls, and takes another pull on the beer, as a deep, sexy-from-years-of-smoking, female voice answers on the other end of the line.

"Oh, hi Mom. It's me Blaze. You remember, your son."

"Why don't I ever hear from you?"

"I've been pretty busy down at the shop."

"Too busy to call your own mother? The woman who brought you kicking and screaming into the world?"

"I'm sorry. And I know I missed Mother's Day."

"I gave up on that a long time ago. You might as well drive a dagger through my heart."

"Have you stopped taking your medication again? You know what the doctor told you."

"Yeah, he told me I was an old lady who had a lousy, good for nothing son, who was wasting his life hanging around good for nothing people at that good for nothing country club. That's what he told me."

"Listen Ma, as much fun as this is, I'm calling you to tell you I'm going to be going away for a bit."

"Are you in trouble again? How much is it this time?"

"No Mom, it's not like that. I'm going to be playing golf. For money."

"You promised me you were through with gambling and golf."

"No, Mom. It's not gambling. They're paying me to play golf."

"Where on earth is that?"

"Well, it is in the desert."

"How long will you be gone?"

"Just 40 days."

"And nights?"

"Yeah, Mom, 40 days and 40 nights."

"Have you joined some kind of religious golfing cult?

"No Mom. It's a kind of crazy golf match."

"Played out in the desert for 40 days and 40 nights?"

"Yeah."

"You lost your job didn't you?"

"No Ma. It's a bet. Not by me, but by four old guys who are hiring us four younger guys to play the match for them."

"Do you need some of my medication, son? It definitely helps with the delusions. You're not hearing voices are you, hon?"

"Listen Ma, I gotta go, someone is at the door." Blaze knocks at the bedside table. "I'll call you from the road. If we pass any phone booths."

"You gotta call me more often Sonny. You're all I got left.

Just me and you kid, and a bottle of booze and a carton of cheap cigarettes. That's all I've got left."

"Just take your pills Mom. I'll be in touch. And Mom, remember I do love you."

"I know you do Sonny. What kind of person doesn't love their mother?"

---

E.Z. is packing his suitcase in Gyll and Giselle's basement where he lives on the fold-out couch in the rec room, next to the laundry. The sounds of the washing machine drone in the background, shifting through its cycles, much like E.Z. and his older brother's often contentious relationship has been since they were kids. It's like they're both permanently stuck in the spin cycle. Over the years, they've single-handedly redefined sibling rivalry to a near death match. But for the moment, Gyll is waxing nostalgic.

"To tell you the truth, I'm envious."

"You think I should take the long johns?" E.Z. asks holding up the old-fashioned red kind with the flap in the back.

"It can get mighty cold in the desert."

"What's to be envious of? I'm going to be working my butt off. You know how far 400 miles is?" E.Z. says as he folds the long johns and packs them in his suitcase.

"By my calculation, approximately 400 miles."

"Playing golf without a course?"

"Don't let me down here, little brother. The Harbingers have got a lot riding on this thing. I want you to have your game face on. This is serious business. These guys don't fool around. Not when it comes to golf and money. These guys made their money from dry cleaners and funeral parlors. Let's just say they're not the kind of guys who take kindly to failure. Think of them as very sore losers."

"That's just great. Not only do I have to play golf for over 400 miles, without a golf course, with a bunch of guys I don't even like, and oh, by the way, if you lose, you might end up on a fishing trip wearing cement golf shoes!"

"Come on, little bro. I'm serious. You gotta figure Pops would be proud. Carry on the Harbinger name."

"Yeah, doing really dumb things."

Giselle yells down from upstairs.

"Gyll, come up here and take out the damned garbage!" You can hear her mumbling under her breath as she walks away.

"Like I said, I'm envious. 400 miles wouldn't be far enough away." Gyll moves upstairs. "I'm coming honey!"

---

Hub Hogle is looking over rows of glistening golf shoes at a sporting goods store where a whole department is devoted to golf. Overlooking the department are hundreds of mounted antlers from all manner of elk, moose, deer, bison and antelope. Cougars, grizzlies and bighorn are all mounted on rocks overlooking the gun department. Apparently the gun department has been very successful. Perhaps it is an eerie precursor of things to come. Hub gets the shivers when he looks at a sneering badger mounted on a log, baring its fangs in all their glory. Truth to tell, going into nature is not exactly Hub Hogle's idea of a good time. He is startled out of his wits when a salesman approaches him and snaps him back to reality.

"Can I help you find something?"

"I'm looking for something comfortable in a 13 wide. I'm going to be doing a lot of walking."

"Not advisable. Not until you break them in. Wear them first around the house. Make love in them. Aerate your lawn with them. But don't take new golf shoes on a golf course before they are ready. Most common mistake a new golfer makes. Always results in blisters. Hands and feet mostly. You wanna try a couple of these on?"

"Yeah. And I might want to get a couple of other things too. Do you carry sleeping bags?"

The salesman gives him a look.

"And how about mosquito netting?"

"Is this one of those exotic golf vacations?"

"Something like that. And how about matching sweater, slacks and sock combos? I'm thinking maybe of something in a Day-Glo orange. So the rescue planes can spot us."

The salesman gives him another look. Is this guy for real?

"Sounds like this is going to be one hell of a vacation."

"I think the operative word there is hell. A hell of a vacation or a vacation in hell. Either way, I need new golf shoes and some camping gear."

"I gotta get the name of this course!"

"Have you ever heard of the Grand Canyon?"

"Well, sure. The big old canyon out west. Do they have a golf course?"

"Not yet. But they will by next week."

The salesman gives him another look like this guy is out of his mind.

Hub's attention is drawn once again to the menacing badger at the edge of the gun department.

"Did he just move?"

The salesman gives him another glance that indicates Hub may be certifiable. Then again, the badger may have cracked a smile, like it knows something that no one else perceives.

———

Ben Ichi is doing tai chi in his Zen garden, full of raked pebbles. He glides effortlessly through his moves, like clouds passing mountain tops. He is form and function all rolled up in his diminutive frame. He is graceful beyond measure. He is strong as steel. As he pushes forward, bending his front knee, he lets out a sonorous fart. He smiles a beatific smile, like a serene Buddha, at peace with the universe. His elderly father sits meditating on a mat in the corner, near the koi fish pond.

"A man who farts freely is a happy man."

"I am a happy man Father. But hiding a fart is a long practiced art."

"But a man who farts in church, must sit in his own pew. You see, the serpent of bad smells slithers a crooked path my son."

"I know father. But if you want to draw a snake, just add two legs."

"And the two fanged snakebite of ambition and ego makes for a potent poison."

"I know Father."

"And a coiled snake in a corner will always strike when it is discovered."

"Yes my Father."

"And a house full of mice is always an invitation to the snake."

"Yes my father. I remember the story."

"Do you remember what it means?"

"Avoid snakes at all costs?"

"Yes, my son. Avoid snakes at all costs. Because if you are bitten once by the snake, you will be afraid even of a rope that looks like a snake. And always remember my son that serpents come in many guises."

"But what, my Father, does any of this have to do with golf?"

"I don't have the slightest clue. But I really hate snakes."

"I will remember that Father. I will make you proud of me."

"I know my son. Just remember to take enough underwear and clean socks. Change them everyday. And always check your suitcase for coiled up snakes. They're sneaky bastards. As for the golf, show them no mercy. Sometimes, in life, you must also become the snake."

A snake in the grass slithers its crooked path past the large rock wall with a bronze plate embedded in stone announcing the home and head offices of the Royal and Ancient Golf Union, better known as RAGU, the official rules keepers of the game of golf. Unbeknownst to the casual weekend golfer, there exists a massive organization responsible for making, keeping and enforcing the many layers of golfing rules and etiquette, not dissimilar to the tangle of spaghetti from which it derives its namesake. This organization created the handicap system, appropriately named as everyone who plays the game is on some level challenged. It consists of a scoring system based on recorded and attested to scores, witnessed and signed by all the players in the round, so that legions of recreational golfers might compete on a level playing field, with each other and with golfers at all levels of expertise. It was an insidious plan which lead to crowds now playing courses which had heretofore been sanctuaries of privilege for the wealthy. There are now more golf courses worldwide than any other form of athletic endeavor combined and you still have to wait on almost every hole. But without the ruling body, you would not have the game of golf as we know it. This is the beating heart of the golfing world, nestled in the woods; it may as well be C.I.A. headquarters. It is just about as secret, controlling and monolithic, but their employees, as opposed to the Central Intelligence Agency, dress in various shades of pastels.

Riley and Wiley sit nervously in the conference room in the inner sanctum of the association. Seated around the table are the executive committee of RAGU, headed by the Smurf-like executive director, Bob Post. He's all hair, all the time. His hair is so firmly in place and lacquered, that even in a hurricane, it never budges. And it's not just his hair that is fixed in place. Let's just call him way north of extremely rigid. He is certainly not a happy farter.

"So, let me get this straight. You want us to sanction a golf match played out in the wilderness, by four ne'er-do-wells you hired in a bar, for 40 days?"

"That's right Bob. It is a one-of-a-kind opportunity to really go back to the earliest days of the game, back to the roots of golf," Riley offers.

"You mean when the Scots in windswept dunes were hitting a goat's bladder with a stick?" Bob says skeptically. The executive committee members grimace at the thought.

"Something like that, but without the bladders," Wiley adds.

"I'm not exactly sure the golfing public will get the concept."

"Oh they'll get it all right. We are convinced it will become a national story. Who knows, it might even go international. Did I mention we are major stockholders of several media outlets?" Riley pauses for affect.

"Ted Turner is a close personal friend. We started growing our mustaches at the same time," Riley twists the end of his mustache to a point. "We lunched just last week with Rupert Murdoch and his lovely wife Wendi. Jack Welch owes us big time. And Sumner Redstone once dated our sister." Riley is a real name dropper.

"And we practically own Disneyland. You know, the Mouse." Wiley knows how to play the game too.

Bob Post rubs his chin with his hand, mulling over the possibilities.

"I guess it could be kind of different. A cross-country golf match. I guess every sport has its extreme version. I mean, who knows, crazier things have happened. I mean, who would have ever predicted that a rolled up tortilla could ever compete with two slices of Wonder Bread? Or that salsa could replace ketchup in popularity in the American diet? These are complicated times in a complicated world. Sometimes people do need to be able to look at things in a new way."

"We just knew you'd be interested." Riley beams.

"I mean, gentlemen, we own the game of golf. At least the rules part. And without the rules, it would just be each man out for himself. We can decide to do any darned thing we want to because we are the ones who are in charge. And as we all know, it's good to be in charge. If there is to be the Greatest Golf Game

Ever Played in the Wild, the greatest golf organization in the world must be a gosh darned part of it."

Riley and Wiley get up from the table and start shaking hands with the executive committee.

"We'll assign you a couple of scorers and rules officials. I guess, it is official, the ruling body has ruled in favor of your match. Just, please gentlemen, don't let us down. We would never want to be embarrassed. Professionalism and decorum must be observed at all times." Bob Post reaches out and shakes the old codgers' hands vigorously.

"Absolutely. And Bob, call us and we'll talk about that little donation to the museum and the hall of fame. Who knows, this could end up an asterisk on the mighty wall itself."

"Gentlemen, good luck and good playing. We'll be closely monitoring the progress."

Riley and Wiley exit the room. Bob Post looks at the other members of the executive committee.

"These guys must be out of their friggin' minds."

"Bob, who are you going to get to keep score for 400 miles and 40 days? It's an assignment from hell."

"I've got just the couple in mind. They're as maniacal as they come. If anybody can do it, it's these two. Husband and wife team. Tough as nails. Nobody gets anything by these two. Ex-KGB, and they really know their stuff."

A slim and trim rear end waves itself in some form of hypnotic dance, back and forth, back and forth. The beautiful derriere belongs to the vivacious blonde television sports diva, the always smiling, at least when the camera is on, Donna Dina. She is in the edit bay of the television studio, leaning over the monitor, as she works with the editor on a football piece featuring a group of linemen known as the hogs. They are grunting and groaning, rhythmically, as the editor moves them in forward and reverse, piling and unpiling in the mud, in search of the ever illusive pigskin covered ellipse.

"Stop, it's making me ill," Donna says, and she really means it. For a person involved in sports she is really quite a softy.

Then we see why, when the editor lets the TV and the hogs footage move past the pile up and on to the quarterback's leg as it snaps in two with a sickening sound not unlike cracking a chicken bone with a meat cleaver.

Just then, an intern opens the edit bay door and pops his head in.

"The old man wants to see you upstairs."

"Did he say what about? Is it the anchor spot? Did he say anything about the anchor spot? I've been waiting for this moment all my life."

Donna turns to the editor. "Let's use the spot where they actually break the leg. Zoom in and slow it down. I want everybody in America to cringe when they see it. And put the car crash sound effects over it. I'll be back in a jiffy. A new woman. An anchor woman."

The executive elevator opens directly into the president of the network's office. It is the inner sanctum where the decisions are made as to what kind of television America is going to be watching. It is a mostly male bastion, with fresh laundered $500 shirts, golden cufflinks, pinstriped suits and enough aftershave to choke a horse.

Donna Dina takes it all in. It is her first time in the inner sanctum and she is in awe. There are various Emmys and assorted awards in a display case glistening their importance, there are Corbusier chairs arranged around a zebra rug, shot personally by the network head honcho in the Serengeti. There are photos of famous people, including many heads of state, presidents and prime ministers, past, present and future. There is a well- stocked and well-used wet bar in the corner and in the middle of the expansive office an olive carpeted putting green with one of those ball return systems at the far end. Harvey Wallbanger stands over his putt as Donna enters the room.

"You wanted to see me, Mr. Wallbanger? You know I've been waiting for this call for a very long time."

He shanks his putt badly.

"What do you know about golf?"

"They hit a little white ball and wear really ugly clothes."

"I like a woman's perspective. What do you know about New Mexico?"

"It is newer than old Mexico? What's this all about?"

"I got a phone call from some old college chums about a crazy golf challenge out in the desert. And I immediately thought of you." He hits another putt which just misses.

"Doesn't sound like much to me. Did I mention I'm supposed to have a root canal?"

"They also happen to be major stockholders of our parent company."

"I guess I could always reschedule."

"I knew you'd be the person for this Dina."

"It's Donna."

"We've got big plans for you here at the network."

"It is sounding more interesting by the minute."

"You see Donna, women don't understand sports the same way men do. We're hoping you could shed some light on the subject, so to speak, you know, from a woman's perspective." He finally makes his putt and the ball bounces right back to him.

"Mr. Wallbanger, I've been waiting for this moment all my life. Really, I'm sure golfing can be a very exciting sport, from a woman's perspective." Donna is a pretty good actress.

"I knew you'd be the right person for this one."

"I'm your man, or, I mean, woman."

Donna gets in the elevator and you can hear her screams recede with each passing floor. Needless to say, this wasn't what she had in mind. Harvey Wallbanger sinks another putt and lets out a little sigh.

"I am so smooth. Nobody can touch the Wallbanger when he's on."

---

A sprinkler head pops up out of a perfectly manicured lawn and starts spraying its life-giving liquid in perfectly formed droplets in a radius about the perfect yard of the perfect couple, Ludmilla and Boris Uzbetukant, the ex-KGB couple who ride roughshod over this little corner of their perfect little world. Boris checks his watch as he and the perfectly quaffed Ludmilla sit beside their perfect swimming pool. They are perfectly fit, perfectly tanned, perfectly insufferable.

"Right on time," Boris says as he plucks a perfect nostril hair from his perfect nose.

"Boris, you are so perfect, my love. Ve so deserve each other. It is so perfect, to be this perfect," Ludmilla purrs.

Just then the cell phone rings. The ring tone is Beethoven's Ninth Symphony, the most perfect music ever written. Boris answers.

"This is Boris."

Bob Post is on the other end. "Boris, I've got a little assignment for you and Ludmilla. We think you'll be the perfect couple for this one."

Boris smiles wide with his perfect white teeth.

"What are you doing for, say, the next 40 days?"

"No real plans. Just ze little gardening and ze 500 sit-ups ze day, our normal regime."

"That's perfect. Do you have a calculator?"

"Yes, of course."

"You'll be needing it for this little assignment."

"I'm not sure I follow you, Mr. Post."

"Oh, don't worry, it's not me you'll be following. Why don't you come by the office and we'll fill you in on all the details."

"That sounds perfect." Boris hangs the phone up.

"Vat vas dat all about darlink?" Ludmilla slurps her perfect drink. She sounds a lot like Zsa Zsa Gabor. Only younger and more perfect.

"I don't know. But I've got ze bad feeling about zis Ludmilla. And you know vhen I have ze bad feeling, nothing good ever comes."

"Maybe it vas ze borscht. Don't vorry darlink, if it vas Bob Post, zen it is only about ze golf game. How bad could it get?"

Boris furrows his perfect brow and knows perfectly well that he should be perfectly worried.

---

The night before the match finds our fearless foursome sound asleep in their own little beds, with each one having a little dream in their heads.

Blaze is riding a beautiful white stallion bareback on the beach. The wind blows through his hair, the surf pounds the sand and he rides the horse effortlessly. And then there is another rider on a jet black horse next to him. In the dream he can't quite make out the other rider, sheathed in a cape, but they ride together. And then another horse and rider join the group. And another. The Four Horsemen of the Apocalypse ride down the beach as the storm clouds gather on the horizon. And then the riders turn their horses from the beach and gallop their way across a velvety green golf course. On the golf course there is a castle. And in the castle, in the top of the tower, Blaze's mother waves to her son. But she is not the same woman we have met. She is younger, healthier and actually quite a babe. Standing outside the castle is a young man, dressed in knickers and a white shirt with a tie. He has a golf bag on his shoulder. He too waves at the four horsemen as they pass in front of the castle. Apparently the Four Horsemen of the Apocalypse are quite popular here. Blaze waves back, but he can't quite make out the young golfer's face as he rides by. And then a bolt of lightning strikes the tower and it catches fire and Blaze wakes with a start, beads of sweat on his face. He's had this dream before, but he can never see the faces of the other riders or the young man with the golf clubs, who looks a lot like Bobby Jones. Blaze rolls over and buries his face in the pillow.

"I think I could use a little vacation," Blaze groans.

Hub Hogle snores loudly in his bed. He's wearing cute little flannel pajamas and he's out cold. In his dream, he's sitting in the seat opposite Larry King. He's a guest on the show and he can't take his eyes off of Larry's suspenders. They have little red devils all over them. Larry King is talking but Hub can't quite make out what he is saying. All he can see are all the little red devils who suddenly start to speak to him. He can hear the devils but not Larry King.

"Double, double, toil and trouble, fire burn and cauldron bubble.

Thrice the brindled cat hath mewed. Thrice and once the hedge-pig whined, tis time, tis time. By the pricking of my thumbs, something wicked this way comes. Open, locks, to whoever knocks."

And then Jack Hanna, the exotic animal handler who is a frequent television guest steps out of the dark and on to the set, with a giant badger in his arms. The same badger from the sporting goods store.

"Don't be afraid, little buddy. Nobody is going to hurt you." Jack turns to hand the badger to Hub and it snarls at him. Larry King breaks into a belly laugh, as does Jack Hanna, who drops the angry badger into Hub's lap, live on television. Even the little red devils on Larry King's suspenders are laughing at him. Hub Hogle wakes from his dream with a start. He sits up straight in bed, pushing the covers into the air, as though they held the snarling creature in their folds.

"I think I could use a little vacation," Hub says as he checks under the covers one last time.

Ben Ichi is asleep on a stone slab with his neck resting in a wooden cradle. His eyes twitch as he is deep in his dream.

He is alone in a huge gothic cathedral. The sunlight splinters the stained glass windows into spectrums of light, floating about the room, like rainbows of butterflies. The church bell begins to ring very loudly and with a strong vibration. As it continues to dong, the inside columns of the cathedral begin to crack and start to crumble. Suddenly Ben Ichi is sitting inside a disintegrating church, violently breaking up with each resounding ring of the bell. He ducks into a doorway, and standing there quietly is David Carradine, dressed and in character as the *Kung Fu* master from his 1970s television series.

"We've got to get that bell fixed," Carradine says. "This happens every hour on the hour, and frankly I'm tired of it. As soon as I get the church put back in order, the damn bell goes off again. It is really exhausting. You at least can leave. Me, I'm stuck here. Wearing this stupid outfit and always speaking in nonsensical riddles. And don't get me started about my hair. Look at this mop top I'm stuck with. Whatever happen to pomade? Even a little mousse or a good gel would have helped. I look like friggin' Roy Orbison on a bad hair day."

Ben Ichi doesn't quite know what to say. "I like your hair."

"And another thing. I hated being called 'Grasshopper'. You know how many people come up to me and say 'Grasshopper'? If I had a dollar for every time, I'd be a rich man."

"I always loved watching your show. My father also loved it."

"Well, isn't that swell. You may not realize this, but I'm not at all Asian. I'm about as Asian as you are."

"But I am Asian. And an American."

"That's exactly my point. Why on earth did they saddle me with it? It would be like you being cast as, say, the Indians in a spaghetti western. It just doesn't work."

Ben Ichi wakes with a start. He sits up on the stone slab.

"I think I could really use a vacation." Ben Ichi rolls over on his stomach and rests his chin back on the wooden cradle.

E.Z. Harbinger is asleep on the fold-out couch in his brother's basement. Despite the stingy mattress and the metal bar driving through his back, E.Z. is sound asleep. Suddenly in his dream, he is underwater, sinking through the murky green flotsam, with the weight of the world pulling him down. He looks down in the dream and realizes he is Houdini sinking to the bottom of the river, with his hands bound by police-issued handcuffs, barely a whiff of air in his lungs, and sinking fast thanks to a pair of brand new cement golf shoes. E.Z. struggles to get free, blowing desperate bubbles past his contorted face as he sinks lower and lower into the icy water. And then the waterfall shows up. The waterfall is a big part of E.Z.'s life and he is always on the verge of going over it. Most nights he wakes up just before he goes over. But not tonight. He's on an underwater adventure. He sinks to the bottom of the river where he breaks free of the shackles and walks into a lush casino, where he is greeted by tall black men waving palm fronds and dressed in tunics and turbans. Suddenly, a large Italian guy approaches him. He's got to be a mobster. All the signs are there. Sharkskin suit. Gold chains. A pinky ring.

"You're Houdini aren't you? I recognize you from your pictures."

"No, I'm E.Z." He's always hated his name for the obvious reasons.

"Sure you are kid. And I'm Babe Ruth. Listen, could you do me a favor?"

"Sure, I guess I could." E.Z. sounds like a little kid.

"Could you take this lucky penny and make sure it gets into the right hands, if you know what I mean?" He even winks in Italian. He passes the coin into E.Z.'s hand.

"I'm not sure I understand?"

"Hey, you're Houdini. I'm sure you'll figure something out. By the way, how do you hold your breath for so long?"

"It's a long story. Perhaps another time."

"All I've got is time. You can fill me in on the details later. Just remember to save the penny and to come up for air occasionally. You'll find it quite refreshing. And one other thing, if you want to get good at golf, don't ever get married." He gives him another Italian wink.

E.Z. wakes up when the washing machine goes into the spin cycle. He's never been one for swimming, but he often finds himself submerged. The cement golf shoes just come with the territory.

"I think I could use a little vacation," he says wearily as he gets up and goes to the bathroom.

---

Our four old duffers are asleep too this big night before the match. And they too are having dreams, but their dreams are more expensive.

Riley Hancock is sleeping atop his lush four-poster bed, alone as usual, in his opulent mansion. He has a strange smile on his face. In his dream, he's back on the golf course, but as a much younger man. And he is a brilliant player. Crowds line the fairways to watch him. As he strolls the course spontaneous applause breaks out and he waves to the crowd. And then he looks down and realizes he is naked as the day he was born. And people are applauding. Suddenly, Riley is embarrassed. He realizes he's a younger man, except down there. South of the border everything remains old and decrepit. He cups his hands over his crotch and starts to run towards the clubhouse. The applause turns to laughter, as his skinny white butt disappears over the horizon.

Wiley Hancock is also dreaming alone in his enormous bedroom. A large old grandfathers clock keeps time ominously in the corner. In Wiley's dream, he is adrift in the ocean on a rag tag raft, like Thor Heyerdahl on the *Kon Tiki*. And then he spots an island. And a large canoe, with a scary looking carved head on the front, being rowed towards him by a group of beefy looking natives, outfitted in necklaces of flowers. They are grunting to the rhythm of their strokes, and as they get closer, he realizes they are singing to him. And then suddenly a canon is fired. Wiley looks behind him and sees a heavily rigged schooner, with its white sails billowing and smoke coming from its gunnels. He can hear the canon ball whistling its way towards him. He tries to shout out a warning, but he can't get the words out. And then the clock strikes the top of the hour and lets out a series of mighty bongs. Wiley wakes up drenched in his own sweat, throws a pillow at the clock, rolls over and tries to go back to sleep.

Sal Gravani is snoring loudly in his gold-plated bed. In his dream he is at the drive-up window of his dry cleaner business. All the plastic wrapped clothes are on the numbered hangers, on the chain conveyor that snakes around the business. Suddenly, a convertible drives up to the window and Marilyn Monroe is behind the wheel. She hands him her ticket, and he presses the button to drive the line of clothes. But the button gets stuck and the clothes start to whirl around the room. Sal tries to shut it off, but the plastic sheathed clothes start to gain momentum. He smiles sheepishly at Marilyn and she smiles back, but by now the clothes are screaming around the room. The machine is overheating and kicking out black smoke. All Sal can do is smile and shrug his shoulders at the beautiful blonde in the convertible.

Monty Delillo is also asleep in his heavily mirrored bedroom. Mirrors, mirrors everywhere. And he's really nothing to look at. In Monty's dream he is surrounded by all his former wives, who are doing synchronized swimming in his Olympic-size swimming pool. Monty floats in the middle of the pool on an inflatable mattress, taking in the moment. He loves synchronized swimmers, in their cute little suits and snappy swim caps. And then he hears the familiar strains of the music from *Jaws*. The women are screaming and making for the edges of the pool. And then he sees the fin in the water and knows he's a goner. Just as the shark surfaces and opens his huge set of teeth, Monty wakes up. He stares at himself in the mirror, lets out a little whimper and tries to go back to sleep.

This is the problem with dreams. You can't control what happens in them. Parts of reality seep in, but so do fantasies. And people and places and things. Sometimes funny and sometimes frightening. Just like life. Everyone has to dream. It comes with the territory. But everyone must also wake up from their dreams, and carry those dim messages with them wherever they go, just like a bad back, hang nail or sprained ankle. Something nagging at you just on the edge of consciousness. That also comes with the territory. Turns out, the territory is a pretty big old sprawling frightful slightly-disconnected mess. Might as well make the best of it. Just like life. Turn your fears into your favor. Turn your weakness into your strength. Turn your challenges into opportunities. Then again you could just roll over and go back to sleep.

# CHAPTER 3

## "LET THE GAME BEGIN, PUT YOUR BEST FOOT FORWARD, EVEN IF YOUR SHOES ARE KILLING YOU"

THE DAY BREAKS LARGE and luxuriant, a chamber of commerce day if there ever was one. The morning dew gathers on the blades of grass as if on cue from some art director in the sky. The flowers are just a little bit bigger and brighter than they were the day before. Even the birds seem to have a little extra song in their throats this particular morning. The world is a happy place. The kind of place where everyone gets along. The kind of place where neighbors help neighbors. The kind of place where gentility and order prevail. Where nature has been tamed only in service of mankind. Where the clocks are all set and the trains run on time. The kind of place where moms still cook, and dads make mixed drinks. It's a perfect country club kind of world. Where everyone is a member in good standing. Where everyone's dues are paid up. Where everyone has a smile and a nod of the head, acknowledging their good fortune, to friend and stranger alike, to be alive in such a glorious community.

And then the music starts. That strange bossa nova beat, with the Lalo Schifrin inspired string section, coming in underneath the lazy guitar, indicating we are hearing the opening strains of a

CBS broadcast of what could only be a golf match like no other golf match we have ever witnessed.

Jim Nantz, the straight-arrow announcer with the soothing drawl and a tie collection second to none, lets us know exactly where we are.

"Welcome to the beautiful Burning Bridges Country Club, to the first ever golf match, officially sanctioned by RAGU, to be played without the benefit of a golf course, played by what can kindly be referred to as a group of rank amateurs, but with all the heart of a group of underprivileged kids being unleashed on an amusement park just after dark. I'm here with my colleague David Feherty to witness this unheralded match, destined to go down in the annals of golfing history as a just crazy event."

"That's right Jim, this wild and crazy foursome, whom we'll meet in a moment, has been selected to play golf over the next 40 days, over a course that has been created just for them, covering 400 miles of the roughest terrain known to mankind." David Feherty's Irish brogue is so thick you could cut it with a friggin' knife. It is as though his tongue is wrapped in a cable knit sweater.

The television introduction shows helicopter shots of teams of surveyors, lines of men rolling out huge sections of AstroTurf in various wilderness settings, RAGU officials, dressed in matching tomato sauce- colored blazers, placing spiked white oversized golf balls indicating tee box areas, in places that look like the Grand Canyon.

"The game starts out here at the prestigious Burning Bridges Country Club, a club with a storied history, a club that has seen the likes of the debonair Bobby Jones, Slammin' Sammy Snead, the Golden Bear Jack Nicklaus, Arnold Palmer's Army, and Vlad, the Impaler, one of the lessor known golfing talents who have graced these wonderful fairways." Jim Nantz looks over his notes, a bit perplexed by the last reference.

"That's right, Jim, there can be little doubt, this match will rank right up there with the Crusades and the Grand Inquisition, in terms of its historic value. Let's take a moment and meet the four old gentlemen who have dreamt this crazy dream, who have spared no expense to realize their dream and who may not be able to wake up from all of its ramifications. These guys have deep pockets and they're not afraid to stick their hands in and pull out big wads of cash. These guys are the lifeblood of Burning Bridges, bringing back some of the old glory to the aging beauty. They are the glue that holds the old horse together. They are the bedrock, the tower and everything in between. They are every silly sports metaphor you could ever think of."

The television hanging in the corner of the men's locker room shows Riley and Wiley, Sal and Monty sitting stiffly like white porcelain poodles in front of a massive fireplace in the club's trophy room as they are interviewed by Jim Nantz. Inside the locker room, Hub Hogle is throwing up in one of the toilet stalls. Blaze Jones stands outside the door.

"I'm sure you're just a little nervous. Hey, everybody will be."

"I just didn't realize how many people would be watching, you know, on the first tee." Hub hurls just thinking about it.

"Hey, you wouldn't be human if you didn't have butterflies in your stomach," Blaze calls through the door.

"These are more like B-52 bombers." Hub groans and hangs on to the toilet bowl for dear life.

In walks Ben Ichi and his partner E.Z. Harbinger, as Hub hurls another round.

"You got a problem Houston?" E.Z. is not the most sympathetic guy on the block.

"He's just a little camera shy, that's all."

Hub hurls again, only louder.

"You know what they say," Ben chimes in. "Sailor who gets sick on land, never gets sick at sea. But the converse is also true: a sailor who gets sick at sea should never become a sailor."

"Bon voyage and happy sailing boys. This is going to be like taking candy from a baby," E.Z. practically oozes cockiness, as he and Ben leave the locker room.

Hub raises his head from the toilet bowl and shouts after them.

"Actually, taking candy from a baby is harder than you think. They scream bloody murder." Hub wipes the spittle from his lips, gets to his feet and exits the stall.

"I'm fine. I'll be fine. I'm just a little light-headed, like I'm seeing stars. I think I stood up too fast."

"Let's get you outside and some fresh air."

Blaze takes Hub by the arm and escorts him out and as they near the exit, in walks Wayne Newton, Mr. Entertainer himself. He slips into one of the stalls.

Hub looks at Blaze. "Like I said, I'm seeing stars. Wasn't that just Wayne Newton?"

"Yeah, I think it was. Maybe he's singing the national anthem or something?"

"Wow, this thing is bigger than I thought. Let me know if you see Siegfried and Roy. They could be planning on feeding us to the tigers."

Donna Dina is getting ready to do her live shot, standing in front of the clubhouse. Her cameraman, a balding hipster with a goatee, Dan Flavin, sets up the tripod, as Donna puts on the final touch of lipstick and checks her teeth in a pocket mirror.

"Why do they pick me for this stuff? I don't like men and I don't like the things men do. Like sports. And gambling. And sweating. Why do men have to bet on sports?" Donna asks rhetorically.

"Because we're men? Sports betting is just part of our DNA. Just like you women like to shop. We like sports and gambling." Dan knows his way around the topic. "You like malls. We like bars with TVs."

"That's right, sports and drinking. Go hand in hand. The more you drink, the more you brag, the more you bet. You'd think someone could figure out the connection and put a stop to it."

"There is one other thing men are interested in. And that does require women." Dan smiles. "Usually."

"Yeah, and that's another thing I don't like about men. That thing dangling between their legs, that has a mind of its own. When you really think about it, men are just plain disgusting." Donna knows her way around this topic too.

Dan adjusts the camera. "Let's shoot this thing."

Donna turns on the charm, like the power switch at the Hoover Dam. The way she so blatantly uses her sexuality, you'd never have an inkling of her deeper feelings. She just loves to hate men, when she isn't trying to seduce them.

"Three, two, one. I'm Donna Dina, here at the beautiful Burning Bridges Country Club, to cover what will go down in the annals of golf as one of the greatest golf challenges known to mankind. Four well-heeled duffers have hired four players to play golf through the wilderness, 400 miles, over 40 days, guaranteed to separate the men from the boys. They play one hole here at Burning Bridges, then will be whisked away to Shiprock, New Mexico where the game will begin in earnest. From Shiprock, they'll play to Dove Creek, Colorado, then to Bluff, Utah and finally into the Navajo Nation at Kayenta, Arizona. After that they return to Burning Bridges, assuming they are still capable of walking, to finish up on historic number 18. It is sure to be a golf match that will be remembered, if not for the actual golf, for the sheer endurance. The total madness of the challenge. Besides, the million dollar bet between the sponsors, the question will be whether these players can handle the challenge of playing golf for so long, over such a great distance and without the benefit of an actual golf course. It will be a crazy game played best by crazy people. Only time, an odometer and a calculator will tell the tale. I'll be giving you a daily update on the players' progress and of course, I'll do my best to show you behind the scenes, the trials, the tears and the tribulations, from a kind of woman's perspective. It takes all kinds to make up this crazy world of golf. I'm Donna Dina, reporting from the Burning Bridges Country Club." She breaks out of her television personality and it is as though she is two different people, both equally offensive, but for very different reasons. "All right, cut. These four assholes must be out of their fucking minds. Why don't they make Al Michaels do this shit?"

Dan Flavin just shrugs his shoulders. "I don't know, between you and me, I could use a little vacation. 40 days sounds just about right."

"Yeah, well remember that when we're lost in the rental car in Bumfuck, Utah."

---

Wayne Newton steps up to the microphone. He clears his throat and hits the first strains of The Star-Spangled Banner. *"Oh, say can you see, by the dawn's early light, what so proudly we hail'd, at the twilight's last gleaming?"*

A crowd of dignitaries and celebrities are gathered around the first tee, as are the four players and their sponsors, all with their hats off and their hands held over their hearts. The song, sometimes sung more like *The Star-Mangled Banner,* is meticulously sung by the great and ever youthful Wayne Newton, who also happens to be an avid golfer. There are many avid golfers, all of them quite famous, gathered around the first tee. The Shark is there, with his trademark straw hat. The Donald is there with his trademark hair. Shaq is there with his trademark smile. Bono is there with his trademark sunglasses. Apparently it helps to be invited if you are known by a singular name. Or for a singular thing. Bill Clinton is there. Michael Jordan. Bill Murray. Pretty much any golfing celebrity worth their putter is gathered around the first tee. There are also dozens of cameras, with reporters from all around the world. As the song ends, the reporters begin the normal whispering golf voice, but in French, Spanish, German, Italian, Hindi, Japanese and Chinese. Donna Dina is doing her stand up, and Jim Nantz and David Feherty are in the announcers booth with all that funny music.

Hub looks around the scene like a snapshot of his worst nightmare. He is sweating profusely, has severe cottonmouth and is trembling in his argyle socks.

"Wow, look at all that camera gear. I had no idea this was going to be such a big deal. I'm so nervous, they all sound like they're speaking gibberish."

"I think those are foreign languages Hub. You know, not English," Blaze tries to explain.

"Well, that explains it then. Whew, I thought I was really losing it before we even started." Hub lets out a nervous laugh. "Really, I couldn't understand a word they were saying. I thought I was having a stroke or something."

"Oh, you're going to be having plenty of strokes, on this little trip, my chubby friend," E.Z. riddles him with sarcasm.

"You have nothing to fear but fear itself," Ben Ichi offers.

"That's what I was afraid of."

Bob Post steps forward and takes the microphone from Mr. Entertainer. "A thousand *Danke Schoens* to you Wayne. Really if you haven't seen his act in Vegas or Branson, you are really missing something special. And speaking of something special, do we have golf match for you? I'm Bob Post, executive director of the Royal and Ancient Golf Union, the man responsible for all those wonderful blazers running around. Players are you ready to rumble? Sponsors, are you ready to write some big fat checks? Before we get started, I'd like to introduce to you the two RAGU officials who will be keeping the scores, making the correct calls, enforcing the rules, to keep the game moving forward and with an absolutely accurate score. Ladies and gentlemen, I give you Boris and Ludmilla Uzbetukant."

Boris and Ludmilla step forward at attention as though they've been selected as the first couple to join the Sputnick spacecraft. They click their heels together, in typical fascist fashion, and actually have to stifle a more familiar arm salute. And they're not even German, they're Russian! A smattering of applause breaks out, at their perfect-ness. Bill Clinton seems particularly impressed with Ludmilla's obvious attributes and applauds perhaps a bit too vigorously.

"And, now, without further ado. What exactly is ado? Besides a new hair cut?" Bob Post looks over at the Donald and winks. The Donald doesn't exactly wink back. "But perhaps I digress. Let's get this party started! First on the tee is Hub Hogle, playing for the team sponsored by Riley and Wiley Hancock. Polite applause breaks out as Hub steps up to the tee box with a wave of the hand, almost as though he is in a dream.

"Well, I guess I'll get started here. This is our last chance to change our minds. I mean, maybe the whole thing is a big mistake. You know, everybody got caught up in the moment, things were said, wagers were made. I'll tell you what, why don't we all go over to the bar, and the drinks are on me. What do you say?" Hub just draws blank stares.

"Just smooth it out there," Blaze encourages his partner.

Donna whispers to her cameraman, Dan. "Where did they find these guys?"

Hub addresses his ball. He sets. He shuffles. He resets. Just as he is about to start his backswing, his ball falls off the tee. He bends down and places it back on the tee, his hand obviously trembling.

"Gee, even my ball is nervous." Hub resets and with a loud crack hits it dead solid perfect down the middle of the fairway. It is a monster of a drive.

"That a boy!" Blaze shouts.

"Next up is Ben Ichi, playing for the team of Sal Gravani and Monty Delillo." Bob Post just loves hearing the sound of his own voice, especially when it is amplified.

Ben Ichi steps up to the tee. He doesn't even take a practice swing. Perfection comes easy to him. He hits a wondrous shot, which falls just shy of Hub's huge drive, proving once again that good things do come in small packages. The crowd applauds like they were at a Broadway show and the star just came on stage.

"Next on the tee is E.Z. Harbinger, also playing for Mr. Gravani and Mr. Delillo."

E.Z. steps up to the tee. He's nervous too, but tries to cover it with his big mouth. He lives by the motto, 'live by the mouth, die by the mouth.'

"Are those cameras rolling? Is everybody ready? Watch closely now." E.Z. takes a big swing and smacks a beauty. The crowd goes crazy as his ball rolls well past Hub's drive. Sal and Monty high-five each other.

E.Z. struts off the tee box like a satisfied rooster in a hen house that hasn't had a rooster around for awhile. He's cocky all right and wants everyone to know it. It is all part of his bluff and bluster.

"Just a matter of full rotation and club head speed."

"The last player is Blaze Jones, playing for the Hancocks. And it looks like he's got his work cut out for him."

Blaze steps up to the tee and carefully places his tiny ball atop the thin wooden tee. He eyes the fairway, then sets himself, adjusting his hands on the shaft. He is all about concentration. As he takes back the large driver, E.Z. lets out a large, rather fake sneeze. Blaze stops in mid-swing and glares at E.Z.

"Sorry, I have allergies." E.Z. winks at his brother Gyll who stands nearby. Gyll winks back at his conniving brother. Boris and Ludmilla notice the exchange and are not happy about it.

Blaze resets himself and now he's pissed. He smashes a drive as though it were E.Z.'s head he was hitting. The crowd oohhs and aahhs as his drive rolls past E.Z.'s.

Donna Dina is doing her stand up. "And there you have the beginning shots of what is destined to become the golf match of the new millennium. These guys might be rough, but they certainly look ready. Not exactly your normal looking foursome, but then again, what normal person would be willing to play golf continuously for 40 days over 400 miles? No matter what your feelings are about golf, or even sports, for that matter, you've got to admit, this is one to go down for the ages. After they complete this hole, we'll be picking up the foursome as they arrive in New Mexico where the game will begin in earnest."

As the foursome strolls to their drives, Ludmilla and Boris approach E.Z. "Perhaps you need ze tissue?" Ludmilla offers one of those little travel packs of carefully folded Kleenex. "Do you have an issue with ze tissue?"

"No, I'm fine, thank you very much."

Boris bores his eyes into E.Z.'s. "If zose allergies are going to be ze problem, ve hope you brought your medication, non-drowsy kind. Because ve von't be tolerating any more sneezing as someone is about to hit zer ball. Ve're going to be vatching you like ze hawk. Ze hawk zat doesn't like sneaky players. Do you get my meanink?"

"Hey, it was an honest sneeze. You don't have to worry about me. I don't need to cheat to win. You'll see I'm the best player out here."

"I am varning you right now. Ve von't be tolerating any shenanigans."

"I read you loud and clear amigo. Now why don't you get out of the way, so we can play our next shots." E.Z sneers at Boris and Ludmilla.

All four players hit safe second shots splattering them all around the expansive undulating green. The sign of any decent golfer is always about how many make-able birdie putts you can have an opportunity to knock down. It is all about the up and down. Get on the green and make your putt. Drive for show, but putt for dough. The amazing thing about golf is, no matter how great the drive and the majesty of the distance it covers, it always costs more strokes around those alluring and deceptively simple little slippery light green surfaces, than it does in the middle of those big open fairways. The axiom is always true, the closer you get to the hole, the harder it is to get the ball to go in it. This is where the three-putt players pay dearly for their amateur status. All around the hole is the costliest real estate in the game of golf.

Hub's shot is outside the others, so he is first to putt. He's about

30 feet away from the hole, with a slight left leaning break towards the ocean. Greens always break towards the ocean. Even if they're in Kansas. He lines up the ball and gives it the old college try. It doesn't have the legs, and lags up to within 10 feet, certainly no 'gimmee.' He marks his ball and next up is Ben Ichi.

Ben's ball is about 20 feet away, but must get over a large hump on the right side of the green. He lines it up carefully and strikes it just right. It's got the perfect speed and is breaking towards the hole, when it rims out and stops about two feet away. Ben groans at the near miss, steps up and taps in for a par.

Next up is E.Z. Harbinger. His ball is about 15 feet away. He strolls up to it and nails it. Back of the cup, for a well earned, if somewhat despised, birdie.

Next up is Blaze. Now the pressure is on. His ball is about 12 feet away, but with a dramatic curve in the middle, reminiscent of the Matterhorn shot at the miniature putt putt. He lines it up, but it is so severe it appears he is aiming 90 degrees the wrong way. He strikes the ball and everyone in the entourage is hushed as it makes its circuitous way towards the hole. It rolls with just the right speed and line, and with barely a wisp of momentum left, reaches the edge of the hole and just rolls in. One half inch more and it would not have made it. Cheers go up, as he matched E.Z.'s birdie.

It is now up to Hub to sink his 10 footer to match Ben's par. By no means is this an easy putt. Ten feet may as well be a hundred. The hole has never looked smaller. Hub takes a deep breath. He sizes it up and as he is about to strike the ball, the putter scuffs the ground first and he badly miss-hits the ball. It teeters and totters its way towards the hole and by some miracle, or combination of luck, divine intervention and sheer good karma, it rims around the cup and drops in with a resounding thud, the most perfect sound there is on a golf course.

"And there you have it folks, we're all tied up after one, and we'll be picking up the foursome as they make their arrival in New Mexico for the next leg of this fascinating journey. Golf as we know it may never be the same again."

"That's right Jim, not even the founders of the game of golf would recognize what will transpire over the next 40 days. They'd be spinning in their kilts if they could follow this one. Just bloody exciting! And I do mean bloody! Before we're through, I do think this one will get bloody!

Bloody good and bloody well!"

A bloody Mary is being swigged by Blaze Jones as the plane makes its final approach to the Shiprock, New Mexico airport.

Hub is throwing up in the barf bag still supplied by the airlines, despite the fact that people rarely actually throw up on flights any more. It is a quaint custom, in this time of cost-cutting, but Hub is thankful for it, as are the numerous passengers around him.

E.Z. and Ben are seated just behind Hub and Blaze. E.Z. is reading a romance novel and Ben is meditating. Or perhaps he is sleeping. It is hard to say as they both share the qualities of slow breathing and closed eyelids. Who is to say that sleepers aren't meditating and the meditators are actually sleeping? Either way, they look very rested.

The stewardess comes on the PA system. "We'd like to welcome you to the Shiprock, New Mexico International Airport. I'm just kidding about the international part. That's just a little flight attendant humor. Set your clocks back about 20 years and I'm sure you'll be fine. Temperature is about 105 degrees in the shade, if you can find any. They cut down the trees a long time ago, to build crosses for the churches and pool tables for the drinking establishments. You might have noticed the big old rock out in the middle of the desert, looks like a ship made out of rocks. That's why they call it Shiprock. Of course there isn't a drop of water for hundreds of miles, but who's to quibble with the founding fathers. We hope you have a wonderful stay here in Shipwreck. Just kidding. Local joke. We flight attendants can have a mean sense of humor. Please remain in your seats until the plane has come to a full stop. And thanks again for flying with, ahh, what's our name this week? Oh yeah, Continental Drift Airlines, where our motto is, 'Even if the earth moves, we'll still get you there.' Of course your bags are another story! Just kidding! Just kidding!"

Blaze turns to Hub. "How you feeling big guy?"

"Do you think they might have forgotten our bags? That would save me a lot of embarrassment." Hub wipes his forehead with a napkin.

Blaze looks out the window of the plane. There on the tarmac is a full-on mariachi band, in all their regalia, playing "El Rancho Grande" and a rather large Conestoga wagon parked nearby complete with a grizzled old-time driver straight out of central casting. Scattered about is a small welcoming committee made up of local officials and avid golfers, at least as many avid golfers as one can find in Shiprock.

"Looks like the welcome wagon is here. I think you're just going to have to grin and bear it," Blaze says to Hub.

Ben Ichi leans forward and addresses an ashen-looking Hub. "You look like you could use a little hair of the dog that bit you."

"Did you get the license plate of that dog?" E.Z. laughs to himself, which is a frequent occurrence, as most of his jokes are lost on mere mortals.

The foursome gathers its formidable belongings together, including backpacks, canteens, duffle bags and tents from the overhead bins. The players all flew coach, and their golf clubs are standing at attention on the tarmac, like brave little soldiers, all shiny and spit-polished.

As they deplane on the tarmac, they are greeted by Mayor Freddy Fender, not the country western singer, but a good facsimile. He is about 6'4" in his snakeskin cowboy boots, has jet black hair and a pencil thin mustache. He's about as slick as a bottle of baby oil at a Mr. Universe contest.

"Buenos dias! Or 'good day' in our second language. Welcome to Shiprock, New Mexico! We, of the welcoming committee, are pleased to welcome you. Welcome!" The mariachi band hits a high note.

"Do you have a bathroom nearby? Cause I've got to take a leak like there is no tomorrow." Blaze drank quite a few Bloody Marys on the flight.

"We, the golfers, are pleased to be here in Shiprock. That is to say, we are pleased to be anywhere on the ground." Hub is still a little green around the gills. "Especially in Shipwreck, I mean rock. Shiprock."

"Welcome to Shiprock, my crazy golfing friends. The gateway to your adventure in the Land of Enchantment." Mayor Freddy slaps Hub on the back. "Your portal into your destiny. Each step you take brings you closer to the fame and fortune you so richly deserve."

"I like this guy." E.Z. grins as he smacks his Doublemint gum.

"Old Chinese saying, beware of lavish praise, it will one day cost you friends and money." Ben knows his way around Confucious.

"We, of the welcoming committee, would like to present you with the key to our wonderful city."

"Does it work for the men's room?" Blaze is a man on a mission.

Just then, Donna Dina and her cameraman Don Flavin rush up to the scene, camera rolling. "Have we missed anything?" A clamor of other journalists follow them.

"Just the welcome from the welcoming committee," Blaze says as the group makes its way towards the terminal entrance.

"Welcome international journalists!" Mayor Freddy beams to the camera. "The whole world is watching us, and we welcome it!"

Inside the airport men's room, Blaze stands at the urinal.

Next to him, the mariachi band continues to play "El Rancho Grande." If looks could kill, these guys would be skeletons in really ridiculous outfits playing large guitars and trumpets.

"Really guys, I appreciate the welcome and all. And I love the outfits and the music and all. But back home, if you followed a guy into the men's room, dressed like that, they might think you were a bunch of gay caballeros." Blaze zips up and washes his hands in the sink. The band plays on as he dries his hands in one of those old-fashioned towel dispensers that go round and round. It is all lost in the translation.

---

Deep inside the Shiprock International Airport sits the Shiprock International Lounge, for jetsetters and the like. It is basically a beige cinderblock room, with twinkling lights around the bar on one end, plastic tables and folding chairs, and Mexican blankets hung randomly on the walls. But the beer is cold, the limes are cut, the glasses are salted, and the welcoming committee is buying the rounds. The tequila flows in these parts like Niagra Falls after a thunderstorm. And at this point in the journey, with the match to begin in earnest tomorrow, the foursome is only too happy to drink itself into the depths of oblivion. Think of it as men in barrels going over the frothy edge.

"Welcome to our cozy lounge!" Mayor Freddy is a boisterous booster. Donna approaches him to get an interview.

"Welcome!" He shakes her hand.

"As the first host city for what is being referred to as 'The Greatest Golf Game Ever Played in the Wild', what do you think of all this Mr. Mayor?"

"We say welcome. Welcome to our city. Welcome to our airport. Welcome to the Land of Enchantment."

"How do you feel about all this attention?"

"We welcome it."

"Do you play the game yourself?"

"Golf? Only the miniature kind. With my kids a couple of times in Albuquerque. Although I am supposed to be a distant relative of Lee Trevino. I do play a little pool once in awhile. Mind you, I'm no hustler or anything." Mayor Freddy smiles at the camera, like all politicians, you know he is lying through his teeth. That's precisely why they call it lying through your teeth. The bigger the smile, the bigger the lie. And Mayor Freddy looks like the alley cat that swallowed the prized canary at the state fair, gulping the last vestiges of Chirpy, just as the owner encounters the empty cage.

---

The pool balls, in all their stripe and solid glory, sit momentarily in limbo, in that perfect triangle on green felt sitting atop blue slate. And then KABOOM, the crack of the cue ball announces we are late into the night in Shipwreck, and in a new bar with a fabled pool table Mayor Freddy is more than familiar with.

"Welcome to my favorite bar and my favorite table. Welcome to my brother's place!" Mayor Freddy announces after he breaks, sinking three solids without even thinking about it. He spins in a full circle, matador-style, waving the cue stick like the sword under the cape. The whole bar full of patrons shouts in unison, "Welcome to the Land of Enchantment!"

The bar is done in what could kindly be called early American or more closely, early Davy Crockett. It has log walls, reminiscent of oversized Lincoln Logs, cheap sirloin steaks which are constantly burning in the kitchen and add to the ambience and smoke factor, as well as the oily residue on all the frequent patrons. One look around the place and it is like the scene out of *Star Wars*, where all the aliens from the furthest fringes of the universe are belly up to the bar. These patrons are as chiseled as the landscape outside the window. Pockets of bikers, hikers, cowboys and Indians who have one thing in common, today at least- no one is feeling any pain. Creedence Clearwater's *Run Through the Jungle* is on the juke box and the place is rocking. Donna Dina and Dan Flavin, with camera in hand, are shooting the local color and taking in the scene, one shot glass at a time.

By this time, of course, the foursome has had enough tequila to sink a ship and though the sun hasn't sunk yet below the horizon, the foursome's eyelids are beginning to look like flags at half mast. But Mayor Freddy is just getting started. Blaze is his current victim on the green felt table. And Hub is at the bar hustling up another round, while Ben and E.Z. pick at a bowl of nachos that has seen better days.

The bartender delivers another round of margaritas to Hub, who is well-versed in serving more drinks to all ready drunk people.

"The drinks are on them," Hub says as he gestures to the group of Hell's Angels seated next to the bar. They wave back.

"Hey, thanks fellas. Mighty neighborly of you." Hub tips his hand.

"Happy to for a fellow duffer," the huskiest of the bikers says. He's really more of a Kodiak bear than a human.

"Some of my happiest times have been out on the golf course," the other biker with an eye patch chimes in.

"I know I don't look like it, but I'm a six handicap," the Kodiak says.

"Oh, you look like a six handicap to me." Hub looks at the guy with the eye patch. "Sorry."

"Hey, maybe we could get a foursome together some time?" The guy with the eye patch says with a smile that reveals several missing teeth.

"Absolutely. Just say the word. I'm in the book," Hub says as he sashays off with the free drinks.

"What book do you think he was referring to?" The guy with the patch turns to the Kodiak bear.

"I have no fucking idea"

Hub delivers the drinks, sloshing all the way to Ben and E.Z., who are watching Mayor Freddy give Blaze a tutorial on the finer points of billiards.

"Hey, the people here are really friendly," Hub says as he puts down the drinks. E.Z. is winking at a couple of girls across the way.

"Well, I sure hope so, because there is nothing like a little down home friendliness to cure what ails you," E.Z. leers, which is seldom appreciated and never returned.

"Have you noticed how many of them are related to Lee Trevino? Ben asks. "That's all I've heard, Lee Trevino this, Lee Trevino that! Lee Trevino! Who knew he was such an icon?"

"You can feel it when you drive," Hub says in Lee Trevino's voice.

Everyone looks puzzled. "It was back when he was doing tire commercials. I guess you had to be there. And have a television."

Suddenly, Mayor Freddy twirls around matador style at the pool table.

"What do you say we double or nothing the bet, my gringo golfing amigo?" Mayor Freddy spins on his heels like an ice skater at the Olympics. He faces what appears to be an impossible shot. The cue ball is tucked behind three stripes, creating a barrier to the two solids left on the table. A virtually impossible shot. Blaze can see it too.

"That looks like a pretty tough shot, your Honor. I don't think you could make that shot but once in a hundred years. The question is, could this be the time?"

"I'll even call it for you. Both balls, corner pockets. One time. What do you say? You already owe me a grand. What have you got to lose?" Those are always the words that get Blaze into trouble. What have you got to lose? When you've got nothing left to lose? He lost it all long ago.

"Sure. Double or nothing, you can't sink both those balls in a single shot. You bet, you're on Mr. Mayor!"

Everyone in the bar is now riveted to the pool table. Donna and Dan are shooting away as Mayor Freddy sizes up the shot.

The beads of sweat are forming on his brow, dropping onto the felt like rain drops from the sky. Everyone is hushed as he takes his position. He strokes the cue ball very low and jumps the ball over the three striped blockade and spins it into the first ball which rockets into the corner and then careens into the second ball which rolls in as though it had radar. The bar erupts with cheering and back slapping, and Blaze just looks at his table of cohorts and shrugs his shoulders. He's been in this position so many times, he wears it like an old shoe. In fact, by this point in the evening, he kind of looks like an old shoe.

"That was some kind of shot your honor. I can tell you've practiced that shot a time or two," Blaze says sheepishly.

"Maybe just a little."

"Very impressive." Blaze looks around the room and spies a small four-paned window at the far end of the bar, just past the dance floor.

"How about if you give us a chance to win some of our gringo green back, by doing something we've practiced a time or two as well?"

Everyone in the bar inches closer.

"What have you got in mind, amigo?"

"What do you think the odds are of each of the four of us hitting a little itty, bitty teeny tiny golf ball through that itsy bitsy teeny tiny window over there?" The bar crowd gasps at the audacity of the proposal.

"All four of you?" Mayor Freddy is giving it serious thought.

'All four of us?' Hub is freaking out. Such a public feat gives him shivers down his spine. Hub is more of a private practitioner of golf. Playing in front of people makes him nervous. Playing in front of this crowd, under these circumstances, is his worst nightmare.

"All four. One time. Double or nothing. You win, we owe you four grand, we win, we walk out of here free and clear. What do you say?"

"You are on Mr. Fancy Pants!" The crowd lets out a roar

not unlike what the Roman Coliseum must have sounded like just before the slaves were fed to the lions. The crowd goes into something akin to a gambling frenzy, with side bets galore. This kind of excitement hasn't been seen in these parts since Evel Knievel ran out of gas in his tour bus just at the edge of town. And that caused a near riot.

The players go to their clubs neatly lined up near the entrance.

"What are you going to use?" Ben asks first.

"I was thinking a 2-iron." E.Z. answers soundly strangely like Yul Brenner in *The Magnificent Seven.*

"No way. 3-iron. You need a little loft." Blaze answers matter-of- factly, like he does this all the time.

"God help us." Hub says, sweating bullets. "We're in a strange town, drinking with the Hell's Angels, gambling with the mayor and I'm supposed to hit a 3-iron through that microfuckingscopic window over there or we owe his honor four grand? How could this happen? We haven't even started this stupid game!"

"I'll go first," E.Z. says assuredly.

E.Z. steps up to the welcome mat they've placed on the bar floor to serve as the tee box. A drunken cowboy at the end of the bar opens the window, just in case they actually make a shot. E.Z. takes a couple of practice swings, eyes the window and steps confidently up to the ball. The crowd settles. You could hear a pin drop, just like on a golf course, such is the reflexive nature of hushed crowds around big golfing moments.

E.Z. takes the club back masterfully and nails it. The ball sails through the center of the window and the crowd goes crazy. Several kids scamper out of the bar to go find the amazing ball.

Blaze and the boys slap E.Z. on the back. "Nice shot."

"It's definitely a 3-iron." E.Z. says as he slams his club back into his bag.

Next up is Ben, who doesn't even take a practice swing. He simply steps up and hits the ball right through. Just another day at the office for the Zen master. People can't believe their eyes. These guys are pretty darned good.

Hub is next up and of course he is the weak link. He is a nervous wreck. His hands are shaking, his face is all sweaty and puffy from all the drinking. He started out the day with a barf bag and it has been all down hill lies ever since.

"Maybe you don't understand what I'm saying. Hitting a 3-iron is a nightmare for me. I've put more smiles on balls with a 3-iron than a hooker's convention at a Motel Six."

"Just keep your head down. Your arm straight. You can do it." Blaze is always an encouraging player, especially when there is four grand at stake. "Just smooth it out there."

"Envision it in your mind," Ben offers stoically. "And it will happen."

Hub steps up to his ball. His hands are obviously trembling and Mayor Freddy cracks a smile, knowing this is his chance to prevail. Hub takes a practice, then digs in and the world pauses for just a moment. He takes the club head back slowly and with a glint of determination in his eye we haven't seen before. He hits the ball with a ferocious swing, topping it badly, putting a savage smile in its dimpled surface as it loops in a high arc through the rafters towards the window. By some miracle, it hits the bottom of the window casing and jumps through. Everyone in the place goes mad. Even Mayor Freddy has to grin.

"That was easy enough! No problema! Si se puede!" Hub is ecstatic.

Now it is Blaze's turn. It all comes down to this. The pressure is on, as it always is in golf. Each shot presents an opportunity for success or failure in equal measures. Pain or pleasure. It all emanates from the same place, at the top of the backswing. At that moment there are still unfolding possibilities, but at impact everything is written, destinies set and courses of action determined. There is a fine line between perfection and disaster, and Blaze knows all the detours and exits. And when you think of yourself as a failure, especially at the top of your backswing, your chances for success go down dramatically. The thing about golf, even if you know you are a fuck up, you've got to be able to put it out of your mind, for a moment at least. This is done by many methods and techniques, called going numb, settling down, staying positive, visualizing the outcome you desire, all in an effort to quiet the restless and wandering mind, so full of self-doubt and ridicule.

All these ideas are rustling through Blaze's mind, like leafs in front of a leaf blower, as he puts his ball down on the welcome mat. He swallows hard and clenches his teeth as he looks towards the window. It may as well be a hundred miles away. Whether it is the effects of the agave plant, the pressure, the crowd or the bowl full of nachos, Blaze feels more than a bit woozy. He steadies himself with his 3-iron, wipes the sweat from his brow and addresses his ball.

"Come on buddy, you can do it," Hub offers as he can sense Blaze is struggling.

"Don't blow it now pal. This was your big fat idea." E.Z. shows no mercy and it is not helpful.

Blaze licks his lips, narrows his eyes and sets himself. Donna Dina and Dan Flavin are on the edge of their seats. Everyone knows this is a big shot and they are absolutely still and silent, kind of like the occupants of a Madame Tussaud's museum if it were set in a Davy Crockett frontier bar.

Even Mayor Freddy is breaking into a sweat, and politicians rarely sweat, unless there is an indictment involved.

Just as Blaze is about to start his backswing, one of the Hell's Angels lights a match that sounds in the hushed silence like a jet engine revving up on the tarmac. Everyone turns on him with glaring eyes and he quickly realizes his mistake and extinguishes the match with a quick breath. He smiles sheepishly and mouths the word, "Sorry."

Blaze resets, looks at the window again, caresses the club, looks down at the ball sitting perfectly on the rough mat and he goes for it. He hits the ball dead solid perfect, producing a clicking sound at impact which may be one of the most beautiful sounds in the world, comparable to the swish sound of a basketball finding only net. All eyes are on the ball as it sails, as if in slow motion, methodically rotating and spinning on its way towards the window. Just as it is about to pass through, the window curtain catches a slight breeze and blows into the path of the ball. The ball gets tangled in the gauzy firmament and drops to the window's ledge, where it teeters and spins as if in a magical vacuum. Suddenly, one of its dimples catches an edge and the ball flies to the siding and spins out the window, falling to the ground and into the waiting hands of anxious children. The crowd goes crazy, hands clapping at the miracle of it. Blaze sighs a big sigh of relief.

"Wow! That was almost curtains!" Blaze breaks into a big grin.

Mayor Freddy shakes his hand in congratulations. "You must be blessed. I didn't think you could do it, but you did. Drinks are on me!"

The kids come in from outside, carrying the four miracle balls. They hand them to each player, with a large Sharpie pen, and the players sign them and then they give them all to Mayor Freddy, who hoists his glass in a toast.

"We will save your balls in a special glass case behind the bar. There they will reside, in a place of honor. Forever known as the Miracle Balls of Mayor Freddy Fender's Brother's Frontier Bar. They will be honored as religious icons, as this had to have been a miracle we have all witnessed this day."

This is the stuff of legends. Legendary hangovers that is. Everyone downs their shot and as the foursome looks on, the entire roomful of people makes the sign of the cross in the Miracle Balls direction.

The night sky is sprinkled with twinkling stars, glittering like bright diamonds on black velvet. A rundown motor court motel sports a flickering red neon sign announcing the vacancy at the

Atomic Motel. Mayor Freddy leads the fearless foursome and their golf clubs to one of the rooms. He fumbles with the key attached to one of those plastic disks that lets you know if you drive off with the key, just drop it in a mailbox and it will be returned no postage required.

"Sshh! I think this is it," Mayor Freddy whispers, slightly slurring his sshhing.

"You mean, we have to all share a room?" Blaze asks incredulously.

"Welcome to my sister's place!" Mayor Freddy opens the door to reveal the 1950s, replete with chintz bedspreads, black velvet paintings screw mounted into the walls, Magic Fingers coin operators next to the two double beds, cigarette burn marks in all the appropriate places on the furniture, and a smell somewhere between death and stale socks.

"Wow. If this is the Best Western, I'd hate to see the Worst Western." Hub remarks, as he steps inside.

"Kind of Early American Radioactive," Blaze offers.

"Oh stop your complaining. This is just like being on the tour. Think of it as paying your dues." E.Z. is a tough cookie and a real touring pro who knows whereof he speaks.

"Speaking of paying. It'll be $60 for the night." Mayor Freddy holds out his hand.

Blaze pays him. "You've got a real corner on the market, don't you Mr. Mayor?"

"Is there a corner on the market? I'm starved." Hub rubs his stomach.

"Yeah, his cousin owns it," E.Z. sneers.

"That's true. But he is closed. There are some vending machines outside. But please keep it down. These are working people here."

Just then a bottle smashes against the wall and we can hear shattering glass and loud voices.

"You know what they say, the early bird gets the worm." Mayor

Freddy shrugs his shoulders, takes his money and says good night to the golfers.

"Welcome to the Land of Enchantment. I think you must be the craziest golfers I've ever met. The desert is going to eat you alive. Welcome to the beginning of your end. Vaya con dios mis amigos!" And with that Mayor Freddy is off into the night like Zorro in a blender.

---

Several packages of Fritos are open on the bedspread, as the four guys let down their hair and start that unique phenomenon known as male bonding. They sit around in their underwear and tube socks, drinking some beer and munching, filling in the blanks in the multiple choice telling of their stories. There is something uniquely leveling as a group of strange men sit around shooting the shit in their dingy grey briefs. Let's just call it a letting down of their guard. There may even be some shrinkage involved.

"So when did the golf bug bite you Blaze?" Hub asks between mouthfuls of corn chips.

"Oh hell, I was just a kid," Blaze says as he takes a long slug on a Dos Equis. He gets a glazed look in his eyes and we are no longer in the Atomic Motel room, we are back in Blaze's youth and he is just a 10 year- old scrawny kid with a crew cut, high top sneakers and sneaking a cigarette.

"My mom used to drop me off at the golf course." We see the Cadillac pulling away as he lights up. "She'd go home and ball some guys brains out. It used to work out pretty nice." We see Blaze's mother, as a beautiful young woman, escorting a man into her room and closing the door.

We see a young Blaze caddying on the course. "Then I started caddying to earn beer and cigarette money. I guess I've been screwing around a golf course ever since." We see Blaze as a teenager with his pants around his ankles and a girl in a Catholic school outfit making it in a sand trap. "I've had a few chances to make something out of golf," Blaze trails off. We see his three putts at the state amateur. "But basically I still just earn beer and cigarette money."

"How about you? How'd the golf bug bite you Hub?"

"Me?" Hub gets all glossy-eyed and we are in his childhood memory.

"I got a job first as a pin setter in a bowling alley." We see a cherubic but still plump Hub as a 10 year-old kid, setting the pins in an old-fashioned bowling alley. "But guys from the high school used to wait until you were down then they'd roll two or three balls down the alley." We see Hub scramble out of the way and big guys in Levis and wife beater t-shirts laughing at him.

"So, I switched to golf. I figured the balls were smaller." We see a young Hub driving in one of those caged tractors picking up golf balls on the driving range. "Got a job on the driving range. Unfortunately, the same guys followed me over there." The same guys bombard the caged tractor with dozens of golf shots and laugh as Hub is pelted.

"But now, I serve them all drinks," Hub says as we see him pouring extra booze into all the drinks. "And it works out pretty good for everybody." We see the bar patrons, the same guys from high school now with their older wives, sound asleep in their clothes in their bedrooms with the TV on the shopping channel.

"Not me!" E.Z. says emphatically. "It wasn't exactly the country club environment for me. It was more like the school of hard knocks." His eyes glaze over and we see him as a 10 year-old boy lying on his back on his parent's living room carpet. "I mean, Gyll was bad enough, but he was nothing compared to my old man. He was a real prick." We see Mr. Harbinger sloshing his scotch and fondling strange women.

"He used to hit Wiffle ball wedge shots off our noses at cocktail parties." We see a young E.Z. with a Wiffle ball on his nose as his drunk dad takes a massive swing. "Everybody thought it was real funny. Except Gyll and me. But Daddy always had a pretty good short game, so we learned to be tough little soldiers. But to this day, I can't stand to look at a Wiffle ball. They give me the heebie jeebies."

"How about you Ben? How'd you get into the game?" Hub asks.

"It was long ago, in a far away place." Ben gets all misty eyed as he remembers. "My grandfather always loved miniature golf, so he used to take the whole family." We see Ben as a tiny boy, with his entire family dressed in traditional Japanese clothing, lined up on the first hole of a miniature golf course. Young Ben bows to his elders and makes a great putt through a rotating windmill. His grandfather smiles. "He taught me to see the deeper meaning in things. To see the ridiculous and the sublime. Once I learned there was more to golf than putting through King Kong's legs, I was hooked."

Back in the reality of the Atomic Motel, the Fritos have been banditoed, the beers drained and the foursome is exhausted.

"As much fun as this has been," Blaze yawns. "We've got to get up pretty early and I hate it when I look all puffy for the cameras."

"Yeah, we've got 40 days of this," E.Z. says as he crawls under the covers.

Blaze turns to his bed mate Hub. "You don't snore do you?"

"Not that I'm aware of."

Lights are out. It is the dead of the night. Hub snores like a freight train at full throttle. Blaze tries to roll over and pull the pillow over his head, to no avail. The runaway train has left the station and the caboose is on the loose.

---

A lonely traffic signal blinks red over a lonely intersection at the outskirts of Shiprock, where a small, ragtag collection of the idle curious are gathered to witness the tee off for our motley foursome, more than a tad hung-over from the previous evening's libations. Mayor Freddy is there, as are Donna and Dan, shooting footage along with several other nationality's TV crews. Boris and Ludmilla are also there, wearing aviator sunglasses, their signature tomato sauce-colored blazers and standing beside a bright yellow dune buggy emblazoned with the RAGU logo. Standing, erect and perfect, they look a bit like the plastic couple found atop a wedding cake, except for the blazers. No one in their right mind would be caught dead wearing one of those blazers unless they absolutely had to.

There is also the welcome wagon, an old Conestoga with a team of horses and driven by an old grizzled runt of a man that we saw earlier at the airport.

Mayor Freddy steps up to a podium situated at the center of the intersection. He speaks into the microphone, which squeals feedback, as all microphones do in these kinds of situations.

"Welcome!"

"Here we go again," Blaze says under his breath.

"We are here today to witness history in the making."

"I thought we saw that last night," Hub whispers.

"But first, I'd like to introduce my sister-in-law Mabel Fender to sing the Star-Spangled Banner."

Donna looks at Dan, rolling her eyes. She checks her watch.

A very large woman steps up to the microphone. She clears her throat. *"Jose can you see, by the dawn's early light, what so proudly we hail'd at the twilight's last gleaming."* She clears her throat again, like she's got a chicken bone lodged in there somewhere. "I'm sorry. Where was I?"

*"Whose broad stripes and bright stars,"* Mayor Freddy whispers under his breath.

"Thank you. *Whose broad stripes and bright stars,"* she clears her throat again, like she swallowed a gnat. "I'm sorry."

*"Through the perilous fight,"* Mayor Freddy coaxes.

By now his sister-in-law is tearing up and hacking like a two pack-a- day smoker. She squeezes the words out between inhalations. *"Through, the, perilous, fight."*

*"O'er the ramparts we watched,"*

*"O'er, the, ramparts…, we watched,"*

"I don't think she's going to make it," Blaze says under his breath.

"I've got 20 bucks, says she gets through it," E.Z. whispers.

*"Were so gallantly streaming."*

*"Were, so, gallantly…, screaming."* By now she is practically choking to death.

*"Streaming, not screaming,"* Mayor Freddy is turning bright red, like the rocket's red glare.

*"Okay, streaming!"* By now she has totally lost the thread of the melody. She stops coughing and starts to cry, big sobbing whelps of tears.

"I think we all know how the song ends, with the red rockets and the bombs bursting and sure enough the flag's still there. Thank you Mabel, for that inspiring rendition, and perhaps you should see a doctor for that cough."

"You owe me 20." Blaze says with a wink.

"I would now like to introduce my nieces to sing a few traditional folk ballads."

"Now wait just a minute, your honor. We're on a bit of a time schedule here. We'd like to get to the golf game." Donna is running out of patience and Dan is running out of tape.

"But they've been practicing all night."

"Look your honor, we're not exactly *American Idol* here."

The kids are all dressed up and look very disappointed.

"Well, then, let me at least introduce my father, the priest to offer a prayer."

The small crowd groans.

"Come on people. The old guy's a priest for heaven's sake," Hub says. "We might need a little spiritual guidance before this is through." Who knew Hub was such a facilitator? Then a thought occurs to him. "How'd your father become a priest? I thought priests never married?"

"He was a slow learner. He became a priest after the 12 children were born. And our dear mother, bless her soul, departed."

"Oh, I'm sorry."

"Don't be. She departed for Las Vegas and never looked back. Who could blame her?" Mayor Freddy shrugs.

His father, the priest, steps to the podium with great effort.

"Dear God, please watch over these poor sonsabitches. They got to be crazy in the head to do what they are doing. Please bless all of us crazy people. We know not what we do. But somehow we do it anyway. Give these men strength in their shafts, length in their putts and the courage of their evictions. And make sure they wear their sunscreen, cause that old sun can be pretty serious in these parts. And make sure they floss. Flossing is terribly important for good dental hygiene. Never underestimate the power of flossing. I guess that's all for now God. Amen"

And with that inauspicious prayer, the game is on. Ben steps up to the welcome mat that came from the bar to tee up his ball. As usual, with no practice swing he nails a perfect drive sending it straight down the street.

"That's my partner!" E.Z. enthuses.

Next up is Blaze who also works quickly. He eyes the horizon, sets and hits a huge drive that screams down the highway like a banshee on a rampage.

"Sweet!" Hub shouts.

Next up is E.Z., who swaggers up to the tee box. "Are all those cameras rolling, cause I'm going to cream this one." Sure enough, he rips a giant shot which rolls just past Blaze's amazing drive. "Put that in your pipe and smoke it."

Finally, it is Hub's turn and as usual, he's nervous hitting in front of a crowd, even one as ragtag as this. He steps up to the mat, places his ball down. "I'm playing a Titlest 2." He sets and swings and the ball slices badly, hitting the side of a building first, ricocheting past the onlookers, off a park bench, off a fire hydrant, off the stop light and lands back at his feet.

"I've always been a slow starter." Hub winces and hurriedly swings again, this time sending the ball down the road and into someone's backyard. Boris and Ludmilla look at each other, jump into the dune buggy and are off after Hub's shot.

Donna Dina is doing her stand up. "And so, the Greatest Golf Game Ever Played in the Wild, begins. We'll be following this unlikely foursome, by land, sea and air as they play their marathon match. I'm Donna Dina with the Wild World of Sports, reporting live from Shipwreck, make that Shiprock, New Mexico."

Blaze, Hub, Ben and E.Z. look around a bit bewildered. Are they supposed to carry their clubs? Are there caddies? "How are we supposed to get around. With our clubs and all?" Blaze asks no one in particular. Funny how they hadn't thought of this before. This will be the first of many such realizations.

The old grizzled runt of a man steps forward. He looks like a cross between Old Father Time and Kris Kringle, with a little bit of Walter Brennan thrown in for good measure. He even has a limp.

"I guess that's where I come in." He reaches for the golf bags and starts loading them into the Conestoga wagon. "Name's Cookie. Gourmet chef to the stars, horse whisperer and wrangler extraordinaire, tamer of lions, lover of ladies, organizer of orgies, and all around jack of all trades. Hell, I'll even do your taxes if you need the help. Here at your service gentlemen." Cookie tips his mangled cowboy hat. "I say we get a move on, though boys. We got a long way to go before sundown and we're burning daylight."

And with that the foursome makes its way down the highway, with a Conestoga wagon carrying their hopes and dreams and leaving a sleepy Shiprock in their dust. Mayor Freddy and his assorted relatives all wave a sad farewell to the craziest golfers known to mankind. His nieces strike up the traditional ballads and begin to dance.

"That desert is going to eat them alive. Crazy sonsabitches." Mayor Freddy Fender actually sheds a tear, whether out of concern, nostalgia or not winning the bet. His father, the priest, makes the sign of the cross. "Bless all the crazy sonsabitches! And bless their balls!"

---

Hub's ball has landed in a fenced backyard, somewhere between the fully-loaded clothesline and a tethered goat with a bad temper. White billowy sheets whip in the breeze and the goat stomps the ground with his hoof at the intruding Titleist 2. Hub hops the fence as the entourage looks on.

"Nice goat. Nice little goaty," he says as he inches forward.

The goat snorts at the ground and kicks up plumes of dust.

"I think he likes you," Blaze intones.

"Go ahead, he won't hurt you." E.Z. is impatient.

"He does look like he's tied up," Ben offers.

"If you play from zere, zere vill be no penalty. If you move ze ball, there vill be penalty." Ludmilla lets it be known who is in charge of this rodeo.

"You guys cover my backside." Hub takes out a fairway wood.

The goat is getting mightily pissed. It charges at Hub, but the tethered rope stops him just short of his target. Hub tries to take a practice swing, but the goat comes at him again. It is impossible to get a shot out of here, so he reaches into his pocket and pulls out another golf ball and tosses it in the goat's direction. The goat pounces on the ball like a Jack Russell terrier after a fat rat in a cheese store. The goat sniffs the ball then delicately lifts it with its lips and swallows it whole. While the goat is distracted, Hub takes his swing and hits a beauty, especially under the circumstances. The ball sails towards the asphalt, on its way out of town, gets a huge bounce off the hard surface, what under normal circumstances would be "a cart path shot" and just rolls on forever down the highway. The goat turns to him and glares. A Titleist 2 isn't normally part of his diet. Now he's pissed and has a bad case of indigestion. He charges at Hub, one last time, and breaks his rope, just as Hub hops over the fence. The goat slams into the chain link fence, bouncing off it like a slingshot in reverse.

"I think he just wanted your autograph," Blaze jokes.

"Do you think he'll be okay?" Hub asks. "I didn't know what else to do." Hub is actually quite considerate of animal welfare, despite all his worst fears and nightmares.

"Ancient Chinese saying," Ben intones. "No matter, garbage in, garbage out. If you have a tethered goat in yard, you'll always have a garbage disposal and mowed lawn. Everything will come out in the end."

"That was a great shot, by the way." Blaze slaps Hub on the back.

The foursome walks down the highway, like the shooters from *High Noon.* Cookie and his Conestoga wagon, full of clanging pots and pans and jangling golf clubs, follows the foursome at a leisurely pace. Boris and Ludmilla roar past the group in their souped-up dune buggy, startling the horses.

"Whoa, Sheba! Get along now!" Cookie shouts to his lead horse.

"Damned road hogs!"

Twangy western music kicks in, and as our group of crazy golfers disappear into the horizon, a western band steps onto the highway, guitars strumming as they yodel up a storm, to the melody of *Gilligan's Island.*

> *"So this is where our story starts,*
> *where the rubber meets the road.*
> *This crazy game of golf begins,*
> *Can these mothers carry the load?*
> *Can these mothers carry the load?*
> *Four strange guys, 400 miles*
> *Through the briars and the brush,*
> *These guys could choke, or drown or die*
> *From eating Cookie's mush.*
> *From eating Cookie's mush.*

*Golf is such an obsessive game,*
*you may as well be on crack cocaine.*
*You'll spend all your hard earned money,*
*just trying to stay sane.*
*Just trying to live down the shame.*
*So when the going starts to get tough,*
*and your buried deep, deep in the rough,*
*just remember to use up all your stupid luck*
*Cause, you never know when things can go to hell.*
*When things can go to hell."*

# CHAPTER 4

### "IF GOLF IS A GAME OF INCHES, THEN LIFE IS A GAME OF FEET. AND IF LIFE IS A JUST A BOWL OF CHERRIES, THEN GOLF MUST BE THE PITS."

BLAZE EXAMINES HIS BALL which is deeply embedded in a towering saguaro cactus, about 4 feet off the ground. The cactus drips and oozes from the wound. The ball is surrounded by spines and tentacles, just daring someone to stick their hand in to retrieve it. Boris and Ludmilla inspect the ball and refer to their rule book, which is about the size of the King James Bible, but with smaller type. They aren't finding too many saguaro cactus rulings.

"I am not finding any of ze references for balls in ze cactus," Boris says, thumbing through the book.

"It is clearly suspended in ze natural object. If he can play ze ball, zere vould be no penalty. If, on ze other hand, he must remove der ball, zen two stroke penalty must ensue." Ludmilla really knows her way around ze rules.

"I'm going to try to play ze ball, I mean, the ball. We've been around you for five hours and I'm starting to talk like you." Blaze pulls out a sand wedge.

"I'll just try my trusty old cactus wedge. I mean, what do you use to hit out of a towering succulent?" Blaze hits the ball and it smushes out of the cactus. A large chunk of the cactus goes flying with the ball. The cactus divot lands with a thud about 20 feet away. The ball however sails about a mile down a canyon. Everybody applauds at the shot. Blaze walks to the chunk of cactus, picks it up with his club head and returns it, just like replacing his divot.

"I like to think of it as good golf karma," he says as he tries to replace the missing piece, without hurting himself.

All of the player's shots are down in the canyon, near the dry stream bed. Cookie and the team of horses make their way slowly through the rocks. Boris and Ludmilla wait up ahead at E.Z.'s shot. With their bright yellow dune buggy, aviator glasses and official tomato sauce-colored blazers, they look like aliens from another planet. A planet where bad taste reigns supreme.

"What do you figure their story is?" Blaze asks his partner Hub, pointing towards the KGB couple, as the foursome stroll to their balls. This is the time when golf means so much to the participants, the strolling conversation between the shots. For many players this is the best part of the game, the socializing part. Many golfers could actually care less about the finer points of the game. They just want to get away from their wives and kids, from mowing the lawn, running errands, doing the normal things that count as life. They just want to smoke a big fat old stogie, have a couple of beers, stroll around a lovely green velvety surface and shoot the shit with their buddies. Who cares how many strokes it takes?

"I don't know. They sound Russian or German. Or Slavic. Some kind of Slavic thing," Hub answers.

"They appear to be a couple," Ben chimes in.

"Yeah, a couple of Slavic nuts," E.Z. chortles. "I mean, who wears blazers all the way out here and in this heat?"

"I'd say they've got their neckties on a little tight," Blaze says.

"It could be a long slog, with the two of them looking over our shoulders." Just as Hub says the words, suddenly a helicopter swoops in over the ridge, getting beauty shots of the landscape and the tiny foursome practically swallowed up by the sheer immensity of the desert. They are but specks of dust in a vast universe.

Inside the helicopter sit Donna Dina and Dan Flavin, who is hanging off the side of the copter, getting some great aerial footage. The pilot dives and banks as Donna holds her hand over her mouth and shuts her eyes.

The copter zooms over the heads of the four golfers as they make their way through the dry stream bed. They wave and laugh and swing their clubs over their heads, like some sort of remote tribe discovered in the jungle. But there is something iconic and ironic in the image of four golfers playing through the immense wilderness with nary a blade of grass to be found for hundreds of miles.

The campfire sends sparks into the night like a box of bottle rockets at a Boy Scout jamboree. The foursome sit around the campfire, swapping stories and shots of whiskey. Cookie cleans up the dishes from dinner. Boris and Ludmilla enter the campfire circle dressed for bed in matching flannel pajamas made up of little hammer and sickle symbols.

"Ve are going to retire early. Ve vant to be fresh for tomorrow. Thank you Mr. Cookie for a vonderful dinner. You know, ze sun comes up pretty early in zees parts. You've got a lot of golf to play tomorrow gentlemen," Ludmilla says.

"Ve vill be in ze pup tent nearby, if you need us," Boris says.

"I've just got one question for you guys," Blaze says with a wink.

"Where on earth did you get those pajamas?"

"These are special issue direct from ze Kremlin. Ve got them ven ve vorked for ze KGB. You've heard of KGB?" Ludmilla purrs like a kitten.

"Oh, yes, of course," Hub offers. "Something like the FBI, CIA, IRS and the Mafia all rolled into one."

"Yes. It vas like von stop shopping for ze spooks."

"So what did you do for them?" Hub asks.

"Ve vorked mostly on counterintelligence. Ve spied on ze spies. Ve vere very good at vhat ve did." Ludmilla looks like she must be very good at many things.

"Why did you stop? How'd you get over here?"

"Ze spies ve vatched eventually took over. Ve needed to get out of Dodge in ze hurry. And voila! Here ve are." Ludmilla laughs girlishly.

"How'd you get into golf?" Even E.Z. is curious.

"It vas something like ze vitness protection program for ze international spies. Golf vas ze perfect ting for us. And vorking with ze Mr. Post, is actually a lot like vorking vith KGB. Both are totalitarian regimes run by ruthless bureaucrats who don't have clue!" Boris stifles a grin. "Our pup tent beckons, gentlemen ve bid you adieu."

The KGB couple, in their hammer and sickle pajamas, shuffle off into the darkness towards their tent. The foursome sits around the campfire, staring up at the night sky, just taking it all in. The fire crackles and glows, sending flickering shadows to dance into the night.

"Wow. The KGB. That's an interesting couple," Hub says.

"Yeah, who knew spies could be so, so attractive?" Blaze adds.

"Just gives me one more reason not to like them. Stuck out here in the middle of nowhere with a couple of Commie pinkos riding roughshod over our game. Ruling body, my ass," E.Z. complains.

"Oh, quit your bellyaching. She's not too hard on the eyes," Cookie says as he towels off the dishes.

"Yeah, she could rule my body," Hub offers.

"But he drives like a bat out of hell," Cookie says as he dunks another dirty dish. "He keeps driving that newfangled buggy like he does and she's going to bust a gut."

"Would you look at all those stars. I don't think I've ever seen so many stars in the sky," Blaze says staring up.

"Yeah, they look like little white golf balls, twinkling in the night," Hub says as he rubs his sore feet. A shooting star streaks across the horizon, momentarily lighting up the entire sky, like some kind of omen or sign.

"Did you see that? Oh my God! That was a shooting star!" Hub yells.

"Yeah, that was really something. I don't think I've ever seen that before," Blaze says scratching his head in amazement.

"Incredible!" Ben adds, staring into the night.

"I sure wouldn't want to be where it landed," E.Z. says looking over his shoulder with more than a little paranoia.

"They usually burn up when they hit the atmosphere. They're not really stars, they're meteors. Space matter. Like boulders and ice chunks floating in space. Some of them are the size of a whole city block." Cookie knows about a lot of stuff, some of it is useful and some of it is not.

"Yeah, well whatever they are, I wouldn't want to be under one."

"You got that right," Hub says. "They say that's what killed off the dinosaurs. One big meteor hit, a huge dust cloud and they starved to death." Hub hates the idea of starving.

"Aren't we supposed to make a wish or something? When you see a falling star? For luck?" Blaze asks.

"Yeah, we could probably use it," Hub says. "I'm going to wish that my golf shoes get broken in. The guy in the store warned me, but I didn't take it seriously. My dogs are killing me."

"I'm going to wish that we get famous and I make a lot of money and join the pro tour, and beat Tiger Woods at the Masters," E.Z. beams.

"I think that was about four wishes," Blaze protests. "I think I'd wish for, I think I'd wish for true love. Because if you've got that you can survive pretty much anything." Who knew Blaze was such a romantic?

"I would wish for good health and lots of hot sake, served by a beautiful geisha," Ben says.

"How about you Cookie? What would you wish for?" Blaze asks.

"Oh hell, I don't know. I'm too old and tired to ask for much. But if I had to, I'd wish for another shot of that Jack Daniels, cause I know that is something that just might come true."

Blaze passes the bottle over to Cookie, who pours another shot into his metal cup.

"So tell us Cookie, what's your story?" Blaze asks.

"Oh hell, not much to tell I guess. I was born in a brothel, raised in a bar, went to school in a one-room schoolhouse, ran away to join the circus, the army, the rodeo. Pretty much in that order. Never got married, always got along better with horses and dogs. Traveled all around the world, twice. I've been shot at, punched more times than I care to remember, chased by headhunting pygmies, nearly froze to death once in Alaska. Been hunted by a bear, attacked by a herd of water buffalo, stepped on by an elephant. That was not a pretty picture. Shook hands once with the Dali Lama, and told him a couple of off-color jokes. He laughed so hard at I thought he was going to pee in his toga. I've crashed more cars, boats and airplanes than your average Joe. That's why I'm partial to traveling by Conestoga. I call it living on Conestoga time. Like I said, really not much to tell about. Just an old cow puncher. Pretty normal life. Except, of course, for that time at Alcatraz, but that'll have to wait for another time, cause those Commies are right about one thing, the sun does come up pretty early in these parts and we do have some miles to travel before we get to Coloradi."

The foursome seems mesmerized by equal parts of Jack Daniels and Cookie's story. And so they should. He's one heck of a talker. How much of it is true may be another matter. The foursome crawls into the sleeping bags around the campfire and snuggle down for the night. Truth to be told, they are all a little afraid of the dark.

In Blaze's nighttime dream, he is in an open field of enormous sunflowers. The sunflowers turn their heads toward him as though they are alive sentient beings. He smiles at them and they smile back. From across the field he spots a beautiful, buxom blonde woman, who might be an Amazon or maybe Wonder Woman. He can't quite tell, because, after all, he is in a dream. Wonder Woman waves at him from across the field. She's even wearing her jeweled tiara. He smiles and waves back. The sunflowers nod their heads in approval. And then Wonder Woman, in wonderful slow motion, starts to run through the fields towards Blaze. And Blaze knows this is the part where he starts to run towards her too. They are both running and smiling and waving, and the sunflowers start to sing their favorite sunflower song, Blaze and Wonder Woman are getting closer and closer and just as they are about to touch, Blaze realizes he has run too far and finds himself running over the edge of a cliff. He looks like Wiley Coyote in the *Roadrunner* cartoons. He starts to fall, floating through the air, with the sounds of the sunflowers receding into the background, supplanted by the sound of the wind whistling through his falling body. Just before Blaze hits the ground, he wakes with a start, sits up in his sleeping bag, pokes at the embers in the campfire, rolls over and tries to go back to sleep.

In Hub's dream, he is back in the golf store, trying to return his golf shoes. Except the store salesman is now a Nazi, dressed in a swastika adorned uniform. He is nodding his head back and forth in the negative, indicating he won't take the shoes back. Hub is pleading with him, showing off his blistered feet, and trying to push the shoes forward towards him. The Nazi salesman is having none of it, when he pulls a Lugar pistol from his bandolier and aims it at Hub, who smiles sheepishly and pulls the shoes back. Then the gun goes off and Hub ducks as the bullet passes by his head. He runs away from the salesman, who begins to chase him. Hub makes his way to the gun department with all the stuffed animals. He reaches for a rifle off the rack, finds a box of bullets and frantically loads the gun, as sirens and searchlights scan the sports store for the escapee. He is literally sweating bullets when the Nazi fiend finds him cowering behind the counter. They point their guns at each other and fire. Just as the guns go off, Hub is startled awake by the popping wood in the campfire. He looks around the camp, doesn't see the Nazi salesman, rolls over and tries to go back to sleep.

In E.Z.'s dream, he is walking up the 18th fairway at the U.S. Masters tournament, with hoards of crowds cheering him on. He waves his cap to the adoring masses and realizes he is strolling up the fairway with Tiger Woods, who also waves and smiles at the applauding crowd.

"This is what it feels like to be a winner," a smiling Tiger says. "You want to be a winner, don't you?"

E.Z. can't answer. He tries to open his mouth, but the words won't come out.

"Everybody loves a winner," Tiger says as he waves to the crowd.

"And nobody likes a loser," a strange voice from behind the players says. E.Z. turns around to discover the voice is actually his brother Gyll, who is caddying for him.

"That's right," Tiger purrs. "Nobody likes a loser." Tiger Woods smiles his patented white-teethed, wall-to-wall smile.

E.Z. whimpers in his sleep like a distressed little puppy dog.

In Ben Ichi's dreamscape, he is floating in a pool of lotus blossoms. He has a long pony tail pulled back tightly in a bun. He looks like a Samurai master. Giddy laughter comes from behind an ornate Oriental screen. Suddenly, a bevy of exquisite geishas, take their tiny footsteps towards Ben carrying trays of hot steaming sake. Their giggles float up into the air, like the steam rising from the sake cups. And then a large black snake slithers through the water and lotus blossoms. The geishas suddenly stop in their tracks. Ben doesn't understand why, as he hasn't noticed the snake. The snake gets closer to him and then the geishas drop their trays of hot sake and run screaming away from the pool. Ben turns to see what it is that has frightened them and comes face to face, only inches apart, with the black mamba. He freezes as he notices every detail of the snake's scaly face. And then the snake smiles at him and he freaks out. Ben jumps up from the campfire, flailing away at the imaginary snake. Making quite a commotion in the process, he awakens Cookie, who is sleeping in the back of the Conestoga. Cookie raises his head, looks toward the campfire and sees the dancing Ben Ichi, swatting at the snake that isn't there.

"First night out under the stars and this bunch of tenderfoots is already falling apart at the seams. They just don't make fellers the way they used to," Cookie says to himself and his horses. He rolls over and goes back to sleep. The moon slowly rises over the horizon, like a giant golf ball hanging on the rim of the cup.

The clanging of the metal triangle with a branding iron announces morning breakfast, as Cookie lays out coffee, danish, fresh fruit, grilled bacon and sausage, scrambled eggs and French toast. How he manages all this out of the back of the Conestoga is something of a mystery. But that is why they call him Cookie.

"Rise and shine, ladies," Cookie shouts out . "We've gotta get a move on. Those mountains aren't getting any closer."

The foursome rustles out of the sleeping bags, a little worse for wear, given the hard alcohol and the hard ground from the night before. Nothing aches more than a body who has slept on the cold, hard bedrock of the desert. The heat of the day held in the rocks is released through the night until you may as well be a cold bloody corpse, with a twisted spine, a crooked neck and a sore gladius maximus. Add a headache and hangover to the mix and you've pretty well got the picture of one motley crew. And now they have to play golf through the desert in what may as well be compared to the Trail of Tears, or The Bataan Death March- no offense to the bearers of those burdens.

Blaze stumbles to the edge of a cliff to relieve himself as the sun is cracking the horizon. He stands in the bright light of day, doing the time honored ritual unique to men: taking a pee in a bush. With the cascading flow illuminated by the sun's rays, it is almost a thing of beauty, if taking a leak could be described in such terms. It is as though a drop of dew could illuminate the entire universe.

Suddenly a whirling sound is heard, a loud thumping of the air and up over the edge of the cliff comes a whirlybird carrying Donna Dina and Dan Flavin hanging out the door of the copter, shooting video of Blaze in what can only be described as a compromised position. Donna Dina is doing a live shot for *Good Morning America*.

"And so, the greatest golf game ever played begins the day anew, as the intrepid golfers will be making their way due north towards the Rocky Mountains. We'll be bringing you up to date on their progress through the course of the day. I'm Donna Dina and I think I'm going to be ill. Back to you in the studio."

Blaze stands there at the cliff edge trying his hardest to finish quickly.

Dan Flavin tries to pan off the embarrassing spectacle but the damage is done. All of America is waking up to their cups of coffee, bacon and eggs watching a man taking a leak on national television.

The helicopter banks off as Blaze zips up and gives them the middle fingered salute. "Damned reporters! I think I just took a leak on national TV."

Hub joins him at the cliff's edge. "I wouldn't worry about it. It's so small, I don't think most people would notice. The TV, I mean."

"Yeah, thanks for that. I just wish they'd leave us alone and let us just play the damned game."

E.Z. and Ben join the party.

"Not me," E.Z. says. "I love the exposure."

"Exposure like that I could live without." Blaze rubs his head with his hands.

"What's the matter? Feeling a little hung-over this morning?" Ben Ichi asks.

"I've got a little headache is all."

"That's the problem with a headache. It usually follows you around. Usually." Ben smiles.

"You need a little hair of the dog that bit you. Bloody Marys always work for me." Hub offers. "Or screwdrivers, Ramos fizzes, mimosas, or tequila sunrises in a pinch."

"We've just got 10 or 12 miles of golf to play today," E.Z. says.

"Should be no problem," Blaze says. "I just wish they hadn't filmed me taking a whiz. Come on, let's rustle up some breakfast and I'm ordering a round of Bloody Marys for everybody. Since we're out here, we may as well enjoy ourselves. I say we live it up. Forty days of a paid golfing vacation. Let the drinking begin!"

---

The foursome tee off the edge of the cliff and into a vast desert, that closely resembles the surface of the moon. Nothing lives out here but scorpions and ants, and both have to dig down deep into the earth to avoid the heat of the day. The sun has beaten down on this desert for millenniums. The heat shimmers on the horizon as the foursome make its way, shot after shot, across the great expanse. Cookie's Conestoga wagon trails the foursome, and Boris and Ludmilla roar around in their yellow dune buggy, running and gunning between the shots and the players. It is like a scene out of a Fellini film or *A Clockwork Orange* meets *Rawhide*, but with golf clubs. The surreal nature of the landscape is juxtaposed by the bizarre idea of playing golf through the wilderness. And yet, somehow they are doing it. And doing it well. Most of the shots are fairway woods, getting maximum loft and distance. And the balls sail through the pristine air like rockets at launch and then bury themselves on landing in the fine mica sand.

Everything is going smashingly well until the foursome meets up with the tumbleweeds. At the edge of this great expanse of desert stands a veritable minefield of tumbleweeds that have gathered together by force of wind and a lack of resistance. The tumbleweeds, some the size of a Volkswagen Bug, form a carpet over the last of the desert floor, like a moat preventing entry to the snow-capped mountains that loom in the far distance.

"Well, what do you suppose we do now? This looks impenetrable," Blaze says. "I say we take a break, mix some more drinks and think about this one."

"Is this the only way through, Cookie?" Ben asks.

"Afraid so fellers. We gotta get on the other side of this ornery mess. And I can tell you from experience you don't want to be messing with no tumbleweeds. They got little thorns that if they get into your socks you're a dead man out here. Or at least a barefoot one."

"What does the RAGU committee think? Have you got anything in the rules about tumbleweeds?" Hub asks gently, already knowing the answer.

"Ve have reviewed all ze rules and no zer is no tumbleweed section. Ze two options are play through ze tumbleweeds and suffer many lost ball penalties and many tiny scratches or play around ze tumbleweeds, which could take long time. Choice is yours," Boris announces and Ludmilla shakes her head and chest in agreement.

"Well, my feet hurt already. I don't want to chance more foot problems. I say we play around," Hub says.

"Wait a minute, fellers," Cookie says as he scratches his beard. "When I was a sailor on the high seas, we used to have a little superstition about whistling up a storm. Nobody but the captain was allowed to whistle on board for fear of whistling up a storm."

Cookie looks towards the clouds massing overhead. "And from the looks of those cumulus clouds, we might want to start whistling right away."

The foursome all look at each other not quite knowing what to do.

"What do you want us to whistle?"

"How about the song *Drifting Along With the Tumblin' Tumbleweeds?*" Cookie answers. "I was always partial to that song."

The foursome puts their lips together and with Cookie's accompaniment starts to whistle the opening refrain from the cowboy classic. Even Boris and Ludmilla join in as the clouds thicken overhead. The horses shift nervously in their bridles, their nostrils flaring at the hint of rain or maybe all the bad whistling. And then a bolt of lightning strikes and the horses rear up on their hind legs. The thunder is deafening but still they all whistle, like Sir Alec Guinness and the prisoners of war in *The Bridge On the River Kwai*.

And then the winds start. Glorious gusts of invisible hands that begin to push on the wall of tumbleweeds. And just as the whistling reaches its crescendo, a small funnel cloud drops from the sky, tornadic activity known in the west as a dust devil. The dust devil cuts a path through the tumbleweeds, all while Cookie stands on the Conestoga's seat, watching in amazement, not unlike Charleston Heston in *The Ten Commandments* as Moses parts the Red Sea, or in this case the Yellow Sea of Tumbleweeds.

"Come on fellers, take your shots quickly now, cause this thing could close up on us like a tumbleweed tsunami!" Cookie yells over the gale.

The foursome tees up and hits almost simultaneously as the dust devil swirls around them, opening a path through the terrible tumbleweeds, which almost come to life in the tornado. They groan and snap and crackle, like a bunch of ornery people in an old folks home forced to move from their rockers. The foursome literally plays through the swath of the tornado, with the dune buggy and the Conestoga trailing behind, as the Gates of Hell swirl to each side, if the Gates of Hell could be conceived as whirling tumbleweeds.

And behind it all, hovers the helicopter, with an airsick Donna Dina and a filming Dan Flavin capturing what looks to the naked eye like a minor miracle.

"Are you getting all this?" Donna shouts out. "This is amazing!"

The helicopter pilot comes on the headset.

"This wind is getting too strong. We're out of here." Whereupon he turns the helicopter on a dime and heads off into sunnier skies, leaving behind our intrepid foursome, who succeeded beyond all expectations in whistling up a storm. Turns out Cookie is a lot more talented than he lets on.

---

Donna Dina is on a pay phone at the dirt airstrip that serves as a fueling station for the big oil and gas exploration outfits. The helicopter is refueling as she tries her best to reach the network offices in New York, as she pours quarters into the coin slot, like a gambler on a binge.

"Yes, Marge, it's me. Donna Dina. I'm calling from a pay phone because my friggin' cell phone doesn't work way out here. So I can't talk for long. Is Charlie available?"

"He's in makeup. He's got the bump coming up."

"Well, I'm telling you to tell him to check out the footage we've just sent back. It is amazing. I'm not religious, but it was like something out of the Bible, if they played golf in the Bible. I think Charlie will want to see it. He may want it for the evening broadcast."

"I'll let him know, dear. I saw your live spot this morning. It was disgusting, but I have to admit, it is all anyone is talking about around here. So keep it up. I knew a women's perspective would be interesting."

"Please deposit another 85 cents," the operator drones.

Donna hangs up the phone, straightens herself, checks herself out in her pocket mirror. She cleans the grit out of her teeth, puts on some lipstick and marches back to the coin-operated snack machine for lunch.

"Do you think they made Diane Sawyer do this kind of stuff?" She says to no one in particular, but she marches like a woman who knows she may be on to the story of her life. If she can just keep lunch down.

Shot glasses of whiskey are being liberally poured, indicating this is not the first round, as the foursome hoists their glasses to the clearing skies and sunnier dispositions.

"Here's to Cookie! A good man to be with in a tight spot!" Blaze raise his glass.

"That sounds so gay," E.Z. sneers. Ben Ichi just winces.

"You know what I mean. He saved our bacon out there."

"Well, I'll admit it was kind of strange. The way that storm whipped up."

"Listen fellars, I don't mean to break up the party, but we've still got some daylight left and I wouldn't mind if we pushed a little further," Cookie suggests.

"Ve sink zat is very good plan. If ve push ve might be able to make ze green before ze dusk." Boris is a tough task master and you wouldn't want to cross him. He could break you in two, like a cheap pencil.

"I'll harness up the horses," Cookie says as he goes about his chores.

"And we'll just take that whiskey. Jim Beam can be my caddy," Blaze says only slightly slurring his words. "And maybe we could get a couple of cold brewskies to wash it down with."

"Coming right up, Mr. Jones. But do you really think alcohol improves your game?" Cookie really would like to know.

"Let me be the judge of that. I always think I play golf better drunk. My rule of thumb is to stay away from the pot, unless I'm already playing bogey golf, then who the hell cares."

"Hey Boris, what is the par on this first hole?" Hub asks.

"By my calculations, ze hole is 22.2 miles, assuming 17 shots per mile, not including ze penalties or hazards, or ze paved roads, ze rules committee has determined par to be in ze neighborhood of 377.4 strokes."

"And what is our score, so far?" E.Z. wants to know, as he lost count a long time ago.

"As it stands now, Harbinger/Ichi are 665 and Hogle/Jones are in at 667. Representing ze two stroke lead."

"I knew we could get you guys. We're the talent and you're the hacks."

"You wouldn't want to put a little side bet on that now would you?"

Blaze just can't help himself, especially when his golfing is impugned.

"Name your figure, wise guy." E.Z. thinks he's so tough, his button practically pops off his golf shirt.

"How about a hundred bucks a hole?"

"You're on. Like taking candy from a baby."

"Like I said, taking candy from a baby can be harder than you think. Believe me I've tried and it is not easy." Hub knows whereof he speaks.

And with that the foursome returns to their balls just where they left them and pick up the game anew. And with each passing shot the looming snow capped mountains get ever closer, looking like Shangri-la after the sun-parched desert.

By now, Blaze is three sheets to the wind and a storm is brewing off the coastline of his brain. He sets the bottle of Jim Beam on a rock as he gets set to hit his next shot. His ball is sitting nicely up on a tuft of cheat grass. He appears to be alone, as the others are just over the ridge. He eyes his shot and the direction of the hole.

"Looks like a 2-iron to me. What do you think?" Blaze turns to a wild burro that stands motionless nearby. It brays a response that could only be described as extreme disapproval.

"Okay, how about a 3-iron?"

The burro honks in approval of his choice of club.

"Now would you just stand still, so I can concentrate. This is not an easy shot. Especially with you twitching."

The burro hasn't moved an inch. It just blinks its big eyelashes at this strange drunken golfer.

Blaze pulls out his 3-iron and addresses the ball. "Hello ball." In his drunken state, the ball appears to be three balls. He steps back, rubs his eyes and tries to concentrate.

"Would you just stand still, so I can see you?"

The burro doesn't move an inch. He's transfixed.

Blaze grips the club, squints his left eye and takes a masterful swing that sends the ball screaming into the atmosphere with such force the wild burro is startled to take action and he high tails it in the other direction, leaving a trail of burro berries in his wake.

"Was it something I said?" Blaze asks as he picks up the bottle of whiskey and gives chase to his ball.

Meanwhile, E.Z. has a difficult shot, as his ball is perched on a rock the size of a house. He's got to get on top of the rock and hit a perfect shot, or risk hitting the rock and possibly ruining his club, not to mention his hands, from the vibration. But first he's got to get on top. He grabs the dead trunk of a tree, wedges it against the rock and scrambles up. Once on top, he spots a little sand, and checking around for any watchful eyes, he improves his lie, moving the ball several inches onto the sand.

Suddenly a whistle goes off and Ludmilla steps out from behind a neighboring rock.

"Zat little trick is going to cost you mister. Von stroke penalty for improving ball."

"Oh hell lady. It was just a couple of inches."

"That's vhat ze all zay."

"I thought we were playing winter rules."

Ludmilla looks around the desert. "Does it look like vinter to you?"

"Well, it's not as though you've never improved any balls, now is it?" E.Z. leers at his double entendre.

"You better vatch your P's and Q's mister. Ve've got your number. And my Boris is very good at teaching ze lessons. So you better watch your potty mouth, or Boris might have to vash it out vith ze dishvashing soap. And ve vill not stand for ze cheating. Do I make myzelf clear?"

"No problem lady. I didn't mean anything by it. I was just kidding. I'm a great kidder."

"Just play ze game and put ze sock in it. And no more ball improvement."

"Absofuckinglutely!" E.Z. takes out his 5-iron and hits a beauty that sails off the rock with some authority and lands in the wild burro berries.

"Zat ball looks like you've landed in ze shit. It couldn't have happened to ze nicer guy."

Ben Ichi and Hub Hogle have hit nice normal shots, the equivalent of hitting down the middle of the fairway and then they see, for the first time, the miraculous putting green shimmering its dark green AstroTurf welcome mat. It beckons like an emerald in the rough, like a beacon of light in the darkness, like a luxurious green carpet in a roomful of broken glass. It represents safety. It represents home. It represents a place the ball is naturally drawn to. What ball in their right mind wouldn't want to find its rightful place on the green? If only balls had free will and education and a mind of its own. Come to think of it, they do have a mind of their own. And it is a mind beyond contempt. And when the golf ball has issued its final insult, contested its final approach, there it sits, staring at you with a big smile on its face. Such is the nature of greens and golf balls. They are like magnets, constantly opposing one another and doing funny, physics-defying anomalies. The harder you try to get them together, the funnier it can get. The closer you are, the harder it gets. Golf is the only sport where it can take fewer strokes to go great distances and many more strokes to go short distances. It is one of the conundrums of golf. The closer you get to the hole, the harder it is to get the damned little white golf ball to fall into that dark little place. Even the pros sometimes miss the short ones. That's why there are no gimmees in this game. Every shot counts and every shot must be counted.

Sometimes though, there are guys, usually pretty good players-we've all played with these guys- who, once they've missed one short one, will backhand the next one. Or hit it with the opposite hand, not taking measure of the hole. It's as if they missed it, they don't expect to count it. It is known as the self-imposed gimmee or the grab gimmee. The other players only grudgingly play along, because everybody knows if they had to actually make those putts, they'd miss as many as they make and their scores would balloon to be what they really should be in the first place. But those kinds of tactics won't work on this course, not with the likes of Boris and Ludmilla around. They are real sticklers for the rules, as all golfers should be. Otherwise, why not just call it field hockey and go home?

Blaze's approach to the vaulted green is a tough one as it is a blind shot. And he isn't seeing too well himself. His ball sits down in a gully a good 100 yards from the green, and a large willow tree stands in between. His lips are cracking from the sun, his tongue is as dry as a package of moth balls in grandma's cedar closet. And he smells like a still that has been working overtime in a tar paper shack. But he is still standing and that speaks volumes for his fortitude and for his liver. He pulls out a 7-iron, eyeballs the willow tree, looks back to the ball and creams a beauty that sails over the tree like a trapeze artist. It drops on the other side of the tree right on the green about 6 feet from the hole. Hub cheers him on and waves at him from across the field.

"Great shot my friend! That's my partner!"

Ben Ichi is next up. His shot is a little bump and run, which he pulls off without a hitch, landing the ball about 10 feet from the flag stick, leaving him a slight uphill putt.

"That's my man!" E.Z. shouts as he approaches his shot, which is buried deep in the side of a hill, with an extreme uphill lie. He pulls out a sand wedge, chokes down on the club, gets his feet into position and grinds them deep into the sand for traction and stability. He pulls the club back quickly and lets fly an enormous shot that pops out of the hill like a cork out of a shaken champagne bottle on New Year's Eve. And he's about as bubbly over the results. The ball sails over the flag and lands 10 feet past the cup and then rolls back towards the hole. It settles about 6 feet from the hole, about the same as Blaze's shot. Ben Ichi applauds his partner.

Finally, it is Hub's turn. He is about 60 feet out with a straight shot to the pin. His feet are wrapped in tattered clothes because of blisters, but he's still a game guy. What's a little blood in your shoes between men? He pulls out a 9-iron, grits his teeth and smashes a beauty which sadly shoots over the green, landing in a natural bunker.

"Damn!" Hub shouts, but it is too late for words to matter much. His fate is sealed. His shot sucked and because he is still away, he is next up.

Hub climbs the hill to the green, sweating and panting and in some pain, not from the physical ailments, though they are many, but from the emotional pain of making such a chump shot from so close. This is known as the longest walk in golf: across the green to the backside, where you are up again. Hub examines his ball, as if by some miracle it wasn't his and his ball actually went in the cup when no one was looking.

"Come on buddy, put her in." Blaze intones, like the father he never had.

"I've always wanted to do this. You know, to chip in, when things looked bleak. It's a million to one, but if you think about it there is only one right way to do it. You just need to find that one right way to the hole. Of course the bandages aren't helping." Hub pulls out his pitching wedge, sizes up the distance, imagines where he wants to have the ball land and goes for it, bandages and all. He chips the ball halfway to the hole, where it runs right towards the cup as if it were on a wire. It drops in with a resounding thud and Hub starts dancing around the green despite his sore feet. He waves his putter in the air and by the looks of it you'd think he just won the Irish sweepstakes.

"Yahoo! I did it. I really did it. Holy moly! What a shot! I knew I had it the minute it left the club."

Ben Ichi is next up and he matter of factly sinks his 10 foot putt as if it were 10 inches. He is like a golfing machine. Precise, automatic and without any emotion.

E.Z. is next up and he eyes his putt carefully, knowing this is what it all comes down to. He steps up to it, as if it were the 18$^{th}$ hole at the Master's and the tourney was riding on this final putt. He strokes it softly and it runs to the hole, breaking slightly to the left and then drops in just at the last second, just before it ran out of steam.

"Beauty! Now don't let that put any pressure on you Blaze" E.Z. and Ben Ichi slap high-fives.

Blaze eyes his putt, which unfortunately is quite similar to his three putt nightmare in the state amateur. He tries to wipe the memory out, but it is as if his muscles had retained the memory for him. He attempts to swallow, but all the booze has dehydrated him to the point of dizziness. The ball is only 6 feet away from the cup, but it may as well be 60 feet. When he looks at the hole, he sees three dark ellipses floating on the green, like UFOs in formation. He closes one eye to improve his vision and he steps up to the putt. He strokes the ball hesitantly and cuffs it, leaving it still two feet short of the hole. This is his worst nightmare. This should be a makeable putt, but once doubt starts to creep in, you are usually a goner. He steps up to the ball, hoping to hear the time honored words, "That's a gimmee." No such words are forthcoming and he knows what he has got to do. He's got to get the ball down, or it has cost him three strokes to move the ball six feet. This is what happens to golfers who are not right in the head. Your brain is like a ping pong ball in a lottery barrel, just plain jumbled and with a really scary number painted on your backside.

Blaze steps up to the putt, takes a deep breath and puts it in the back of the cup with some authority, the ball rolling over the lip like a long jumper. Lucky for him, because if the ball hadn't found the back of the cup, it would have rolled well past 6 feet slightly downhill beyond the cup, leaving him with an even worse shot than where he started. Such is the nature of greens and golf balls and the fragile state of the human mind. Everybody does love a winner, but for the rest of us, settling for a double or even triple bogey, in golf and in life, is more the norm.

---

Blaze lies flat on his stomach, drool coming out of his mouth, passed out dead drunk back at camp. Everyone else is finishing up one of Cookie's particular treats, filet mignon with a bearnaise sauce, potatoes au gratin and haricot vert. With a bottle of Chateau Lefite to wash it all down with. Cookie failed to mention he'd been a French sailor. And he definitely knows his way around a pound of unsalted butter.

"Looks like your partner lost out in his match with Jim Beam," E.Z. observes as he cleans his plate with his index finger and nods in Blazes' direction.

"Yeah, I think somewhere between the Bloody Marys, the beer chasers and the whiskey-inspired afternoon, he lost his way. He'll sleep it off and be fine in the morning. I've seen him do this hundreds of times before. I think his drinking releases some tension."

"Or it helps him forget." Ben offers.

"Forget what? We've all had our share of abuse. It's called growing up in a family." E.Z knows what he's talking about.

"Maybe that's the reason. The family that wasn't a family." Ben is good at this. "Old Chinese saying, man spend too much time in dog house, eventually make way to cat house."

"I don't think this guy is going to make it to any house. He's out cold."

"I'll tuck him in." Hub retrieves a blanket and covers up his numbskull partner. "Hey Cookie, is there any more of that chocolate mousse left?" Hub returns to the campfire as the embers float into the night like cherries jubilee on the wings of butterflies.

Meanwhile, back at the network office, Harvey Wallbanger is watching the video footage of the Parting of the Tumbleweeds on a giant flat screen in a conference room full of network executives. He's got Donna Dina on speaker phone from somewhere between New Mexico and Colorado.

"Donna, darling, we've been watching your amazing footage."

"Dan did a wonderful job."

"Dan who?"

"Dan, our cameraman. Dan Flavin. He's worked for the network for over 18 years. You remember the Bosnian footage that you won an Emmy for?

"Oh, sure, sure. Guy with a ponytail."

"That was a couple of years back. He's mostly bald now."

"Besides the point Donna. We're just very impressed with what you've come up with here, and the overnight's look like this is a story with some legs."

"Nice to know my legs are appreciated."

"Donna, so far everything we've seen is just a beauty shot. A chamber of commerce sort of thing. We need to dig deeper into the minds of these golfers, how they live, how they compete, how they survive. What makes them tick. We need you to get up close and personal with them."

"We're trying our best out here but the conditions don't make it easy. I haven't bathed in days."

"Just do whatever it takes to fill in the blanks of the story. You've got a nose for it and we want to feel like we know who these guys are. This crazy bunch of golfers, taking on the wild. We'll call it *A Walk on the Wild Side* or something else equally catchy. We've got ratings week coming up and quite frankly we need to sex it up a bit. You know, find some controversy we can endlessly hype. I mean the tumbleweeds were great, but we need to dig deeper."

"Sounds good Harve. We'll see how close we can get to these guys. It shouldn't be too hard, after all, they are guys." You can practically hear the feminine wile and charm oozing out of the speaker phone.

"I knew you'd be the woman for this Donna. Keep it up and there could be a very bright future here for you. Of course, then again, we could all be fired tomorrow." Harvey lets out a furious howl, rocking back on his haunches and banging the walls. Everyone at the table just sits stone-faced and silent staring into the void of life and job security at network television.

---

Meanwhile, back at the bar at the Burning Bridges Country Club, our original foursome is watching the havoc they have created on the television set perched over the bar. They are all there- Riley, Wiley, Sal and Monty, Gyll Harbinger and the lady still playing the golden harp. They are all enraptured by the footage of the Parting of the Tumbleweeds.

"I've never seen anything like it. Imagine playing through a miracle," Riley says dumbfounded.

Sal makes the sign of the cross. "I told you I always hated nature."

"These guys are pretty good golfers, under the circumstances," Wiley adds.

"Yeah, but my little brother is clearly the cream of the crop.

The Harbingers rule!" Gyll guzzles his beer. "Set me up another one will you? I'm in the mood to celebrate."

"What do you figure this is going to cost us?" Monty always has a mind for numbers, especially when the numbers are going out the door.

"What's the matter now, Monty, getting cold feet?" Riley knows how to push everyone's buttons, but Monty's are especially well used.

Another day brings the snow capped mountains ever closer to our heroic foursome and their traveling companions. They are now more like a traveling circus show than a professional golfing event. The players take their shots in the grandeur of the green valleys, and enter the land of the quaking aspens. It is as though they are playing golf where the hills are alive to the sounds of music. You can practically hear Julie Andrews singing to full orchestral accompaniment. Wait a minute, you can actually hear her singing and so does everyone else on the trail.

"Do you hear that music?" Cookie stops the horses.

Boris cuts the engine to his dune buggy.

"Ve do hear it. It zounds like ze zinging. It zounds like *Ze Zound of Music*."

"I think we must be losing it. What would Julie Andrews be doing out here?" Blaze asks. Just as the words leave his mouth, over the rise comes a large black S.U.V., with the windows down and *The Sound of Music* blaring out of the car stereo. The giant Escalade rolls up to the scene and Donna Dina leans out of the window.

"Hey, you guys weren't easy to find. We've been driving around for hours. What's for lunch fellas?" Donna flashes her biggest smile and bats her eyelashes in time-honored fashion.

"Well pretty lady, there is a nice little spot just up ahead where we could set up a nice little picnic. I've got some lovely fried chicken and potato salad. Fresh ears of corn and a very lively

California chardonnay, with strawberry shortcake for dessert." Cookie is very good at menu planning.

"That sounds great!" Dan Flavin yells from inside the car. "We've been living on vending machines and I'm starved."

"Just head on up to that little rise, by those rocks up ahead. We've got a pretty little view from there down to the Rocky Mountains."

The Escalade pulls ahead, Cookie nudges the horses, Boris revs up the dune buggy and the four players take their next shots, positioning themselves all near the idyllic picnic spot.

Dan Flavin sets up the camera tripod and is shooting the view from the spot looking up the spine of the Rockies. It is a breathtaking view, like some kind of verdant paradise. White-tailed deer graze in the meadow, red-winged blackbirds sing in the trees, and busy little beavers clog up streams building their version of waterfront property. It is as though the foursome has entered into a Disney movie and all we need is Bambi to complete the scene.

Cookie pulls the wagon around and begins to set up camp for lunch. There are some five-star restaurants that don't put on such a spread. He's got white linen tablecloths, silver buckets of ice with champagne and wine at the ready. Fine silverware, china and crystal goblets are laid out in a flash.

"Wow! This looks spectacular. Do you do this everyday?" Donna asks. "Dan, come get a shot of this."

"Three times a day. Breakfast, lunch and dinner. And if the boys need a little midnight snack, I'll throw a little something together impromptu-like. You know how boys are. Eat you out of house and wagon."

Dan Flavin has the camera on his shoulder as Donna gets some face time with the immutable Cookie.

"So, how do you pull all this off? I mean, we are out in the middle of nowhere. It is a beautiful bit of nowhere, mind you, but still, it is nowhere.

How do you come up with all this food and stuff. Isn't that fine china?"

"Yes it is. It belonged to my grandmother, rest her soul. She made a mean meatloaf. Well, first off, the Conestoga is a lot bigger than it looks. Second, it is totally tricked out with modern refrigeration. Third, the fellars that hired me gave me carte blanche. And these golfer dudes put out so much energy all day, everyday, without a day off, they need their nutrition. And that's my middle name."

"Well, where on earth did you learn to cook like this?"

Cookie keeps working as he talks. "I've picked it up, here and there.

Cordon Bleu. C.I.A."

This gets Boris and Ludmilla's attention as they load their plates.

"You ver vith ze C.I.A.?"

"Not the one you are thinking of. That's the Culinary Institute of America, up the Hudson River."

"Vas cover for clandestine activities?" Ludmilla is naturally suspicious.

"No, no, just a fancy cooking school. The only secrets they have are about French sauces and pastry dough."

"And when you aren't doing this, Cookie, what do you do?"

"Well, that is pretty much a mystery. That's why I try to travel light, you know, with the wagon and horses and all."

"Is there a lot of, how should I say this, need for great chefs riding around in refrigerated Conestoga wagons with a team of horses?"

"Oh, you'd be surprised. Plus, I've got a corner on that market, cause I'm pretty much the only one there is."

"Well, you are a one of a kind, I'll say that Cookie." Donna Dina turns to the camera and speaks directly into the lens. "This is just one of the many colorful figures we've met along the way of this epic golf match. I'm Donna Dina reporting from somewhere near the Rocky Mountains. And I'm here to tell you, they are really rocky mountains!"

The foursome enters the camp, leaving their bags near their balls lying in the meadow.

"I am starved!" Hub announces as he starts to fill his plate.

"And I'm thirsty. What have we got to drink Cookie?" Blaze says, wiping sweat from his brow.

"Cold beers, Italian lemonade, a lovely chilled chardonnay and of course, still champagne left over from this morning."

Blaze pops a cold beer, drains it in a single gulp and pops another. Then another. He's had three beers, in about 30 seconds, before having a bite of lunch. Dan Flavin gets it all on video.

"Wow! You must be thirsty. Why don't you just inject the beer directly into your veins?" Donna asks impertinently.

"Can you do that?"

"I don't think medical science, and the food and beverage business have come up with anything yet"

"Well, let me know when they do."

"So, how is it going out there?"

"Well, it is a lot harder than it looks."

"Oh, it looks pretty difficult."

"The lies are horrible. The weeds, the rocks. You can never be sure which way we are playing. The sun, the weather, the wind. We've had cactus the size of skyscrapers, you've got wildlife around every nook and crannie. You've got sore hands and feet and your back feels like you've been tortured on the rack. And don't get me started about having to go, you know, to the bathroom!" Blaze is on a riff.

"I am awfully sorry about that."

"Was that actually on TV?"

"I'm afraid so, sport. It was a live shot." Dan speaks up from behind the camera. "But I don't think you have much to worry about. Given the size and all, I mean of the shot. It was a pretty wide angle." Dan Flavin smiles knowingly.

"Well, at least here, your surface is improving. You know, this is almost like grass," Donna says as she gestures to the beautiful nature.

"Yeah, grass that has never encountered a steel blade whipping at 60 rpms. Some of this grass is two feet tall. Try finding your ball in that lady."

"Are you all having as many problems as your teammate here?"

"Not us," E.Z. boasts. "We're just moving along, singing our song, side by side. These are the guys that are spraying the ball all over the place."

"I saw you in that stream, that didn't look so fun," Hub says between gulps of food.

"Yeah, I had a little problem today in the water. So what? One hole does not a golf score make."

"Ancient Chinese saying, when bird of paradise flies up your nose, takes very large box of Kleenex to get him out," Ben smiles.

"I don't know from Kleenex, but I do know we are going to bury these guys. They don't stand a chance. Hub is too fat and out of shape, and Blaze, there, well, let's just say he just doesn't know when to say when, if you get my meaning." E.Z. knows how to hurl an insult with the best of them. Donna and Dan are soaking up all this inside stuff.

Donna turns again to the camera. "So, as you can tell, there is no love lost between these teams. It is mano y mano out here. And man oh man, the foursome still has hundreds of miles to go. I've got a feeling this could get interesting before it is over. I'm Donna Dina, enjoying a bite of lunch with our fearsome foursome."

---

After lunch, the foursome returns to their shots and begin to make their way towards those big old Rocky Mountains. The meadow actually is an improvement over the conditions they've faced. E.Z. hits his fairway wood into a herd of deer that scatter at the interruption. Hub hits his ball through a pine tree that sends out a rush of birds on the wing. Ben Ichi hits a beauty that bounces off a rock, zings past a forest service trail marker sign and rolls down the trail for about half a mile.

"Nice shot there Benny boy," Blaze tips his hand. He steps up to his shot, eyes the horizon and lets fly with a crusher that veers into the quaking aspens and bounces off four of them pinball-style, before settling under a large rock, at the entrance to what appears to be a den of some sort. But not the kind of den most golfers are familiar with. This one has twigs and branches built up around the edges, has a dusty, well-used entrance and in the middle of the entrance sits Blaze's ball. It sits defiantly, practically begging its owner to come in and take a penalty. A shot would require Blaze to get down on his knees and swing the club blindly under the rock. He'd be lucky to get the ball out at all. But that is exactly what he decides to do. In golf, a person of a certain talent can decide to play each shot conservatively or to go for the gusto and push the edges of what their swing, club and ball can physically do. Blaze has always been one of the go-for-the-gusto kind of guys. That's why he works in the golf repair shop, repairing the clubs of other go-for-the-gusto guys. Not to mention the girls. There are plenty of them too, and Blaze knows them all on a first-name basis.

Blaze pounds down another cold beer, crushes the can with one hand, dumps it in his bag, pulls out a 3-iron, belches loudly and gets down on his knees as if in prayer.

"Here kitty, kitty. Anybody in there?" Blaze moves cautiously towards his ball. He gets into place and just as he is about to strike the ball, there is a deep growl coming from inside the den. Blaze gulps. Then two yellow eyes appear in the darkness.

"Nice little kitty." Blaze takes his shot and miraculously hits the ball out of the bunker and it sputters to a stop, like a bird shot out of the air, just 50 feet away. Suddenly, a young cougar comes screaming out of the den, claws churning, fangs flaring and rushes past Blaze like he wasn't even there. Instead the big cat chases after the golf ball like a household pet working on a SuperBall. The big cat swipes at it, sending it into the air, tosses it from paw to paw then sends it scurrying down the trail, pouncing after it like a cat on a pogo stick. The big cat and the ball finally settle in the field, under a big tree, where the cat curls up with the ball.

"Where's Tiger Woods when you need him?" Blaze asks.

"Vat do you vant to do Mr. Jones? Take relief and zave your life or do you vant to play it vhere it lies?" Ludmilla and Boris saw the whole thing. So did Dan Flavin, who got it all on tape.

"Well, I've always been more of a dog person. Wait a minute, I've got an idea. Cookie, is there any more of that champagne leftover?"

"Coming to ya, partner."

"And bring a big old bowl."

Blaze pours the champagne into the bowl, saving the last sip for himself, and moves towards the sleeping big cat.

"My dog always used to love this."

Blaze inches towards the cougar. It breathes deeply sending up dust and ants. He is close enough to smell its breath and trust me, that is never a good thing. It has clearly not been eating healthy. He puts the bowl of champagne down in front of the cougar, and backs away cautiously, never turning his back on the big cat.

The cougar opens an eye, smelling the brut. The cougar really prefers extra dry, but in this case makes an exception. The cougar's tongue, which looks more like an infant's arm, laps up the nectar of the gods until the bowl is finished and licked dry. Then it rolls over and falls into a deep champagne-induced sleep.

"Do you think he is out?" Hub asks his partner.

"He guzzled it down pretty fast."

"Ancient saying, goes something like, better to take two stroke penalty than wake up drunken cougar with hangover." Ben Ichi is quick on his feet with all the sayings.

"Still, I'd rather not take the strokes, if I can help it. We're already down a couple. I don't want to add to the load. I'm going in with my pitching wedge. If I don't make it, let my Mom know, just let her know, I died with my golf shoes on."

Blaze moves within range of the cougar who is stone cold passed out. Who knew cougars could be such lightweights? Blaze gets up to his ball, sets his stance, looks towards where he wants to go and hits a perfect shot, barely grazing the top of the grass- an almost silent shot. The cougar rolls over and snores like the groom after the honeymoon. Champagne does that to people and some of the larger vertebrates.

Blaze and the other players move cautiously away from the cougar in the clearing and the game continues as though it were just another day at the office. You've got to say one thing for our foursome- they are a game bunch, real foot soldiers down in the trenches. Real golfers, willing to endure any kind of indignity, foul weather, unfair play, uncut rough, and sandy, perforated greens just to pursue the crazy, incoherent game of golf- the only game where the lowest score wins, the only game where the penalties are self-induced. The only game whose acronym was rumored to originally stand for Gentlemen Only, Ladies Forbidden.

Donna Dina is doing a stand up as the foursome makes its way through the meadow.

"We've just witnessed another miracle moment on our incredible journey with these gallant golfers. Like a moment out of a National Geographic nature film, a playful cougar nudges the ball forward and our players show great courage in the face of adversity, aided and abetted by a bottle of the bubbly. I'm Donna Dina, reporting from somewhere in mile- high Colorado."

Somewhere in America, in one of the many dank, dark drinking establishments that dot and define our country, amidst the smell of stale cigarette smoke and sour beer, with jars of pickled eggs and pain relievers sold two at a time, sit a pair of old friends. Dressed in white socks, with red necks and drinking Blue Ribbon beer, they watch, with some intensity, the golf coverage on the television set behind the bar. The set shows a compilation of Donna's coverage, most prominent is the beer guzzling episode by Blaze, just before he encounters the cougar.

"Isn't that the guy who peed on *Good Morning America* the other day?"

"It sure looks like him."

"What time do you figure it is out there?"

"It's got to be earlier than here."

"That guy starts drinking at breakfast and just keeps it a going."

"You'd think, what with being on the TV, that he could wait at least until noon, like we do?"

"That guy is out of control. I don't know how he can keep this up. I've got five bucks says his liver gives out before they finish."

"You're on. And I don't think the fat guy can keep it up either. My money's on the jerks. We may not like 'em, but what the hell. You've got to go with your head, not your heart."

Thanks to the worldwide media coverage, this conversation is taking place, millions of times over, in hundreds of languages in all the dank, dark drinking establishments in the world. Morning, noon and night.

---

Meanwhile, back at the RAGU national headquarters, Bob Post is having a bad day. He too is looking at the media coverage and is more than a bit concerned about how the match is being portrayed. More importantly, how RAGU is being portrayed. It looks more like a moveable feast than a rigorous golf match. No one wants to link binge drinking to the game of golf, whether it is the cause or the effect.

"This whole thing is just a love fest to the players. Where are Boris and Ludmilla? They're not being tough enough. This shouldn't just be a walk in the fucking park! They need to grow some balls!" Bob Post is speaking to an empty room, until we look down at his lap, and there sits his furry little Cockapoodle, who looks up at him affectionately, but without a clue what his owner is shouting about.

---

Blaze's mother is alone in her apartment, sitting in the dark, watching the TV, with a highball in one hand and a lit cigarette in the other. She too is watching the coverage of her son and his crazy game of golf. She's seen all the ups and downs. She's lived all the ups and downs. A tear wells up in her eye, when she hears Blaze say, "Tell my Mom, I died with my golf shoes on."

Ben Ichi's father sits cross-legged in front of his television set, also watching the coverage. He lets out a little squeaker and smiles beneficently, when he hears Ben's comment about "the bird of paradise flying up your nose."

The salesman at the sporting good store is watching the coverage on the TV in the store. He sees Hub Hogle gorging himself at the food table.

"Hey, I know that guy! Son of a gun, I know that guy!"

The Harbingers are also watching the television at home, with Gyll transfixed and Giselle doing her nails.

"Aren't you glad sweetie, that it's E.Z. and not you out there? It doesn't exactly look like a bowl of cherries. I think it looks more like the pits."

"If anybody would know, it would be you Giselle."

# CHAPTER 5

## "GO WITH THE FLOW, AND FLOW WITH THE GO"

A MAJESTIC WATERFALL SENDS rivulets of water cascading over rocks into an emerald pool of water. At the base of the waterfall, stands our foursome, staring at the beauty as the twilight sunset frames the scene. Cookie is setting up camp, and Boris and Ludmilla are pitching their tent as they settle in for the night.

Suddenly, from behind the waterfall, a siren is singing her siren song, and the boys all hear it at the same moment.

"Do you hear that?" Hub asks.

"Yeah. What in the hell is it?" Blaze answers.

"Sounds like singing," E.Z. states the obvious.

"We should all be careful," Ben says with a glint in his brow. "Witches and spirits live behind waterfalls."

From behind the veil of water an image emerges. It is a beautiful woman, with a long blonde mantle of hair, riding naked on a white horse. She sings a beautiful song as she rides from behind the waterfall. She sees the foursome and abruptly stops. Apparently even sirens can be embarrassed by their singing. She stops the white horse in front of the foursome.

"Well, what do we have here? Trespassers?"

"No ma'am. We're just a bunch of crazy golfers," Hub answers too enthusiastically. This is as close to a naked woman as he has been in a very long time.

Cookie joins the fray. "We're just passin' through missy. We'll be out of here at first light. I just put on a kettle for some tea, would you care to join us?"

"Well, I'm not exactly dressed for high tea, so I'll take a rain check. I live just over the rise there, why don't you all drop by for some neighborly hospitality. I'll change into something more comfortable."

"Well, you look pretty comfortable to me," E.Z. says.

"How nice of you to notice. We are known in these parts as the Bear Naked Ranch and Day Spa. We're kind of like a nudist commune, where you can get facials and mud wraps, and just kind of let it all hang out. Feel free to drop by later. You all look like you could use a little R & R. Just remember to bring a towel. No swimsuits required."

She begins to ride away.

"Wait a minute," Hub shouts out after her. "What's your name?"

"If anyone asks you, tell them Lady Godiva sent you."

She goes back to her beautiful song as the horse follows the trail home.

"I love ze day spas," Ludmilla announces.

"I love ze naked bodies," Boris answers.

"I don't know about you guys, but there is no way in hell I am going to take off my clothes in front of complete strangers," E.Z. says.

"If I had your body, I wouldn't want to be seen in it either," Hub retorts. " I, on the other hand, am very comfortable with my body. Besides, I think she kind of liked me. What do you say, Cookie, we'll all go over for some R & R?"

Cookie thinks about it, rubbing his whiskers. "Oh what the hell, I haven't had a facial in years. What do you figure a mud wrap entails exactly?"

After dinner, the foursome, along with Cookie, Boris and Ludmilla, all travel just over the rise, to a gate that announces in bold day-glow lettering BEAR NAKED RANCH - DAY SPA AND YOGA CENTER - WHERE NATURE MEETS NURTURE -A CLOTHING-OPTIONAL DUDE RANCH ENTERPRISE. The foursome isn't sure what to make of the sign.

"I am not taking off my clothes," E.Z. huffs.

"But what if there are naked women in there, like Lady Godiva?" Hub was impressed with her natural attitude.

"What do you think Cookie? Do you think it's a trap?" Blaze is always dubious of naked women offering R & R.

"It's hard to say for sure. She was definitely naked. We can't be certain there are others."

"Vell, I don't know about you boys, but I'm going in. I vant to get ze facial," Ludmilla announces and starts to undress. She's got a body that would put many movie starlets to shame.

"If Ludmilla is going, then I vill be going as vell. Vhat the hell fellas, you only live vonce!" Boris rips his shirt off. He looks like a blonde Tarzan with a tan line.

"I guess that settles it." Cookie starts to take off his boots and Levis. "If you can't beat 'em, you might as well join 'em. If you fellars are too modest, what with your celebrity and being a bunch of uptight golfers and all, I'm sure Lady Godiva wouldn't object if you just arrived in your skivvies, with a towel. You know, as a sign of respect."

The foursome all look at each other and Hub is the first one to strip down to his skivvies. Blaze and Ben are next. Finally, E.Z. relents stripping down to his white bikini BVDs. At least the other guys wore boxers, with fun shapes and colors. E.Z. looks like he belongs in one of those naughty Calvin Klein ads.

"Hey, this is what I wear, okay?" E.Z. is clearly embarrassed.

He wraps the towel around his waist. "But I am interested in a mud wrap!"

---

Inside the compound, it looks like a collection of buildings made by an ancient and primitive Stone-age people who were indeed very stoned. There are teetering rock walls, molded earth homes, straw bales and teepees. It is like an old fashioned hippie commune or kibbutz, or a place where very blissed-out people come together to get naked and enjoy the benefits of sunshine and fresh air. Like *The Flintstone's* Bedrock, but without the animal skin togas. Our foursome looks oddly out of place, like aliens who just landed from outer space wearing only cotton towels. Lady Godiva approaches them.

"Nice to see you again. Why don't you all take a swim in the hot springs. It has natural healing powers." Lady Godiva smiles at Hub. "Just watch out for the mosquitoes. They're the size of Buicks."

"Thanks for the tip. A mosquito in a nudist colony must be a very happy mosquito! Mosquitoes just love me. I guess I have sweet blood." Hub is cute when he is trying to be flirtatious. He drops his towel and his skivvies and runs to the hot springs where he yells, "Geronimo!" as he jumps in with a thunderous cannonball.

"He's just a great big kid at heart," Blaze remarks after his friend.

"This is quite a spread you've got here." Lady Godiva looks at him funny.

"I mean, the ranch and all."

"Yeah, well, we've been working on it for awhile. I came out here in the 70's. Turned on, tuned in and dropped out. And that was all just in the first week!" Lady Godiva laughs a belly laugh that shakes her breasts like suspended bowls of jello. "You all make yourselves at home. Facials and mud wraps are in the two teepees. Sweat lodge is down by the creek. And the merlot is flowing around the campfire. Just don't get too close, cause it can fry your pubes. The drum circle starts when the moon comes up. I think Yongo is coming down from the mountain. It should be an interesting night."

"Who is Yongo?" Ben asks.

"Yongo is the oldest hippie out here. He's something of a legend. He was a world class mountain climber until he took a bad fall. Nearly killed him. Somehow, though, the fall knocked some kind of wicked good sense into him and now he is just a wandering mountain man. He plays a mean bongo. If he shows up tonight, you're in for a mighty good time."

On the hillside above the nudist colony, Donna Dina looks through binoculars with Dan Flavin recording with the camera what they can of the proceedings. With night settling in and the distance involved, the images are a bit blurry, but the whole thing has a tawdry tabloid quality to it, with the guys all standing around in their skivvies and towels in front of Lady Godiva in all her naked glory.

"The guys in the tower are going to love this!" Donna says as she puts down the binoculars. "I think these guys have been out in the wilderness too long."

"I don't know," Dan says. "I think it looks kind of fun. But what's up with the one guy's underwear?"

"I have no fucking idea. Who could play golf in bikinis BVDs?"

Later that night, with the moon rising, with the merlot flowing, with all the muscles healed and the mud wrapped, the drum circle is well on its way to frenzy, and the foursome and crew are all well on their way to nirvana. At the center of the circle is the mountain man Yongo. He has long hair, a braided beard and eyes that look like aquamarine stones. He hammers on his bongo like a man possessed by demons. But he has a big shit-eating grin on his face.

"Whoa!" Yongo shouts at the top of his lungs as he brings his playing to a conclusion. "Let's take a break so we can get up our energies for the last set. Smoke 'em if you've got 'em folks." He wipes the sweat from his brow. He pulls out a joint from behind his headband and lights it up. He takes a huge toke and passes it on to the boys. E.Z. takes it and holds it uncomfortably.

"Is this what I think it is?"

"Natural herb for what ails you, brother."

"I think I'll pass, and don't call me brother."

"Don't mind him. He's got brother issues," Blaze says as he takes a hit. He passes it on to Ben.

"I've never tried this herb. What will it do to me?"

"It will open up your mind, man. It will help you see everything clearly. You'll be in synch with the time space continuum, man, with the whole friggin' universe, dude."

"Sounds good," Ben inhales and holds it, then slowly lets it out.

"Wow. I see what you mean. Is this what they call a Rocky Mountain high?"

"You'll be extremely hungry in about an hour," Hub says as he takes a hit. He goes into a coughing seizure. "Yeah, I think, it opened, something up, all right!"

Hub sidles up to Lady Godiva. They smile at each other, almost as though they were the only two people on the planet.

"So, what are you guys doing out here again? Lady G told me, but I don't watch much TV out here, so I wasn't sure I understood." Yongo takes another big hit.

"We're playing a golf game over 400 miles through the wilderness, in 40 days," Blaze says.

"Far out man!"

"That's pretty much what it is. Far out." E.Z. grumbles.

"These four old rich guys hired us to do it."

"I've never been much for golf. Could never understand why

grown- ups would put themselves through it. It's like make-believe nature. But then again, I climbed mountains, and pretty much everybody agrees that defies logic."

"Everyone must climb their own mountain. Even when it is flat," Ben says in a stoned voice.

"I see you are something of a mystic," Yongo says turning to Ben.

"I try in my modest way," Ben answers.

"Have you heard this one? Virginity is just like a bubble. One prick, and it is all gone!" Yongo rolls his head back and roars with laughter. Ben and the boys are laughing hysterically, from the smoke, the night and the company.

"I've got one more, brother. A man who eats cookies in bed will always wake up feeling crummy!" Yongo howls with laughter.

The whole camp roars with laughter that echoes into the night as the drumbeat picks back up and the fire embers glow into the darkness, rising ever upward towards the stars and the heavens. Who knew a bunch of naked hippies could be so much fun. And it was true, Yongo could play a mean bongo.

---

The next morning finds the foursome feeling a little crummy themselves. Somewhere between the merlot, the herb, the dancing and the mostly naked bodies, the crew moved into the land of headaches and hangovers, exacerbated by the "high" altitude. Cookie is brushing his teeth near the waterfall, as the camp rustles to life. Boris and Ludmilla look radiant after their facials and wraps. The foursome pops a bottle of champagne to try to take the edge off their hangovers.

"Hey, that was a riot last night," Blaze says as he sips his bubbly.

"Yeah, I haven't danced like that since high school," Ben says.

"I have to admit, it was more fun than I thought it would be,"

E.Z. agrees. "And I think lover boy got lucky last night." E.Z. turns to Hub, who is turning from bright red to deep crimson.

"Hey, I can't help it, women just find me terribly attractive. We swapped phone numbers. She's coming over this morning to say goodbye."

"You know, I have a little headache, but my body feels better. My muscles aren't as sore. I think that hot spring soak really worked. I feel like playing some golf today," Blaze says stretching his back.

"I know what you mean. I really slept well last night. I think it was the sound of the waterfall. It lulled me to sleep," Ben says.

"You know guys, I haven't exactly been one of the gang," E.Z. says adjusting his shirt collar. "But after last night, seeing what can become of people in this big old scary world, I just am glad to say we are golfers."

"What do you mean?" Blaze asks.

"Well, I'm just saying I take comfort in the fact that we are all bound together through golf. Like a kind of brotherhood."

"Coming from you, I guess that's saying something," Blaze answers.

"I think I know what you mean," Ben says, drawing closer. "Golfers are a certain breed. Not fly-by-nighters, not a bunch of drug- crazed hippies, howling at the moon, as fun as they were to hang out with."

"I think I know what you mean," Blaze ruminates. "Golfers are pretty much a conservative bunch. Steady. Straight forward. Mostly honest."

"You're not saying golfers are all Republicans are you?" Hub hates Republicans.

"No, not at all. Though they probably are the majority at most country clubs. It's the Democrats on the public courses." Blaze offers his political analysis. "But, golfers represent more of a lifestyle. More of a belief system. Almost like a religion."

"A religion where they wear really ugly clothes," Cookie says as he joins the conversation. "Like most religions."

"I'm just glad to be a part of it. I'm proud to be a golfer!" E.Z. is actually getting choked up about it. He raises his glass in a toast.

"Here's to us golfers. A brotherhood of players who share honest values, where we call our own penalties on ourselves, just because it is the right thing to do!" E.Z. hoists his glass.

"To us golfers! May we always wear dorky clothes!" Blaze raises his glass.

"To golfers around the world!" Ben raises his glass.

"Hey, I don't know about you guys, but I kind of had fun with the hippies. Here's to hippies and to golf! May the world unite in peace and harmony! Even Republicans and Democrats get along on a golf course!"

"Here, here!" All the glasses go clink and our merry foursome, feeling bright-eyed and bushy-tailed, sufficiently male-bonded and free of the aches and pains, compliments of Lady Godiva and the day spa, begin the next leg of their journey full of optimism and comraderie.

Lady Godiva riding on her white horse and Yongo with his bongo, come over the rise, to bid them farewell. Hub jumps up when he sees her.

"Hey, I was hoping you'd come by before we teed off."

"I wouldn't miss it for the world," Lady Godiva says.

The guys all retrieve their golf bags and set their shots in the tee area, with the magnificent waterfall in the background.

Yongo approaches Blaze, who is taking practice swings with his driver.

"You mind if I try it?" Yongo asks, putting down his bongo.

"Sure. In fact, why don't you hit a practice shot. Go ahead and tee it up." Blaze hands Yongo a ball and a tee.

"I haven't done this since the 60s, when I was in a fraternity."

"Somehow, I don't see you in a fraternity," Blaze says.

"Oh yeah. Krappa Zappa Pi. Named for our spiritual leader Frank Zappa and his Mothers of Invention. But we used to love to play golf. Drop acid and then giggle a lot around the golf course. It was a lot of fun." Yongo sets his ball, looks off into the horizon, steps up, sets himself, stiffens his arm, cocks his chin and takes the club back slowly and deliberately. He brings the mighty club head down in a masterful swing and he creams the ball, sending it shuddering into the cloudless sky.

"Smokin!" Blaze high-fives Yongo.

"You know, I just might have to find my way back to golf. One thing for sure, it is a lot softer landing than mountain climbing. And I've got to say, I think you guys are on to something here, playing golf through the wilderness. It takes the best part of nature and the best part of sport and turns it into a test of endurance. In that sense, it is a lot like mountain climbing, but with much smaller mountains. Do you think when you are finished I could be your agent or something? I'd even come out of semi-retirement."

"I'll tell you what Yongo, when this is all through, look us up and we'll give you a hearing. Nobody really knows how this is all going to end, least of all us." Blaze takes his club back, sets his ball and smacks a drive down the meadow that rolls well past Yongo's massive shot.

"I see good things in your future. That's what old Yongo sees."

E.Z. steps up next and hits his normal blast into the stratosphere.

"It's all in the hips gentlemen."

Next up, Ben hits a beauty like he always does, without breaking a sweat. "If you are in a hurry, you will never get there."

"One can only stand up from the place one fell," Yongo replies.

Hub blows Lady Godiva a kiss as he steps up to the tee. "Parting is such sweet sorrow. I feel like a new man."

"Would you just put a cork in it, Mr. Lovey Dovey and hit your shot," E.Z. says pointedly.

"So much for brotherly love," Hub murmurs as he hits a long ball way past any of the other shots.

"Now there's a real man's shot. You keep it up sugar! We'll be watching you from the ranch. Come back and visit or who knows, maybe one day I'll get a wild hair up my ass and come visit you at Burning Bridges. You can buy me a big ol' margarita!"

"You're on! I'll call and write when I can."

"We'll be watching you on the TV!"

The foursome moves on down the dirt road leading down the meadow and to the west. Boris and Ludmilla roar off in the dune buggy chasing after the players' balls. Cookie mounts the wagon and takes the reins in one hand and waves at Lady Godiva and Yongo.

"Thanks again ma'am for all the hospitality. This is one that will go down in the memory banks for some time to come. It kinda gives you hope for humanity." And with that the game of golf, like no other in the world, goes on around the next bend.

Harvey Wallbanger sits in his office with the tabloid footage running on the monitor in front of him. He looks extremely worried. Seated across from him are Bob Post, from the Royal and Ancient Golf Union, as well as Wiley, Riley, Sal and Monty.

"Gentlemen, we may have a problem here. Thanks to our crack investigative team, the players may have stepped over the bounds of propriety and I wanted to alert you at the earliest possible moment."

"I just knew this was going to happen!" Bob Post chews on his nails.

"I'm not really sure I follow you," Riley intones, tugging on the ends of his mustache.

"Gentlemen, this golf match has caught the country- forget the country- the whole world by storm. Our ratings are through the roof. But if this gets out, that the golfers were naked, or ingesting illegal substances, or taking advantage of loose women, why it might not look so good to say to the youth of the world."

"No, I'm pretty sure, they'd be behind the nudity, sex and drugs. They're kids. What else do they believe in?" Sal retorts.

"Probably the only thing missing is rock and roll!" Monty adds.

"No gentlemen, this is bad. This is really, really bad. Our professional organization will be tarnished if this gets out." Bob Post paces the floor. "I mean we represent the game of golf! We can't have nudity and drugs. Golf is not professional basketball for Christ's sake! We have standards to keep. Professional golfers never have problems. We make sure of that!"

"Listen, from what I can see it was really nothing more than a little skinny-dipping. Who's to say what was in the cigarettes they were smoking? As for the naked woman on the horse, what can I say? People are usually naked at least once a day. She just stays naked." Wiley makes an attempt at damage control.

"That's an excellent point you make there Mr. Hancock," Harvey rocks back in his chair, as if brainstorming. "We can always black out the parts of the body everyone really wants to see. That shouldn't pose a problem for you, should it Bob?"

"You're not seriously thinking of broadcasting this footage?"

"This could send the ratings into the stratosphere! People love this kind of stuff, you know, people caught with their pants down. And we'll get Donna in there to fuel the controversy, you know, asking how they could have disappointed so many kids. It'll be fantastic. It adds the elements of Greek tragedy to the game of golf." Harvey is brimming with pride.

"This whole thing is a disaster. From the moment you came into my office, I should have hidden under the desk."

"Oh buck up Bobby! It's only a friendly game of golf. So what if the guys turn out to be human. You should try it sometime," Riley says with a grin.

"This just better not get any worse. From here on out, these guys better be on their best behavior. Or I'll make sure they never get out on a golf course ever again! And I don't just mean country clubs and touring. I mean every municipal and county course. Christ, I'll even get them banned from putt-putt. I have that kind of power!" Bob Post is going postal.

"We'll be very discreet with the footage, Bob. We'll never mention RAGU while we are showing any kind of nudity, you have my word on it."

---

The next thing we see is the television in Blaze's mom's house. She sits in her normal spot, sipping her cocktail and smoking her cigarette. The local news is on. They are showing the shadowy images of the nudist colony, with the players standing around in ther skivvies, drinking, smoking and generally raising hell. When Lady Godiva shows up, with her private parts blacked out, Blaze's mom shrieks at the sight.

"Oh my God! What have you done now?"

The reporter on the TV is standing outside the RAGU headquarters.

"After several requests, for the Royal and Ancient Golf Union to make a statement, we did finally get this from the executive director." She rolls the footage of Bob Post standing nervously outside the headquarters' sign.

"We realize this may not look good to the average golfer, but we want to assure golfers everywhere that nudity does happen, sometimes several times a day, in this great big country of ours. These guys are human, after all. We should all try it sometime, I mean the humanity, not, not the nudity, of course. No golfer in his right mind would want to attempt to play the game naked. I mean, if you think about it, lining up the putts would be murder. So, we are monitoring the situation and just hopeful the game can continue without any more controversy. I mean, golf is almost never controversial. So we are in all new terrain here." Bob Post looks like a deer caught in the headlights of an 18-wheeler and it is not a pretty sight to behold.

# CHAPTER 6

## "WHEN LIFE PRESENTS YOU WITH A THREE-LEGGED DOG, YOU SHOULD PAY ATTENTION, BECAUSE NEITHER ONE OF YOU HAVE A LEG TO STAND ON"

DONNA DINA IS DOING her standup routine, with the foursome playing through a place known as Paradox Valley, which is made up of long canyons forming a kind of giant maze. The terrain is new as the ground gives way from the Rocky Mountains down to the high deserts of Utah.

"We are watching closely as the match nears its halfway point, with the players nearing the turn at the 9th hole. As it stands right now, and I do mean right now, Hogle and Jones are trailing Harbinger and Ichi by just two strokes, 6,245 to 6,247 strokes. It is hard to believe, but the foursome has been playing golf now for a continous 20 some days, nearly 200 miles, over some of the roughest, toughest terrain known to mankind, let alone to a crazy bunch of golfers. Despite their recent problems, they've proven to be worthy gamesmen. They've broken only a few clubs, not to mention a few hearts along the way. But that is really what the game of golf is all about. At this level, it is all about the pain. And as they say, no pain, no gain. For the next couple of days, I'm going to be following the foursome, hoping to get a more personal glimpse, into their competitive heads, into their shoes, so to speak, so we might know what it is really like to be playing golf at this level, for this long and over this geography. Stay tuned, as this turns into a marathon match unparalleled in the annals of sports history. If golf wasn't an Olympic event before, golf played like this, just might be vying for the gold one day in a wilderness near you. I'm Donna Dina reporting from somewhere on the Colorado plateau, on our way into the Canyonlands of Utah."

Our now controversial foursome is playing along smoothly in a large sagebrush field, with the Conestoga wagon trailing alongside in a two-track dirt rut that stands in for a road in these parts. The dune buggy follows behind the wagon, proving once again that actual horses always beat mechanical horsepower. And Donna Dina and Dan Flavin are trailing behind the whole shebang in their black Escalade, shooting everything, bump for bump and shot for shot.

"Jeez, Donna, can you just try to hit every other bump. This footage could make people carsick in their own living rooms."

"I'm doing the best I can, Dan. I told you I wasn't a very good driver. I mean, I live in New York City for Christ's sake. Who ever drives when you can take cabs and subways?"

"Not too many cabs out here, that's for damn sure."

"How am I ever going to get these guys to open up to me? It's like they are some kind of secret club to which I can never become a member."

"Hey, guys are like that. Especially when they've bonded through adversity and gamesmanship. Even if they are just watching a game, the men's attention bubble is hard to penetrate. And if they are actually playing a game, forget about it."

"I've got to find a way."

"Why don't you try using some of your feminine charms? That's really the only way to break into the circle of camaraderie. That, or share a genuine experience that proves your worth. It's just the way guys are built. They say the way to a guy's heart is through his stomach, but that's not quite right. You have to aim a little bit lower."

A cowboy sits on what can only be described as a well-endowed horse, who is taking a long leak on a scruff of cheat grass. The cowboy and horse don't seem to be in much of a hurry. Behind the cowboy stands our foursome, golf clubs in hand, and behind them sit Cookie and the wagon, Boris and Ludmilla idling in the dune buggy and last but certainly not least, Donna and Dan in their Escalade.

In front of the cowboy and his long dong Hi Ho Silver, stands a herd of cattle moving very slowly over what passes for a road. You've never really traveled out west unless you've been at the rear end of a cattle drive. You have little choice but to wait it out or simply move through, albeit very carefully, unless you want to buy a whole mountain of steaks. The cows shift on their haunches, flick their tails at the black flies and drool a seemingly endless supply of phlegm that elongates all the way to the ground. These are the hamburgers of the future and at the moment they are blocking the progress of the game like a Great Wall of Rawhide. And with each passing hoove, the players' balls get buried a little deeper in the loam of the earth.

"So, what's the protocol out here buddy? Do we try to play through or should we wait for you to move the little doggies?" Blaze asks naively. He really has never referred to a cow before as a little doggie, but when out west, you kind of learn these things naturally. Then of course, sometimes you risk sounding just like the rube you know yourself to be.

"Well, that's hard to say," the cowboy offers as he lights up a hand rolled cigarette he takes from behind his ear. If he isn't the Marlboro Man, he must be his kid brother, before the lung cells started to mutate.

"Some people are afraid the cows might decide to stampede once they get into the middle of the herd. But most cows are stupid and it takes quite a bit to spook 'em. Then again, you might run into an ornery one who woke up this morning on the wrong side of the rock and decide to take out her animosity on your hindquarters. So, what are you fellas doing way out here? You look like you're kinda lost."

"We are actually playing a golf game," Hub answers and then laughs nervously, knowing it sounds kind of crazy.

"Well, I've been cowboying for over 50 years out here and I have to say, you are the first golfers I've ever run into. How's the game goin'?"

"We're leading by two strokes," E.Z. beams.

"What hole are you on?" The cowboy looks off towards the horizon.

"We're about to make the turn at 9," Ben Ichi offers.

"How long have you been playing out here?" The cowboy spits into the dirt.

"It's been 20 days, so far."

"Looks like you're pretty well outfitted. Who are the jokers in the dune buggy?"

"They're the scorekeepers."

"And behind them? The couple with the camera?"

"Oh, they're the television journalists covering our game," Blaze says. "You probably don't get much TV out here."

"I haven't seen a television set since 1988, when I went into town for a haircut. But I have to confess to you, I've always fancied myself to be a pretty good actor. Who knows, maybe this is my big chance at stardom." The cowboy laughs, like a guy who hasn't been into town in 20 years. "You just never know what twists and turns will take you to your destiny. Maybe this was all meant to happen. I can honestly tell you I have always had a powerful hankering to be on TV."

"Well, I just bet we could help you out there partner. Let me go talk to the TV people and see what they can do for us." Blaze walks to the back of the line. Donna Dina rolls down her window.

"What's up boss? Can't they get the cows to move any faster?"

"Well, we've got a star-struck cowboy, and we're hoping you might be able to help."

"Sure, that is just so cute. What does he want an autograph or something? I have this happen all the time."

"It's a little more complicated than that. He's thinking more of a screen test or something. He fancies himself to be a pretty good actor."

"Well, don't we all? We'll get the camera set up and see what he can do. Everybody wants to get in on the act. What the hell, we're not getting any good footage looking at these cows' rear ends, that's for sure."

---

Dan Flavin has his camera set up and the cowboy is off his horse, standing awkwardly in the kleig light, squinting his eyes.

"I didn't realize the lights are so bright. And I don't mind telling you, I am more than a little nervous. I didn't know the camera would be that big. Seriously, I can hardly breath."

"Don't worry about it. Just be yourself. Act natural."

"Okay, are we rolling?"

"Yep. This is a screen test for, I'm sorry I never got your name," Dan says as he looks through the lens.

"They call me Hop-A-Long, cause I've got a bum leg. But my real name's Bud. Bud Weiser."

"Like the beer?"

"Yep. I was named for my daddy's favorite beverage."

"That's interesting."

"Yeah. I did better than my sister though."

"How's that?"

"She was named after his favorite snack food. Dorito. Dorito Weiser."

"Sounds like an interesting family, Bud. So what have you got for us today?" Donna wants to cut to the chase.

"Well, I'm kind of known in these parts as a pretty good

entertainer. I do some impressions and I've got a pretty fair voice. I'm not much of a dancer though, due mostly to the bum leg."

"Let 'er rip, cowboy."

Bud Weiser stands up a little taller, throws his shoulders back and starts to sound just like John Wayne.

"Well, pilgrim, I think you better start walking or my fists are going to start talking."

"Who was that?"

"That was John Wayne."

"Oh sure. What else have you got?"

Bud rolls his shoulders forward and shifts his weight from side to side. "You talkin' to me? Are you talkin' to me? Cause there's nobody else here? Are you talkin' to me?"

"Hey I know that one. That was Al Pacino"

"No. That was Robert De Niro. In *Taxi Driver.*"

"Oh sure. Sure. I always get the two of them mixed up."

"I do a pretty good Al Pacino too." Bud gets a crazed look on his face. "You want to meet my little friend? Do you really want to meet my little friend?"

"Hey that was pretty good. From *Scent of a Woman*, right?"

"No. That was from *Scarface.*"

"Oh yeah. Sure. Sure. Anything else?"

"I do some show tunes, a little bit of yodeling and I'm pretty good with the lariat."

"That all sounds very good. I'm sure the network honchos will find all this very fascinating." Donna rolls her eyes as Bud starts to yodel and jump in and out of a circle with his twirling lariat.

"I don't mean to say anything, but it looks like your cattle are on the move," Donna mentions as the cows begin to stir. Bud Weiser keeps yodeling and it would appear the cows are not impressed. Suddenly a dust devil kicks up and before you can say filet mignon, the cows are in full panic mode, mooing and groaning. Another cowboy rides up from the front of the herd, just in time to yell at the top of his lungs, "STAMPEDE!"

And with that, all the cows are running at full speed. It is to the bovine world what yelling "Fire!" in a crowded theater would do. Cookie hides behind the wagon. Boris and Ludmilla fire up the dune buggy and go off in pursuit. Bud Weiser jumps on his horse, Hi Ho Silver and is off after the misbehaving meatloaf. Dan Flavin picks up the tripod and swoops it into the Escalade, just as he and Donna dodge several mad cows. The foursome doesn't know what to do, this being their first stampede. They wave their clubs over their heads and yell "Fore!" but to little avail. The cows are simply not conversant with the finer points of the game and its etiquette. The foursome run and hide behind the Conestoga, just before they are trampled.

As Bud Weiser rides off into the dust cloud, he shouts back at the golfers. "Have your people call my people and we'll set up a little pow wow! Giddyup!" And with that, the cowboys and the cattle drive are over the next ridge, and the golfers and their entourage are left in the settling dust.

"That was strange. I've never seen meat move that fast before," Blaze says as he dusts himself off.

"Yeah. And how about those impersonations? It was enough to make the cows start jogging," Hub says.

"I don't know, I thought he nailed the Pacino," E.Z. says.

The dune buggy pulls up.

"You boys have only three minutes to find your balls, or you vill all have to take ze penalties. And I don't mind telling you, those cows vere scared ze shitless, so you vill have many cowpies to look under. Ze clock is running and so should you," Boris says as he looks at his watch.

The boys all start their own stampede trying to find their respective balls in all those acres of steaming manure and stringy phlegm. Such is the life of the wilderness golfer. It gives new meaning to the term "play it as it lays."

---

The afternoon's sun casts long shadows across the 9th green.

The emerald surface sits in all its AstroTurf glory, on the edge of a cliff overlooking a breathtaking panorama that most closely resembles a valley on the moon. There are hoodoos and arches, strange outgrowths and remnants from an ancient sea, the biggest water hazard ever known, now a surreal maze of grottos, tunnels and dunes. It's the biggest kitty box that ever was.

The foursome, having found their balls and positioned themselves for decent approaches, all eye their respective shots. Blaze's ball is tucked under a purple sagebrush about 90 yards to the stick. Hub is in a better position, in the sand about 60 yards from the cup. Ben Ichi is also in good shape, resting between two stones about 25 yards to the pin, just a little bump and run, with the proviso that if it runs too far, it runs to the Pacific Ocean. Finally, E.Z.'s ball sits atop a massive ant hill, a good 120 yards to the green. If anyone deserved it, it would be E.Z., as his tongue lashes out like an anteater on an eating binge.

"Jeez! Why does this shit always happen to me?" E.Z. laments to himself. He's out, so he approaches his shot. He's got an 8-iron in his hand, but it is a tough uphill lie. He's fortunate though- the ball sits up perfectly at the ant hole entrance. Just as he addresses the ball, a couple of red ants from the welcoming committee let him know what's up by biting him through his socks. He jumps back and swipes at his feet, like they are on fire. He reaches down and pinches the little devils out of his socks. He tries again, this time getting the club head back, before he succumbs to the bites, this time up his calves. Again, he backs off and dances like a man being electrocuted. Finally he runs up to the ball, doesn't bother to settle, and takes a running swing at it. He catches the ball nicely, sending it high into the air, only to see it land hard in the bunker, just shy of the green. E.Z. runs like a crazy man, pulling his clothes off, until he is stripped down to his now famous briefs. Screaming, he pulls them down around his ankles, plucks the biting red ants out of his underwear, pulls them back up and casually makes his way to his next shot as though nothing had happened, except he is stripped down to his underwear and has dozens of red bite marks all over his body.

"Tough break! That bites!" Blaze yells at him. He's up next and he hits a solid 9-iron with just enough backspin to keep it from rolling off the green. He lands within 25 feet of the pin.

"That's my partner!" Hub says as he steps up to his shot. He's got a pitching wedge out and he globbers it, sending the ball to within 10 feet of the cup. It curls back towards the cup as though it was magnetized.

Finally, Ben Ichi is up. He hits a 3-iron, to keep it flat and low, and it bumps and runs to the pin. It is headed right to the cup, then rolls past and stops 10 feet past the cup, coming to rest just inside Hub's ball.

"These fellars make it look pretty easy," Cookie says to his favorite horse, Selma. She brays her agreement, as if horses understood things like golf. The understanding of golf is strictly limited to the human animal, and we all know that the human animal is strictly limited in its understanding of pretty much everything, especially golf. In fact, the very invention of golf is testimony to the acknowledgement of man's imperfection and the struggle to overcome it. By weighing risk and reward, the human animal is uniquely qualified to make determinations commensurate with ability, and decide when to go for the driver, when to hold back and hit a fairway wood, or when to hit a wedge or putt from just beyond the fringe. That makes golf a uniquely human endeavor. The human brain was uniquely formed to create games of all kinds- games of chance, games of athleticism, head games, game theory, and war games. Leave it up to humans and we'll make a game of it every time,

As E.Z. approaches his deeply buried bunker shot, he knows he is facing the bowels of Hades itself. The ball is so submerged in the sand that he can barely see the top of the ball. And the lip surrounding the AstroTurf is about two feet straight up, making the shot nearly impossible to jump over the lip and get anywhere near the hole. E.Z. clears the area of any debris, as he is allowed to do. Boris and Ludmilla are watching his every move. He takes out his sand wedge, hoping the extra weight in the head and the severely open face of the club might be enough to lift the ball out of the dirt and propel it upward, but without too much momentum to drive the ball past the hole and over the cliff. This is really every hacker's nightmare shot and E.Z. knows it.

"Take your time, bro," Ben says by way of encouragement, knowing full well that time is not the problem here.

"Yeah, take all the time you need. It isn't going to change that lie though," Blaze says, trying his best to rub it in. And this is a ball that doesn't need any more rubbing in.

"Just get under it and follow through. But not too much," Ben winces.

"How are those ant bites?" Hub winks at Blaze, knowing this is one of those time-honored golfing strategies where you try to needle your opponent into a bad shot.

"They sting like hell, thanks for asking," E.Z. says grimacing through his teeth. He's sized up his shot and steps up to address the barely visible ball. He grinds his feet into the hillside, looks over the lip to the flag stick, bends his wrists, cocks his chin and takes the club head back sharply and thrusts downward at the ball more like a sledgehammer than a golf swing. He hits two inches behind the ball and an explosion of sand bursts straight up, lifting the ball over the edge of the berm and sending it rolling amidst the sand pebbles disappearing into the AstroTurf. Despite the aggressive assault, the ball rolls gently towards the hole. For one brief moment everyone stands transfixed, in that way unique to golf and golfers, on the precipice between total success and abject failure, that endless moment when everything has potential. It's not unlike watching a car crash or a comedian slip and fall. You simply can't take your eyes off of it. The ball rolls, as if in slow motion, towards the cup and the players are all frozen in time. These are the moments of golf that will always be remembered. The proverbial pulling the rabbit out of the hat shot. The ball rolls at the hole, like a bunny at a bunny hop. The flag stick is still in the cup and the ball hits it with a unique sound that is at once hollow and sickening. The ball rolls around the cup, as only a recalcitrant golf ball can do. If not for the flag stick the ball would have easily rolled in. Instead, the stick caused the ball to roll about two feet away.

"Oh man!" E.Z. yells.

"I thought you had it. That was a beautiful out, my friend," Ben says, slapping his partner on the back, for what was an amazing shot out of an impossible circumstance. Not to mention the red ant bites.

"Hey, I'm not sorry you missed it, but you were robbed. No doubt about it," Hub says, moving on the green.

"I thought that little sucker was going down, but I guess it only proves the adage that it is very slippery between the lip and the cup. Nice try, though man," Blaze says as he eyes his 25-yard putt.

Despite gentle ribbing and normal competitive rivalry, nobody likes to see a fellow duffer miss a great shot. One may secretly enjoy the failure of others, but at the same time, even on the same course, everyone wants to see the success of others. We may suffer in silence and solitude, but we celebrate in boisterous unity when we witness a true thing of beauty. This also makes golf a unique exercise in bonding and camaraderie, always hoping for the best, but planning for the worst, and usually finding only varying degrees of mediocrity.

Blaze steps up to his putt, just as the late afternoon sun is casting the whole scene in a wonderous light. These are the moments on the golf course, or in this case, in the wilderness, where the mixture of light and nature makes for reverential magic. Blaze strikes his ball, and as if through divine intervention or manifest destiny, the ball, from the moment it is struck, is going to go in the hole. And it does with a wonderous thud, a sound only a golf ball falling 2½ inches into a plastic cup can make. Blaze and Hub dance around the green like leprechauns who have landed the pot of gold at the end of the rainbow. And Ben and E.Z. look like two bumps on a log. Two very depressed bumps on a log. Such is the game of golf and life, one minute you're up and the next minute you are down, way, way down.

Ben, Hub and E.Z. all make their short putts just as the sun is slipping over the horizon. Donna Dina is doing her stand up at the edge of the green.

"And there you have it ladies and gentlemen, as the foursome make the turn at the 9th hole, after 20 days and 200 miles, incredibly, Harbinger/Ichi lead by a single stroke over Hogle/Jones, a combined 6,446 to 6,447. Imagine. Playing over the kind of terrain these guys have had to endure and being separated by only a single stroke is nothing short of miraculous. It is a testament to the talent and tenacity of these players, their competitive natures, not to mention the stellar work of the scorekeepers, that it is this close a match. Stay tuned folks, cause it will only get better from here. To remind the audience, they play eight more holes in the great out-of-doors, then return to Burning Bridges Country Club to play the final 18th hole. When they stroll up the fairway on 18, with the magnificent clubhouse in the background, it will be a sight to behold. These golfers will have accomplished what no others have ever done before them. This marks the halfway point and I've got to tell you, from a personal standpoint, I can't wait for it to be over. I'm Donna Dina, reporting from the Canyonlands of Utah."

---

Later that night around the campfire, the foursome are on their eighth or ninth bottle of Bordeaux, with Donna, Dan, Boris and Ludmilla all sharing in the conviviality and Cookie serving up his usual culinary treats. Donna and Blaze are engaged in a deep and drunken kind of conversation, the kind of conversation that can only come from strong drink and sexual tension.

"That was an amazing putt today. You're pretty good at this aren't you?" Donna says, batting her eyelashes ever so casually.

"I got lucky. It happens every now and then."

"And the way E.Z.'s shot just missed. It could have been a three-stroke swing, if his went in and your shot missed."

"That's the game of golf. Sometimes you win, sometimes you lose."

"So are you a winner or a loser?"

"Oh, I'm a loser. That's for sure."

"Why do you say that? You looked like a winner out there today."

"Well, let's just say I have a long history of losing. I'm one of those rare breeds of people who are able to snatch defeat from the jaws of victory. It's been that way as long as I can remember. How about you? You seem like a sure winner at pretty much everything you do?"

"Well, isn't that sweet of you to notice. But honestly, I haven't always been like this, you know, so put together. Oh no. Believe it or not, I used to be a slob."

"You? I find that hard to believe."

"Oh no. When I lost my dad, I went through a serious depression."

"I'm sorry. I didn't know," Blaze says genuinely touched.

"Yeah, we were pretty close. He taught me a lot. And it was pretty tough for me when he died."

"I kind of lost my old man too. I mean, I never really knew him, so it wasn't quite the same, but I think I know what you mean. I'm very close to my mother, although she probably doesn't realize it."

"You should try to remedy that."

"What about your mom? Where's she?

"Oh, she died years before my dad. That's why losing him was so tough. He was all I had left."

"That definitely sucks. I guess sometimes its better to not know who your parents were than to actually know them, because it is so painful to lose them. If that makes any sense."

"I think I know what you mean. Better to have loved and lost than to have never loved at all. Except in reverse."

"So, we're both only children. Totally spoiled, right?"

"Absolutely. Wouldn't have it any other way."

"How about another round, bartender?" Blaze hoists his perpetually empty glass. Cookie obliges by popping another bottle and pouring freely.

"So, not to bring up a sore subject, but what was that nudity thing all about?" Donna tries to slink up to her subject.

"Oh that. It was nothing really."

"I think we all saw that." Donna smiles demurely.

"I mean, we just happened on to a nudist colony. It wasn't like we talked them in to taking off all their clothes. Colorado is different that way."

"I don't know if you realized it, but the whole country was captivated by it. From what they tell me, the ratings went through the roof. Right now, you guys are hotter than a pistol at an NRA convention."

"I had no idea."

"Yeah. You play your cards right, mister, and the whole world is going to be your oyster."

"That's perfect, because I love oysters. I had no idea. You're completely serious? How could the four of us ever be a big deal?" Blaze looks around the campfire. Hub is singing drunkenly into an empty bottle. E.Z. is scratching his many ant bites. Ben is helping Cookie with the dishes. Boris and Ludmilla are lifting weights in the light of the campfire and reminiscing about the good old bad days.

"We're just a bunch of crazy golfers. We really don't deserve much attention. If you really think about it, except for maybe Ben Ichi, we're all just a bunch of losers. Who else could they get to play this game? Who else could take the time off? Only people who didn't have much going on in the first place."

"Well, you might be pleasantly surprised."

"I've never been pleasantly surprised by anything. Surprise, in my mind, is uniquely reserved for unpleasant things." Blaze drains the last of his drink. "And with that I think I had better retire before I get any more morose. I hate to be puffy in the morning. It was a pleasure speaking with you however. I bid you good night." Blaze takes Donna by the hand and kisses her hand gallantly.

From behind the Conestoga wagon, we can see Dan Flavin has been taping the whole conversation. As Blaze stumbles off to bed, we can see Dan give Donna the thumbs up sign. She sheepishly returns the gesture, but she also doesn't want to betray the trust she is developing. Sometimes being a beautiful, top-notch sports reporter is harder than it looks.

From behind the Conestoga, at the edge of the glow from the campfire, the singer Leon Russell sits at his lonely piano like an apparition. He has long white flowing hair, wears a stars and stripes stove pipe glitter hat and he sings the bittersweet love song *A Song For You.*

> *"I love you in a place where there's no space and time,*
> *I love you for in my life you are a friend of mine,*
> *And when my life is over, remember when we were together,*
> *We were alone and I was singing this song for you.*
> *We were alone and I was singing this song for you."*

The footage of Blaze and Donna's conversation is playing on the television set over the bar in one of the millions of bars that exist in all the dank, dark corners of the world. The bartender, bar maid, cook and five patrons are all glued to the set as Blaze describes his loser mentality and his love for his mother. The bar maid wipes a tear from her eye. This is being repeated throughout the world and the coverage is starting to take on the look and feel of a reality TV sports show, or even a soap opera with golf clubs. And the foursome has no idea of their growing celebrity.

That is until they stumble on a remote trading post, the last gas station for a hundred miles, a little place called Fry Canyon. Set in the middle of absolutely nowhere, it is a rundown, ramshackle rock shop kind of a place, where you can get Vienna sausages in a can, Wonder Bread in a loaf, ice cream in a drumstick in the cooler by the door, and a cold beer, a pack of smokes and maybe even a girlie magazine behind the counter. Over the cash register, the old punch button kind, a dim little black and white TV flickers in the corner.

As Blaze, Hub, E.Z. and Ben burst through the well-worn screen door, the little geezer behind the counter, with a beard that makes him look like Moses himself, pulls a shotgun from behind the counter.

"Hold it right there amigos. Do you usually just burst in like that without announcing yourselves? I didn't hear a car pull up." He spits some chew juice into a spitoon.

"Sorry about that. We're out playing golf and we came upon your place and I guess we got a little excited cause we haven't seen anything like civilization for quite some time," Hub says enthusiastically.

"Wait a minute. I know you guys. You're on the TV."

Sure enough, there in black and white and grainy all over is Blaze's conversation that through the miracle of editing sounds more like a confessional than it really was.

"Hey! That's me!"

"You sound like a real sad sack, pal," Moses with the beard says.

"I can't believe she did this. That woman deliberately got me drunk and took advantage of the situation. I feel totally betrayed." Blaze looks away from the TV.

"I don't blame you. It is kind of embarrassing. It's like being on Oprah or something. You'll have to forgive me, but you can't be too careful out here. What with gun runners, smugglers and the occasional station wagon full of tourists with children and strollers. Name's Abbey. Moses Abbey. What can I do you for?"

"We'll take some cigars. Couple of packs of chewing gum-Doublemint," E.Z. calls out.

"I'd love an ice cream bar. Got any Eskimo Pies?" Hub asks, moving to the freezer unit.

"I just can't believe she did that to me. Why don't you give me a six-pack," Blaze says.

"What flavor?"

"Whatever's coldest."

Moses puts a six-pack up on the counter.

"Can't believe you fellars would end up in my place. I've got a camera, would you mind if we got a picture together? I sometimes go for weeks without anybody stopping in. That's why I collect all these rocks. Not much else to do out here. Just watch the rocks getting older by the minute. I like to think of it as my own rock opera. Get it?"

"Yeah. That's funny. So, are we in Utah yet?"

"Absolutely. Home of the Beehive. Busy little bees, we are here. All organized, each according to its need. Each according to its talents. So, is this everything?" Moses rings up the merchandise. "Plus the government's share, comes to $23.96."

Blaze hands him a 20 and a five.

"You got anything smaller? I'm not sure I can make that kind of change."

"Oh go ahead and keep the change."

"Well, I'll tell you what I'm going to do. Don't know if you noticed outside when you came in, but there is a three-legged dog that's been hanging around here for awhile. I call him Peabody. I'll let you have him for the difference."

"You want to sell us your dog for a dollar and four cents?" Blaze asks incredulous.

"First of all, he's not my dog. He just showed up here one day. Second, I'm not selling him to you. If, when you leave, he follows you, then so be it. If he decides to stay here, that's fine too. But I'm getting pretty old to care for a dog, and you look like you could probably use a good friend."

Blaze has already drowned three of his six beers. He pops another and drowns away his sorrows.

"Women will do that to you. Take your heart in their hands and then just mangle it into a sausage. I know firsthand. That's how I ended up here with my rock opera. There's always a woman behind every sad story."

Outside the trading post, Moses Abbey lines up the camera on a hitching post, sets the timer and joins in the picture of the famous golfers, now with a three-legged runt in the shot. Turns out, Peabody is more than ready to move on down the road. His limp will be no worse than anyone else's. In fact, he may get around better on three legs than our golfers do on two. Where there is a will, there is a way. And when there is a way, Peabody will have his little nose to the ground searching for it. Our rag-tag bunch of losers has just acquired its newest member, a three-legged runt, with a heart of gold, named Peabody.

# CHAPTER 7
## "DOUBLE YOUR PLEASURE, DOUBLE YOUR FUN"

E.Z. UNWRAPS HIS DOUBLEMINT gum and offers it around.

"Gum?"

Hub takes a stick.

"You want some gum?"

"No thanks. I've got sharp teeth and fat cheeks. Makes for a bad combination. Plus, gum gets in the way of my drinking," Blaze says with a Bloody Mary in hand. He points towards Peabody, standing inquisitively on his three legs.

"You think we should rename him, or stick with Peabody?"

"I think Peabody suits him. Besides, there is an old Chinese saying, changing name is not like changing underwear. Even a bad name is better than dirty shorts." Ben Ichi really does have a vast inventory of old adages.

"So, I think I may have come up with a little plan," Blaze says.

"Oh yeah, what's that partner?" E.Z. asks, always the skeptic.

"I say, at our first opportunity, we try to lose the TV crew."

"Why would we want to do that? I like being on TV, even if we can't see it," E.Z. answers.

"I think the TV people are just in the way. We don't need

them to play our game. Or at least, they could just report the day's results, not be there for every friggin' shot. I'm tired of having to always be 'up' for the camera."

"Well, you've got a good point there. I've really had to hold back on my insults and cursing with the camera running." E.Z. has a point. "I'm in."

"Sure, why not. I'm in. Honestly, I'm really tired of looking at that Escalade." Ben says with a smile on his face. "I've always been more partial to Japanese models."

"Okay, but how will we know when the right time to ditch them is?" Hub asks conspiratorially.

"Somehow, I think we'll just know. Keep your eyes out and we'll give each other the high sign. I'll let Cookie know."

"I'll tell the Rooskies. This could actually be fun." Hub says with a twinkle in his eye and an extra kick in his step.

---

The foursome is making its way down a dry stream bed, lined with giant cottonwood trees, stretching to low hillsides of purple sagebrush and black volcanic rocks, deposited from long ago volcanoes. The aspen-choked remnants of those volcanoes still stand proudly in the distance with whole sides of their faces missing. Nature is never kind, not even to itself. But at the moment, the golf is being played at a leisurely pace, despite the rocky terrain. Cookie and the wagon follow behind the players, with Ludmilla and Boris riding ahead to survey the shots. Donna and Dan in the Escalade trail behind the whole bunch, with Dan occasionally getting out to shoot some beauty shots and to get a long distance perspective on the game.

"So that was pretty harsh, the way she used you just to get a story," Hub says as he and Blaze walk up the sandy beach.

"Let's just say it didn't come as a surprise. I don't have a great record when it comes to relationships. Besides, what am I to her?

Someone in her position? Like we were really going to dig each other? Come on, I may look young, but I wasn't born yesterday."

"I've never trusted women," E.Z. blurts out. "Then again, I've never trusted anybody. Not even pets."

"My old man used to say, when you learn to trust, you learn to breath. When you learn to breath, you learn to live. And when you learn to live, you learn to love, and when you learn to love, you learn to trust," Ben Ichi chips in like a pro.

"I've got to meet your old man," Blaze says.

"Yeah, he's pretty cool."

"Not my old man. He'd never let you breath. He kept his foot pretty well over your windpipe, all the time." E.Z. isn't making it up.

"That's sad, man. No wonder your brother is such a jerk."

"He's like Mahatma Gandhi compared to my old man."

"Hey, you guys are lucky. Both my folks are passed. They were big people, with big hearts, that one day just clogged up and they keeled over. Within six months of each other. They just left me and my kid sister. It was no picnic." Hub gets wistful about his family history.

"I guess we've all got our crosses to bear," Blaze says.

"Or our bears to cross!" Hub laughs at his little joke. "Wait a minute! Did you see that rock move? Up ahead, look! Those rocks are moving!"

In the foreground, in the shadow of the sagebrush, the rocks are moving. But they aren't rocks. They are sheep. Thousands of them moving across the plateau.

"If I'm not mistaken, those rocks are wooly," Blaze says.

"Not again. We had cows the other day. Today it's sheep," E.Z. complains.

"At least their poops are smaller," Hub offers.

Before you can say lamb chops, the foursome is surrounded by thousands of sheep as they bleat and clang bells tied around their necks.

"Don't move and we won't get hurt," Hub says nervously.

"Whatever you do, don't fall down. It would be like being smothered by thousands of wool sweaters."

Eventually a cowboy rides up on a big black horse. He is the sheepherder and goes by the name of Bo. He has long blonde curly hair and looks like Custer before the last stand.

"Howdy! Hope you're not in too big a hurry. We'll be through here in about 10-15 minutes." He's definitely not Bud Weiser. He's more like Little Bo Peep, but in leather chaps. He nods at Cookie and winks.

"That's a lot of lambies you've got there," Hub says.

"Yep. Gotta keep sheep moving or they'll eat everything in sight."

"What are they dining on here?"

"Well, besides the normal prairie grasses, they've been eating some foreign species, things like leafy spurge, knapweed and dalmation toadflax."

"That sounds kind of like the salad bar."

"If it doesn't move, they'll eat it." The cowboy's shepherd dog runs up and smells at Peabody's rear end. "What happened to your dog?"

"We're not sure. That's how he came."

"Ain't no place out here for a three-legged dog. Little fellar barely has a leg to stand on."

Peabody growls, more at the owner than the shepherd.

"So, what are you fellows doing out here, are you on some kind of religious pilgrimmage or something? What's with the staffs? You know, the walking sticks?"

"These? These are golf clubs. We're out here playing a golf game," Hub says.

"Golf? Ain't that something? Hoity-toity game all the way out here. Who knew you could play golf through a sheep herd? I just hope the sheep don't find your golf balls, because if they do, they are going to eat them."

The whole crazy enterprise is surrounded by thousands of fleecy little critters moving on their spindly little four legs. All legs of lamb in waiting, baahing and braying like little future morsels of chops, roasts and stews in protest of their destinies, the end of the line, as it were. Let's face it, no one wants to end up a sausage, not matter how much fennel you put in. You'd eat everything in sight too if someone shaved your skin twice a year, ate your young and made you walk for miles in search of food and water. And then the coup de grace; at the end of the line, they slit your throat, slice your body into prized and prime selections of meat, and grill you over a hot flame. And still the sheep follow the leader. Such is the power of the clanging bell. In the end, we are all sheep heading gleefully to slaughter. Sports may be our collective clanging bell. Golf can only be a distraction from the awareness of our eventual demise. But what a distraction it can be. Just ask any golf widow. She'll tell you golfers are all like sheep, dressed in polyester and driving around in those cute little carts, smoking stogies and pounding Silver Bullets, but all headed to the same killing floor, one stroke at a time. Enjoy it while you can fellow duffers. Eat, drink and be merry, for tomorrow you may be in Utah.

"Listen, I'm wondering if you and all your sheep might give us a little hand here," Blaze says to Little Bo Peep.

"Sure. What you got in mind?"

"You see that Escalade back there?"

"Sure. I've always hated people who drive those damned things. I'm a Prius guy all the way."

"Good, because we'd like you to delay them with your herd, while we make a break for the canyons."

"Nothing I like better than getting in people's way. And if I were you, I'd take a left at the second canyon. They'll never find you back in there. They call it Hell's Backbone and it won't be kind to a Cadillac."

"Much obliged to you Bo," Cookie says as he moves the Conestoga past the sheep. "And by the way, I love the perm. Giddyup now! Let's go!"

And with that the golfers make a hasty exit from the river of sheep, with Cookie and the dune buggy in hot pursuit. The golfers all take a drop, with an equal penalty and they hit quick shots, almost in unison to move themselves and the game away from the herd of sheep and the incessant bleating of the media.

Inside the Escalade, Donna is behind the wheel and not sure what to do. Dan is shooting beauty shots of the cuter sheep.

"What's going on? Where are they going? We're trapped!" Donna honks the horn, but the sheep just stare at her, like it was music to their ears.

In fact, the more she honks the horn, the more sheep gather to hear the cacophony. Sheep are naturally curious with excellent hearing and figure all the honking must mean dinner and dancing. The Escalade is swarmed by sheep looking for a good time. All dressed up and no place to go.

---

The campfire is aglow as the moon peeks over the canyon rim. The boys are gathered around drinking as usual, insulting each other and generally entertaining the peanut gallery, consisting of Cookie, Boris, Ludmilla, and the perky little fellow with three legs, Peabody. Things are getting downright chummy.

"That was pretty good today, ditching the TV people," Cookie says.

"Yeah, it worked out pretty good. I've got to say, though, it seemed almost like you knew Little Bo Peep," Blaze says.

"Well, our paths may have crossed a time or two. It's a small world."

"I loved vhat he'd done vith his hair. It vas gorgeous!" Ludmilla croons.

"Yeah, he's good at that kind of stuff, which is kind of unique for a cowboy. But a good cowboy has got to be a jack of all trades out here. Even when it comes to hairstyles."

"It is amazing what you can do with curlers," E.Z. offers.

The guys all look at him funny.

"Hey, I live with Gyll and Giselle and we all share the same

147

bathroom. I'm telling you, Giselle could work miracles with bobby pins and a blow dryer."

"So, we're not lost here or anything are we?" Hub asks nervously.

"Of course not. Come sunrise I'll get my bearings and we'll get right back on track. Don't you worry about a thing. I know this damned country like the back of my hand," Cookie says with brio he may come to regret.

---

At a lonely phone booth, off the side of the road, Donna is talking with Harvey Wallbanger in New York. Whether it is because of the great distance or the old gum stuck in the receiver, neither of them can hear very well.

"I don't know how to tell you this, but we've lost them," Donna says breathlessly.

"What do you mean lost?"

"I mean they're gone. Vamoosed."

"I can barely hear you."

"My cell phone doesn't work out here."

"Did you say you were lost?"

"No. I said they are lost. The golfers. I lost them."

"How could they be lost?"

"They were there one minute and then they weren't. They ditched us."

"There was a ditch?"

"Yes, there was a ditch. We were trapped by a herd of sheep. By the time we got out, they were gone. We couldn't find them and we don't quite know what to do?"

"This sounds serious. These guys are a bigger deal than Alex Trebek, Donald Trump, Howie Mandel and Regis Philbin all rolled together. We've got to find them!"

Harvey Wallbanger hangs up the phone with Donna. He immediately makes another call.

"Hello, Bob. I wanted to get to you as soon as I knew. We need an emergency meeting. I've got some difficult news. The golfers are lost!"

You can hear screaming on the other end of the phone.

"That's right. They are missing and I'm hanging up and calling the authorities. This has moved from being a big sports story to being a big news story. Everybody in the world is going to be paying attention now. It's like an Amber Alert for a missing foursome for Christ's sake! Heads could roll if we don't play this right. You call the boys for a meeting tonight at my office. Time is of the essence."

Later that night, at a super secret meeting in the black tower that houses the television network, like a black Escalade inverted in the sky, Wiley, Riley, Sal, Monty and Bob Post from RAGU are all meeting with Harvey Wallbanger and his staff. They are mulling over the various possibilities. None of them are good.

"How on earth could they have disappeared?" Riley asks perplexed.

"I told you this was going to cost us a lot of money," Monty retorts.

"I knew I should have hidden under my desk when you guys walked into my office," Bob Post says, his face buried in his hands.

"Now, wait just a minute fellows, before we jump to too many conclusions. Have they found their bodies?" Wiley is the voice of reason.

"No."

"Have they found any missing clubs or bags?"

"No."

"Have they found the Conestoga wagon? No sign of Indians on the war path?"

"No, thank God!" Harvey pours another scotch.

"No signs of a struggle?"

"You don't think they could have been kidnapped? Or met with foul play?" Sal wonders aloud.

"The only foul play is their god damned game!" Bob moans.

"They have simply vanished into thin air." Harvey pounds down his scotch.

"You don't think they could have been abducted by aliens, you know, UFOs?" Riley asks.

"We could only hope." Monty says. "It would save us a ton."

"Highly doubtful, though it would be intriguing. Do you think they've invented golf on other planets?" Wiley is always thinking outside the box.

"Bob, can't you get through to your KGB people?"

"You mean through telepathy or something?" Bob says. "I'll call Yuri Geller and see if he can take some god damned time out from bending spoons! Of course, if we could get through, we would get through. No communication devices work out there. There isn't a cell tower for hundreds of miles. They may as well be in a gulag in Siberia. Let's face it, we're fucked!"

"Gentlemen, I'm afraid we have little recourse other than to let the world in on our little catastrophe. And we'll move heaven on earth to find them. Let there be no doubt, we will find them. Dead or alive."

Donna Dina is doing her live stand-up at the edge of an alkaline desert, where mirage shadows of heat and atmosphere shimmer in the distance. Dan Flavin shoots video from a tripod.

"This is Donna Dina reporting live on a breaking news story. The famous foursome, playing the golf game of the century, has mysteriously disappeared into the labyrinth of canyons somewhere in Southern Utah."

A man in a bar, as men in bars all around the world repeat,

suddenly sits up and takes notice. "Hey, quiet down. Turn this up!"

"It was mid-afternoon yesterday, when the group was passing through a sheep herd, when something must have spooked the horses and the Conestoga wagon took off, with the golfers in tow. Despite our best efforts and with law enforcement now on the scene, the foursome seems to be lost somewhere west of here. We'll be working closely with state officials from a command post set up in the local high school, and we will keep you posted on the progress of this developing story. What started out a courageous adventure, may yet end up a tragic event. It is certainly not just another day out on a golf course. I'm Donna Dina reporting live from somewhere in Utah."

Hub Hogle is wearing a discarded hubcap tied under his chin, to shield him from the murderous sun. His lips are blistered, his clothing tattered and he looks like an apparition from a shipwreck. He stumbles forward, golf club in hand, looking for his ball in a landscape that looks remarkably like another planet. It is a disengorged mud flat, spit up from the bowels of hell itself, known locally as Goblin Valley, for all the misshapen globs of mud, hardened over millenia, in various shapes all resembling Richard Nixon's face on acid.

Hub spies his ball tucked neatly in a sandstone formation. He has little option but to putt the ball out. He takes his putter and hits a shot that rolls as if on an amazing miniature golf course. It loops and runs, jumps and curves, zooms and rushes across the bizarre landscape as though it were a steel ball bearing being bounced by rubber bumpers in a pinball machine in God's den. And when God plays pinball, there is no tilting and he never runs out of quarters. The ball rolls for what seems like an eternity and as we all know, that can be a very long time.

Hub nonchalantly rounds a hoodoo and comes upon a family

having a picnic, replete with burgers on the government grill. The little boy and girl stop in their tracks when they see the bear of a man, looking like a crazed lunatic, wearing a hubcap for a hat, with a golf club in his hand. The kids both start to cry. The mother spots Hub and takes the children by the hand.

"I thought I smelled barbecue!" Hub takes in a deep breath. "Those burgers sure smell good."

"Honey!" The wife says in a high-pitched voice. The husband looks up from his newspaper. He spots the golf club in Hub's hand and gets genuinely nervous. He joins his wife and crying children. Hub notices their concern.

"Oh, don't mind me. We're just playing a little golf game. I know I must look like hell, but really I'm perfectly harmless. You have nothing to fear, but fear itself."

The wife starts to cry now too. Her husband takes her hand and draws his children near.

"Really, I'm just a normal guy. Actually, I'm a bartender. Four rich old geezers got drunk and here I am!" Hub takes in the smell of the charcoaling burger. "You don't think I could talk you out of one of those burgers do you?"

The husband inches his wife and kids towards the Winnebago parked nearby. As Hub reaches for a burger with all the fixins, the little family runs into the Winnebago and locks the door. The husband starts up the vehicle and roars out of the parking spot. Hub shrugs it off and scoops up another burger for the road.

Blaze is getting set to hit an iron shot, as his ball is buried in a grey sand trap. He too looks the worse for wear. His hair is noticeably longer, he has a scraggly beard and he is deeply suntanned. He looks more like a homeless person than a somewhat infamous golfer. Blaze nonchalantly hits his iron and it bounces off one of Richard Nixon's noses, ricochets past one of his loping ears, creases a couple of his smirking lips and settles in his receding hairline. Not a bad shot at all, given the crooked topography.

Ben Ichi's ball is sitting pretty in the middle of Goblin Valley, but Ben is mesmerized by all the contorted shapes and hallucinatory faces. He's never seen anything remotely like this place. He passes one of the goblins and bows kindly to it, as though it were a distant relative, a sentry of sorts guarding this sacred space. Judging from Ben Ichi's threadbare clothing, he may as well be a beggar in the court of the emperor. He pulls out of his bag a wonderous old club, a classic niblick, which belonged to his grandfather. He hits a near perfect shot with it, something his ancestors would have been proud of, as the ball screams along the middle of the valley, undisturbed by the hoodoos and gurus that line the way.

E.Z.'s ball has found its way into a sink hole, left over from an ancient river. He has to slick rock himself down into the pit, getting down on his butt and slowly shimmying his way down. Once inside the pit, he pulls out a 9-iron to gain some major loft to get himself out of this hole.

He hits a powerful shot, popping the ball well into the blue sky and high over the edge of the rim. From his vantage point he has no idea where the ball has landed. It's like the blind leading the blind. And E.Z., like everyone else on the tour, looks the part. His pants are torn, his shirt is ripped and his socks have gaping holes in them. He continues to shave on most days and miraculously maintains a military approved haircut, but other than that, he's a wreck. He's like a bull in a china shop after the party has ended and all the dishes are broken. He slowly realizes, after hitting his shot out of the hole, that he now can't get out of the sinkhole himself. He tries all the angles, like a cat trapped in the basement. After several futile attempts, he knows there is no way out. He resorts to shouting and as he does there is a distinct echo that resounds off the canyon walls.

"H-E-L-P! H-e-l-p!"

"GET OUT OF HERE! Get me out of here!"

"I'M TRAPPED! I'm trapped!"

"I AM THE BEST GOLFER IN THE WORLD! I am the best golfer in the world!"

"NO YOU AREN'T! No, you aren't!" The boys have found E.Z. and the echo.

"YOU ARE A DUMBSHIT WHO IS STUCK IN A HOLE! You are a dumbshit who is stuck in a hole!"

The boys are standing over the ledge and peering into the pit. E.Z. stands there with his golf bag stuck about twenty feet down.

"How'd you manage to get down there?" Hub asks.

"It was easy. And don't make a wisecrack about that being my name. Just get me out of here."

"That isn't going to be so easy, E.Z.," Blaze says. "Do I hear an echo?"

"It must be an echo chamber."

"E.Z. SUCKS THE BIG ONE! E.Z. sucks the big one!" Blaze shouts at the top of his lungs.

"E.Z. DOES IT AGAIN! E.Z. does it again!" Hub laughs.

"E.Z. COME, E.Z. GO! E.Z. come, E.Z. go!" Ben Ichi gets in on the act too.

"E.Z. FOR YOU TO SAY! E.Z. for you to say!" E.Z. shouts. "Just get me the hell out of here."

"And how do you propose we do that?" Blaze asks, surveying the situation.

"Anybody have a rope?" Blank stares all around.

"How about a tree branch? I saw that once in a movie," Hub says.

They all look around the desolate landscape. It would be like finding a tree branch on the moon.

"Wait a minute! I've got an idea. TAKE OFF YOUR PANTS AND THROW THEM UP HERE," Ben shouts. "Take off your pants and throw them up here."

"You've got to be kidding?"

"What's the matter, don't you trust me?"

"Sure, I trust you."

"I couldn't hear you."

"SURE, I TRUST YOU! Sure, I trust you."

"Now you guys drop your drawers too." Ben says.

"What in the hell have you got in mind?" Hub wonders.

"We're going to tie the legs of all our pants end-to-end and drop it into the hole and hopefully they will be long enough for him to grab. Do you guys have any better ideas?"

They all pull off their pants, or what's left of them, and Ben quickly ties them together. He tosses the line of pants down toward E.Z. He stretches on his tip toes to reach the end and has just enough momentum to reach up and pull himself up hand-over-hand. He reaches the top with great effort and excellent stitching. As he does, with all the guys standing in their underwear, a stranger dressed all in black, with a long flowing beard and a preacher's hat, appears from behind one of the hoodoos.

"I heard your shouting. Do you need my help?" The stranger makes note of the foursome's attire, or lack thereof. "Or perhaps my spiritual guidance?"

"Oh, we're fine now. Our friend was just down in a hole," Hub answers nervously as most men in their underwear will in front of a strange preacher who has an uncanny resemblance to Johnny Cash.

"Are you one of those gay tour groups? I've heard about those, you know, getting it on in nature?" The stranger raises an eyebrow.

"Oh no sirree! We're definitely not gay. We're just a bunch of golfers who happen to be standing around in our underwear," E.Z. attempts a lame answer. "And Ben, if you'd be so kind as to untie our pants, we'll all be getting dressed now."

"Gay golfers huh? Are you fellas on drugs too? Are you all hyped up on poppers?"

"No sir. I think you've got the wrong impression. We were just having some fun with the echo and all. I'm Blaze. This is my partner, I mean my friend Hub. And these two no goods are Ben and E.Z."

"Pleasure to make your acquaintence. Name's Jo-Seph."

From behind another hoodoo steps another stranger also dressed in head-to-toe black clothing and also having a striking resemblance to Johnny Cash.

"And this is my brother, Jo-Hann."

"Pleasure to make your acquaintence," Jo-Hann says as he spits on the ground in a slightly menacing way.

From behind yet another hoodoo steps a third stranger, the spitting image of the other two.

"And this here is my other brother Jo-Bob."

"Apparently, we've run into the Echo People," Blaze says under his breath.

"And their parents started to run out of names starting with Joe," Hub answers.

By now Ben has untied all the pants and the boys all pull them on hurriedly.

"Our cook should be around here somewhere. He'll fill you in," Blaze offers.

The three strangers all look skeptical. What kind of guys travel with their own chef? I think we all know the answer to that one.

"And we've got the rules committee bopping around here somewhere in a bright yellow dune buggy, a lovely heterosexual husband and wife team who used to work for the KGB," Hub offers trailing off, recognizing the absurdity of his statement under the stern eyes of three Johnny Cashes. He laughs nervously and kicks the ground like a guilty man who can't stand up to the scrutiny.

---

The three Johnny Cashes lead the golf caravan into the compound, a well-fortified collection of buildings, all resembling each other, in a cinder block kind of way, centered on the Temple House, a magnificent looking structure which is as ornate as the others are plain. Streams of women and children, dressed in long, gingham dresses and worn-denim bib overalls come running out of the houses to gawk at the strangers as the elders march them into the town square. The women all wear their hair in a distinct way, a kind of modest beehive and the children are all toeheads.

The golfers look at the gawkers like they were strangers from a strange land. A land where everyone looks like everyone else, almost as if they were all related in some way. And in tiny Gospel, Utah they are all related because they are all polygamists.

This is a place where men who happen to look like Johnny Cash are allowed, nay, in fact required, to take more than one woman in holy matrimony. And not just any other woman- mostly sisters, cousins and daughters. It is not uncommon for an uncle to marry one of his nieces, as a third or fourth wife. And the men who look like Johnny Cash don't always make the decisions. That responsibility falls only on one person. The most senior elder of the bunch, the one known as Joe the Prophet, or Joe the Pro to his friends.

Joe the Pro, ancient and decrepit, sits in his pimped out camper van with the green racing stripes, swivel recliners and the plastic pop-top roof, with the side sliding door open. Because of a mule kick to his windpipe, he now must speak through an electronic vocalizer pressed against his vocal chord, which makes his voice sound like an alien in a bad sci-fi movie. The bedraggled golfing entourage is delivered to Joe the Pro's feet, like so many explorers in the heart of darkness, brought to the tribal elder by the restless natives looking for a free meal.

The first Johnny Cash steps forward. "We found these people in Echo Canyon. They were standing around in their underwear, with their pants all tied together in some kind of ritual ceremony. They claim to be golfers, just out for a good time."

Joe the Pro eyeballs the unlikely bunch. He presses the vocalizer to his throat. "Who is the good looking couple?"

"They are a heterosexual couple who claim to have worked for the KGB. They say they are the scorekeepers sent from an organization known as RAGU.

"How about the old codger?" Joe the Pro points his vocalizer at Cookie, who has a growling Peabody on a leash.

"Apparently he is their guide, cook and chief bottle washer.

A purveyor of good things who travels by horse and wagon and makes witty observations along the way."

"And the dog?"

"He's just a puny three-legged runt who started following along," Cookie offers. "He's completely harmless!" Peabody growls even harder.

Joe the Pro takes in the group. "Welcome to our little corner of the world. We don't get many strangers here. We're kind of isolated and we like it that way. We don't cuddle up to strangers who have strange beliefs and strange customs and strange sexual practices. We don't like strange. We only like familiar."

Blaze steps forward. "I'm afraid there has been some kind of misunderstanding. We really are just a bunch of golfers, who took a wrong turn, who kind of got lost, who I am sure could never find our way back here, if we even wanted to, which I can assure you we don't. And won't, if we are allowed to leave."

"What about the strange sexual practices?"

"We had to take our pants off, to tie together to form a rope line, to get our friend E.Z. out of a sinkhole. It was all very innocent and above board. It had nothing to do with sex of any kind. We really are just playing a golf match. A nice heterosexual golf match."

"Like I said, we don't take kindly to strangers. But we do know that the Lord does work in some mighty mysterious ways. And if it has been His wish to bring you to us, who am I to question the Knower of All Things?" Joe the Pro purses a wicked smile revealing a set of green, rotting teeth, the result of his addiction to apple flavored hard candies. "We always welcome the opportunity to increase the gene pool."

"What did he say?" Blaze asks quietly.

"Something about a pool for our jeans?" Hub answers under his breath.

Donna Dina is stretched over, looking at a table strewn with USGS maps, in the center of the search and rescue effort. Standing next to her is the head of the highway patrol, Bernie Calderwood, a suntanned fellow with the requisite aviator sunglasses and telegenic teeth; standing next to him is the head of public safety for the state of Utah, the overseer of all police activities and the corrections department, the big, bald giant of a man, Leigh Sauerbrauten. Donna is doing her best to identify the last place she saw the foursome. Dan Flavin shoots video over her shoulder.

"I think it was somewhere near here," Donna points with her finger.

"Goblin Valley."

Leigh and Bernie both wince and look at each other with real trepidation. "That could be bad," Bernie says.

"That could be very bad," Leigh adds.

"What's so bad about it?" Donna asks.

"Well, first of all, there aren't many roads out there," Bernie starts out.

"Second of all, you've got all manner of ornery critter, from scorpions to desert cougar. Not to mention, mountains of man-eating red ants. And rattlers. Tons of rattlers," Leigh adds. "And snapping turtles that can bite a man's finger off clear through the bone like it was a celery stick stuffed with pimento cream cheese at a church social."

"Plus you've got the old uranium mines. Hotter than a fuel rod at Chernobyl."

"And very nasty weather. We're talkin' lightning storms, hailstorms, flash floods. Hot as Hades itself during the daytime and cold as a witch's tit at night. S'cuse me, ma'am, for saying that last part. But it is true."

"Doesn't anybody live out there?" Donna asks.

"Just a crazy bunch of polygamists. And God help them if they got a hold of them. It could be death by green Jello," Bernie says without a hint of irony.

"Or worse. They could make them marry some of the... how

shall I say this? Some of the homelier girls, if you know what I mean. The girls who might have a harder time finding a husband, if you get my drift." Leigh winks at Donna.

"Your drift is duly noted. But we have got to find these guys. I don't care if we have to call in the National Guard. All of America is anxious about their whereabouts. We have got to find them! This is the most important thing any of us has ever done!"

---

The single polygamist women are lined up against the wall, more like potential victims of a firing squad than the wallflowers they actually are. Displayed are all manner of facial warts, weeping pimples, twisted noses, hairy lips and cauliflowered ears. There may be more moles per capita in Gospel than any other place on earth, and that's the gospel truth. Standing in a parallel line, like birds on a wire, are our fearless foursome, all cleaned up, freshly shaven and wearing clean white shirts. Music is playing from a fiddler, a piano player and an accordionist, all playing in a small bandstand in the corner.

Joe the Pro steps between the lines. "Gentlemen, I'd like to present my daughters, first, the adorable Jo-Anne, my oldest daughter." Jo-Anne is the size of a buffalo. She takes a step forward and paws the ground.

"Next, is my second daughter, the beautiful Jo-Beth." Jo-Beth looks like a grey stick in a gingham dress. She steps forward and yawns, then smiles, revealing a set of teeth worthy of a beaver in advanced age.

"Next, is my third daughter, the captivating Jo-Cell. She's the coquette of the bunch." She is in fact rather coquettish, for someone who resembles a peanut still in the shell. She steps forward and giggles, pulling down the sides of her dress over her knobby knees.

"Finally, last but certainly not least, is the divine Jo-Dawn, the baby of the bunch." Jo-Dawn steps forward and she is even bigger than her three sisters combined with all their livestock. She is a formidable fortress of a woman, a veritable flying buttress of a gal. She steps forward and grunts and snorts like a bellows on a wet fire.

A man who looks like Johnny Cash steps forward with the microphone.

"Gentlemen, honor your partners," the square dance caller announces. The four golfers all look at each other not knowing what to do. Cookie steps forward to coach them.

"That means you bow to your partner." The foursome bows awkwardly. The homely sisters curtsy in return.

"Allamande right and do-si-do."

The foursome looks to Cookie. "Face your partner and take their right hand and kinda walk around each other." The foursome takes their partners' hands and the homely sisters guide them around the circle.

"Then fold your arms and kinda skip in place around each of your ladies." The guys look at Cookie like he must be crazy. "Go on, it ain't that hard." The guys all do it but they look like a bunch of lunatics at the asylum social, freshly scrubbed, and in white shirts and padded cells.

"And ladies promenade," the caller sings out.

The foursome do-si-does and the homely sisters promenade. The guys look about as comfortable as eighth graders at an etiquette class, but the homely girls are all having the time of their lives. They haven't been around this many eligible bachelors since, well, since eighth grade etiquette class.

At the folding table on one side of the room sits mountains of green Jello in various incarnations and exotic molds. One, in the shape of a cowboy hat, is filled with shredded carrots. Another, in the shape of a giant heart is filled with raspberries and sliced red grapes. Another in the shape of male genitalia is filled with walnuts and tiny white marshmallows. Boris and Ludmilla are enjoying the Jello and conversing with Joe the Pro.

"Ve love ze Jello. How did it become so popular?" Ludmilla asks.

Joe the Pro holds the vocalizer to his throat. "Because we live in a desert, anything cold and jiggly gets our attention. Plus you've got so many pretty colors. Just like all our pretty girls."

"Ve can zee vith our own eyes, you've got some beauties. It reminds me of ze fatherland, with all ze toeheaded children," Boris announces.

"We would sure be honored if you all decided to stick around and join us in our merry making. I can pretty much guarantee you could have the pick of the litter."

Ludmilla just about chokes on her marshmallow Jello. "I don't think that vill be happening. Isn't that right my darlink Boris?"

"Yah. Right. As much as ve enjoy sex, ve vouldn't vant to enjoy it with others. I'm pretty much a von voman kind of guy."

"And ve vouldn't vant it any other vay. No sirree bub." Ludmilla devours her marshmallow Jello indignantly.

Back on the dance floor the foursome is doing its best to square dance, but just barely managing to keep up with their more experienced partners. It's like trying to put square legs in round holes.

"Gentlemen, form a star and allamande left and ladies, the grand chain, and back the same."

---

Back at the search party headquarters, the phone rings and Bernie Calderwood answers. Donna Dina and Dan Flavin are sleeping in the corner.

"Search party headquarters, Calderwood speaking."

"We were camping out past Goblin Valley, when a deranged guy with a golf club came into our camp and demanded our hamburgers," the voice on the phone says.

Bernie sits up. "This sounds like our guys. Deranged guy with a golf club demanding hamburgers." Donna and Dan jump to their feet.

"Where did he say he saw them?" Donna asks, camera rolling.

"Out past Goblin Valley."

"We already knew they were in Goblin Valley!"

"Well now they are past Goblin Valley. And they are hungry! What else have you got buddy?"

"I think he was carrying a putter. I'm pretty sure it was a putter," the guy on the phone says. "And he was a big guy. A big guy with a putter."

"Then we'll have to consider him armed and dangerous."

"He scared the hell out of my wife and kids. A big guy comes out of the wilderness with a golf club and demands your hamburgers, you can bet the farm, we're going to give him anything he wants. I'm pretty sure it was a putter, but with my wife and kids crying and all, I could be wrong. We made a beeline to the Winnebago and didn't look back."

"We appreciate the call, but honestly, and I don't enjoy being the bearer of bad news, the chances of getting the burgers back are practically nil."

Bernie hangs up the phone. "Sometimes this job gets to you in ways you never expected." He wipes a tear from the corner of his eye.

"We can see that. What time did you say the helicopter was coming?"

"It should be here any minute. Leigh just had to check with the governor's office and the church, of course. Meaning the Mormon Church."

"What on earth does the Mormon Church have to do with getting a state helicopter for a search and rescue?"

"Well, I don't know how it works where you come from, but somebody has got to be in charge. And out here, when the Church sneezes, we all catch cold. Plus, they're not real fond of national media attention that focuses on an embarrassing part of their history by flying over some religious renegades with a state helicopter, if you know what I mean. There is actually a little guy who sits in a little office and makes sure the Church is portrayed in a favorable light when it comes to the media. And I can tell you they are not real keen on acknowledging the pligs in their midst. Even if there are four lost golfers involved."

"Pligs?"

"Polygamists. Practically every good Mormon, if they really are a good Mormon, has them in their family histories."

---

It is late at night and Cookie, Boris and Ludmilla are crawling on their stomachs through the Temple House to get to the foursome's room. A group of Johnny Cashes passes by in a nearby hallway.

"It sure is a blessing those fellas showed up when they did, or we'd be having to marrying all those ugly ducklings. Our prayers have been answered!"

"Amen to that Brother Thurgood. Amen to that. And did you see the rack on that Russian girl? Now there's a reason to get up every morning!"

"And a reason to go to bed at night!" The Johnny Cashes all laugh together in a bawdy sort of religious way and slap each other on the back.

Cookie has to restrain Boris and Ludmilla from raining down their patented KGB death moves on the unsuspecting brethren. But they are on a mission. A mission to escape the compound and get back to the wagon and dune buggy and the game of golf.

The trio enters the foursome's room where they are all dressed for bed.

"Why are you guys crawling on your stomachs like that?" E.Z. asks.

"We're making a break for it tonight. These people have all got plans for you guys and it involves some very long-term relationships with some very challenging women. Women half your age but twice your size."

"I don't know, I thought one of them was kind of cute. And, man, could she square dance," E.Z. beams.

"Do you really want to become a sex slave at a religious compound where all the women look like NFL linemen and the men all look like Johnny Cash?"

"Well, you put it that way," Hub says.

"I really don't think I could take too much more square dancing. I actually think I pulled a muscle," Blaze says as he rubs his back.

"Ve have got to get out of siz place. If it's ze last zhing ve ever do!"

"Hey, vasn't, wasn't that an Animals' song? Eric Burdon?" Blaze asks Boris, who just shrugs his shoulders not having any idea what he is talking about.

"We understand," Ben Ichi says quickly changing into his clothes. "Ancient Chinese saying, goes something like, it takes many nails to build a crib, but only one screw to fill it."

"You think we can get out here without them catching us?" Hub asks.

"Ve have trained all our lives for siz kind of zink. Siz is like KGB von-oh-von. Just follow us closely and don't make any of ze noise. If zey catch us, zer is no tellink vhat kinds of kinky stuff zey might do to us." Ludmilla knows whereof she speaks. That was KGB von-oh-two.

The golfing entourage crawls out of the room in the Temple House on their stomachs. They look more like a bunch of GI Joes than a bunch of golfers. The ultimate SWAT team. Who knew golfing could be this exciting?

The Church-approved helicopter comes screaming over the horizon, a maze-like system of gooseneck canyons and horseshoe bends. Donna Dina and Dan Flavin have wrangled themselves seats despite Donna's aversion to anything higher than stiletto heels. Dan shoots footage out the open side door. Suddenly the pilot gestures down below and, sure enough, there is a group of people, some in bright white shirts, all crawling in a line on their stomachs across the desert floor. A little three-legged dog runs alongside the slithering mass. When the group sees the helicopter, they all get to their feet and start waving wildly. The helicopter circles overhead.

Suddenly, from behind a rock formation, a phalanx of state troopers jump out with their guns drawn.

"Hold it right there folks! Keep those hands up where we can see them or we'll make Swiss cheese out of the bunch of you!"

The golf entourage turns towards the state troopers, astounded to be rescued and arrested at the same time.

"Hands on your heads and spread them," the lead trooper shouts.

"They must take their golf pretty seriously out here," Blaze says.

"If this is about that parking ticket from a couple of years back, I pleaded not guilty and never heard back," Cookie tries to take the heat. He turns to the group. "Have you ever tried to feed the meter when you're parallel parking a Conestoga wagon?"

"I guess you folks know why we're here?" the trooper asks.

"Because we're lost and were almost abducted by a bunch of sex crazed lunatics?" Blaze asks.

"Is it because of all the golf balls we've lost out here?" Hub asks.

"No, it's because of a crazed golfer who brandished a weapon as he purloined a bunch of hamburgers from a terrified family."

"Oops," Hub says. "They told me I could have them! And it wasn't a weapon, it was my putter!"

"Honestly officers, I think this is all a big misunderstanding," Blaze offers. "I can assure you, he's no menace with a putter. The guy is a very lousy putter."

Inside the hovering helicopter, Donna is reporting live as Dan shoots video of the encounter with the cops from the open helicopter door.

"And so today, after several days missing in action, our intrepid foursome wandered out of the wilderness and were immediately arrested by the authorities. We've got a developing story here folks, stay tuned to find out the fate of our foursome as we get to the bottom of this latest twist in an already twisted tale. As we get more information, we'll be breaking into your normally scheduled programs. I'm Donna Dina reporting live over the badlands of Utah, and right now they are looking pretty bad indeed."

The large television monitor in Bob Post's office at RAGU headquarters has the live broadcast on as it goes to a commercial for Cialis, the one with the couples in bathtubs overlooking the wilderness.

Bob Post sits crying at his desk.

A strange man with a strong Scottish brogue, who looks and sounds just like Sean Connery sits across from Bob. In fact, it is Sean Connery, in all his manliness, dressed in a dashing kilt. It is a little known fact but Sean Connery has very lovely legs with lots of very fine black hairs.

"This is as bad as it ever gets Bob. Golfers arrested. RAGU officials in a perp walk on national fucking television. Take a deep breath, my friend. Get a hold of yourself, man. Your reputation is down the friggin' drain, man. Let's just hope it doesn't take the whole damned sport down with it! And if it does, my wily little bastard friend, you can be assured there will be a large contingent of giant Scottish men brandishing clubs and wearing kilts knocking at your fine door. If I were you, I would not let that happen. Then again, if I were you, this bloody fiasco wouldn't be happening in the first place. Have I made myself perfectly clear?"

Bob Post just sobs uncontrollably with his head in his hands. His worst nightmare has just happened. On the television, the announcer admonishes, "For erections lasting longer than 4 hours, seek immediate medical attention."

---

Back at search party headquarters, Bernie Calderwood is having his picture taken with the golfers. Donna and Dan are among the celebrating throngs, which now includes Leigh Sauerbraten and all the members of the highway patrol that just arrested the foursome.

"We're very sorry about the confusion this morning," Bernie says slapping Hub on the back. "But these days, you just can't be too careful. You'd be surprised how many calls we get, deranged people running around with golf clubs."

"Oh, that's all right. Who knew a cheeseburger could get you into so much trouble."

"We're just glad it all worked out so well. We've still got a little bit of golf to play out here," Blaze says as he turns to the camera for another shot with a patrolman.

"Well, I've got to say, it helped that you had the TV people vouch for you. You know, if it weren't for them, we might not have found you in the first place, and then when we did find you we still would have arrested you. Funny how that works out."

Blaze looks over at Donna, who catches her eye. He winks at her and mouths the words, "Thank you."

---

The footage of the lost golfers being found is on the television in the Burning Bridges bar. Riley, Wiley, Sal and Monty are all glued to the television coverage. A small crowd gathers around, including the lady in the corner who plays the harp.

"Thank God they found them!" the lady says.

"Thank God they found them alive!" Monty says.

"Thank God they're not injured," Sal says.

"Thank God they're not a bunch of lawyers!" Riley says.

"Thank God they'll be able to finish the game!" Wiley says. "We've all still got a lot riding on this little puppy!"

"You know, that's the problem with you guys. You care more about games than you do about the people who play them," the lady says as she goes back to her harp.

"That's not true. We care about the people too. As long as they finish the game. It's a contract," Wiley says.

"And we all really love the puny little three-legged dog. We're all dog people and that little guy just breaks your heart. He's such a trouper!" Sal says.

"Yeah, the dog's a real gamer. He kind of reminds me of my third wife, may she rest in peace, in her condo in Florida," Monty says.

# CHAPTER 8

## "NEVER LOOK A GIFT HORSE IN THE MOUTH, OR ANYWHERE ELSE FOR THAT MATTER"

THE CONESTOGA WAGON IS rolling again, with Cookie behind the reins and Peabody riding shotgun. The guys have all teed it up and hit nice solid old man shots right down the middle of Monument Valley, so named for the mighty red sandstone formations that sit like islands in the middle of a sagebrush ocean. The formations are also known as John Ford's mittens, for their filmic status as American icons which happen to resemble two stone gloves. In our case, they may as well be known as John Ford's golf gloves. You can practically see John Wayne leading the cavalry or Ward Bond riding a stagecoach coming over the horizon. Out here, even the sagebrush looks famous.

Given the wide open space, the game is being played at a leisurely pace. Things have settled back into a nice rhythm, the way golf was meant to be played: walking and talking interrupted occasionally by the sweet swing of the golf club working its magic on the tiny little white ball. Thriving and driving. Strolling and rolling. Strutting and putting. The walk and talk is almost more important than the strokes and pokes.

"Wow, this is really pretty out here," Hub says.

"It reminds me of all those old Western movies. You know,

John Wayne and all," Blaze says as he walks along a sandy strip. He sips on a Bloody Mary as he talks. He slips into a John Wayne hip swiveling imitation, "Well, listen up pilgrim," he nearly spills his drink. "Why do you think he called them pilgrims?"

"Because they were all farmers, moving across the prairies. They weren't all cowboys and Indians. They were more familiar with the business end of a pitchfork than with a six shooter."

"I think that whole cowboy and Indian thing was overrated. You know, it was romanticized by Hollywood."

"Yeah, that Hollywood is pretty much to blame for everything."

"I was always a sucker for comedies. You know, W.C. Fields, Harold Lloyd, Buster Keaton and the Marx Brothers, of course."

"I always loved the Little Tramp."

"My mom always used to drop me off at the movie house, so she could entertain her dates back at the house."

"That must have been tough."

"That's why I always loved comedies. They helped me to forget."

"I know what you mean. My old man used to make me mow the lawn every Saturday, even if it didn't need it."

"Well, no offense, but mowing the lawn and having your mom balling every guy that came down the block isn't quite the same thing."

"Maybe not, but it was a really big yard."

---

E.Z. and Ben Ichi are strolling along the valley floor, shooting the shit as they play.

"If we keep playing like this, we'll bury these guys. Blaze isn't as good as he thinks he is. He's a big choker."

"A joker?" Ben asks.

"No, a choker. It's cho, cho, not jo, jo."

"Well, he's a joker too. I think that is part of his problem. He doesn't take anything seriously."

"Yeah, well, if Blaze keeps drinking as much as he does, I think we've got a pretty fair chance of winning this little turkey."

Just as E.Z. says this, a flock of wild turkeys emerges from the underbrush, and cackles and clucks disapproval over the disparaging use of their name and the golf ball sitting in their nest. In the mythical West, even the wildlife have property rights.

"Speaking of turkeys, I think that looks like your ball E.Z. I'd be careful if I were you, nothing worse than a tough old turkey, especially one who's been insulted."

"Go on, now git!" E.Z. attempts to reclaim his ball, but the turkey has other ideas.

Boris and Ludmilla pull up in the dune buggy. "Vhat have ve got here? Ball in ze nest? Von stroke penalty and drop ze ball two club lengths away from ze hazard. And vatch out vhen you get ze ball because ze turkey has ze very sharp beak."

E.Z. moves cautiously towards his ball and the tough Tom Turkey jumps up and down, filling out his full plumage, as a warning sign.

From behind a large bush, Donna Dina inches forward, microphone in hand, in the classic whispering voice known only to golf coverage.

"It looks like the team of Harbinger/Ichi has run into a different kind of birdie opportunity than they are accustomed to. This is the national birdie. And from the looks of it, this turkey is not real happy about it. RAGU officials are on the scene, just ruling a penalty drop is in order, providing E.Z. can retrieve his ball. As of right now, with just two remaining holes to go, before the final hole back at Burning Bridges, we've got Harbinger/Ichi leading by four strokes, but with Hogle/Jones in a position to pick up a stroke here at the turkey fortress. I'm Donna Dina reporting live from the Utah-Arizona border."

The bright green AstroTurf sits atop a bluff, like a bad toupe on a short, overweight man with sagebrush for whiskers. The players are each about 150 yards from their approach shots. A little too far away and with too tough a target to be able to land a screamer on the putting surface, the intelligent play is to lay up. But with this bunch, intelligence has never been their strong suit.

Hub is down a small ravine, hidden from the others. He has to run up the side of the hill to eyeball the green, then run back down the ravine to his ball. He pulls out a club and sizes up his ball. Suddenly he hears the sound of a horse naying. A horse that is very close by. The horse's mouth is practically in Hub's ear. He turns around to find two stoic Indians, Navajos to be exact, sitting atop their mangy looking horses without benefit of saddles. They look like they just rode up from a John Ford classic. The taller one is wearing a black sombrero-like hat which makes him look like a giant. The other one has a dead left eye and a scar running down his face that resembles sections of the Grand Canyon. Hub isn't sure what to think of them, are they going to kill him and scalp him or try to sell him torquoise jewelry? No one says anything for the longest time. The horses shift their weight heavily on their feet. Their tails flick at buzzing flies. Finally, one of the Indians, known as Black Head, because of the hat he lives in, speaks up.

"What are you planning to hit?"

"I was thinking of a 5-iron," Hub answers timidly.

"That's a pretty tough shot from there. Are you sure you shouldn't play it safe and lay up?"

"Well, we're behind by four strokes and running out of time and holes still to be played. I figure if we're going to make a move, this may be the time to do it."

"I don't think a 5-iron is going to get you there."

"Do you play a lot of golf out here, Chief?"

"Oh, you know how it is. We get out every chance we get, isn't that right Crazy Horse?"

"Yep," Crazy Horse says. "Though getting tee times can be a real hassle."

Both the Indians turn to each other and break out in a great big belly laugh. They laugh so hard, the horses start to get nervous. Hub doesn't know what to do but laugh meekly along with them. Before you know it, Hub and two Navajos are sharing a belly laugh in the middle of the Arizona desert, over the absurdity of what golf club to use to hit toward an AstroTurf carpet serving as a putting green, in a golf game being played in the Navajo Nation. Is this a great country or what?

"I guess I should heed local knowledge," Hub says as he pulls out his 3-iron.

Black Head winces at his choice of club.

"What?"

"Not enough loft to keep it on the green, if you're lucky enough to get to the green."

"What do you want me to hit?" Hub asks in exasperation.

"I've always been partial to the 5-fairway wood in this situation."

"What do you think? Do you agree?" Hub says to Crazy Horse.

"Just make sure you get under it," Crazy Horse says with a glint in his one good eye.

Hub pulls out the fairway wood and addresses the ball. "Can you guys see the green from there? Can you give me something to aim for?"

"Try aiming a little more left. Just past the juniper tree."

"And get under it," Crazy Horse adds.

Hub adjusts his stance, eyeballs the juniper tree and lets fly with a mighty swing which instantly elevates the ball out of the ravine, heading just left of the juniper tree. A perfect shot that hits the green hard with enough backspin to hold on the surface. A risky shot that paid off.

"You're on!"

"That was a beauty."

"Thanks fellas. It's all in the wrists."

Meanwhile, Ben Ichi and E.Z. lie side by side, about 225 yards from the pin. Ben pulls out a 5-iron.

"Why don't you go for it?" E.Z. asks.

"I'll play up and then hope to be up and down. No shame in that."

"Not me. I'm going for the gusto. Let's take it to these guys."

"You can have the gusto. I'll settle for a nice little old par."

Ben steps up and as is his fashion, creams the ball without any kind of practice swing. The balls lands comfortably 60 yards from the green with a nice approach to the pin.

Next, E.Z. is up and he aggressively pulls out his 3-iron. He eyeballs the green, takes a couple of practice swings, addresses the ball, sets and unleashes a wallop that sends the ball in a low flight directly at the flag. His shot hits the flag stick and bounces hard going over the backside of the green.

Ben just shakes his head in dismay.

"Ancient Chinese golf saying, man who goes for gusto, better prepare for busto. Man who settles for par, always will go far."

"Ancient American saying goes something like, keep your big trap shut or I'll give you a knuckle sandwich. You capiche?"

"Yeah, I capiche. But that shot still sucked."

Meanwhile, Blaze is looking at his difficult shot, mainly due to the large buffalo that stands between him and his ball. It snorts plumes of dust and pounds the ground with its front hoof.

"Nice little buddy. Why don't you go run off where the deer and the antelope play?" Blaze says as he tries to approach the 2000 pound muscle. "Don't you have a herd that is looking for you?"

The buffalo stands its ground unconvinced by Blaze's entreaties. Hub saunters up with his new found friends, Black Head and Crazy Horse on their mangy ponies.

"Looks like you've met our mascot," Black Head says indicating the buffalo.

"I met these guys a couple of minutes ago. This is Ted Black Head and Bill Crazy Horse. They really know the course."

"Pleased to meet you. What do you mean mascot?"

"You think just because we're Indians, we don't have stereotyped bigoted sports mascots too? That there is Mike Tyson, the friendly bison. He's the mascot for the high school. The Running Bisons."

"Well, he doesn't look real friendly to me."

"That's because you're not a Running Bison."

"Well, could you ask him to run along like a nice little bison, so I can get to my ball?"

Crazy Horse rides up to Mike Tyson, and pats him on the head. "How did you get all the way out here Mike?" He nudges the buffalo out of the way. Mike Tyson moves along like a trained cocker spaniel.

"Thanks," Blaze says as he retrieves his 5-iron. Black Head frowns at the selection and Blaze notices.

"What?"

"He's kind of partial to the fairway wood," Hub offers before Black Head has a chance to answer. "He gave me the tip a minute ago just over the hill and I'm on the green. The man knows what he's talking about."

Black Head just smiles.

"All right, I'll hit the fairway wood. But this better land on the green and stay there or we're going to have to have a little pow wow back at the watering hole."

Blaze takes out his fairway wood. He steps up to the ball, looks towards the green and launches a glorious shot that fades perfectly towards the flag. It lands with a crisp thud on the AstroTurf, takes a couple of hops and comes to a rest about four feet from the hole.

"That was a pretty good shot," Black Head says.

"It didn't go in," Crazy Horse answers.

"Hey, thanks for the suggestion. You guys play out here often?"

"Hey, once they put the green in, we hated to see it go to waste."

"We try to be sneaky about it."

"These guys sure sneaked up on me, I can say that for sure. Practically scared me to death," Hub says clutching his heart.

"I think you may have seen too many Western movies," Black Head winks at Hub. "We're just your average bunch of fun loving Native Americans. When it comes to golf, we're really just a couple of weekend warriors."

Ben puts his shot on the green, inside Blaze's ball. E.Z. lobs his errant miss back to the putting surface and the foursome take their places on the green, lining up their individual putts as their shadows cast long silhouettes over the AstroTurf. Black Head and Crazy Horse watch on, as do Boris and Ludmilla, and Cookie and Peabody, the three-legged dog. Donna Dina and Dan Flavin are filming the entire scene. It's like a frigging postcard for the chamber of commerce, that is, if the Navajo Nation had a chamber of commerce.

Everybody sinks their respective putt just as the sun is sinking on the horizon.

Donna whispers into the microphone. "Incredible as it seems, with Harbinger/Ichi dropping two strokes, with the penalty and overshooting the green, the team of Hogle/Jones have pulled within two just as the sun disappears. Folks, they've been out here for nearly 36 days and, with just a single hole to go, before heading back to the magnificent Burning Bridges Country Club for the final hole on the historic 18th fairway, only two shots out of the thousands these fellows have taken over the month separate these two teams. It looks to be an incredible finish to an incredible match. Looking at these players, no matter what you thought of them going into this match, they have earned your respect for the sheer lunacy of their effort and the style in which they have carried it out. Whether you love golf or hate it, you've got to feel for these guys and what they have done. I'm Donna Dina reporting live from near Kayenta, Arizona."

Large pitchers of beer are being poured from a tap at the local Elks club. All the usual suspects are there enjoying the respite from the rigors of the game. Who knew golf was such a popular game on the reservation?

Black Head, still in his hat, steps to the stage and takes the microphone.

"A big ya'at'eeh to everyone. We're delighted to have the four famous golfers in our midst, and their support team. We also welcome the international media to our little corner of the world. I'd like to introduce my father, Chief Got Rocks, a man who has been very important in my life. The man who introduced the game of golf to me. Who has taught me the lessons of life. Who has taught me the stories of our tribe. Who has shown me the shining path. He's a heck of a good dancer too, my father, Chief Johnny Got Rocks."

The audience applauds as an ancient man, shriveled and hunched over, gets up from his seat and approaches the stage. He waves cordially to the crowd, even though he can barely see. In fact, he can barely wave. He is wearing all manner of turquoise jewelry, which weighs down his slight frame. He is so laden with glittering jewels he practically tips over as he climbs to the stage. Black Head gives him a hand as he turns over the microphone to the illustrious leader.

"Ya'at'eeh." The old man speaks in a barely audible whisper. "It is a pleasure to see you all out here today. We welcome our fellow duffers. As many of you know, I've always been a fan of the game. I would have loved to have played the game, but that would be impossible with all this hardware I have to wear around. But many years ago I did have a vision. I was chewing Juicy Fruit gum. I always chew Juicy Fruit when I'm having visions. The vision included this very moment. I saw four men on the horizon, like the Four Horsemen of the Apocalypse. But instead of horses, they had golf clubs. And in this vision, I saw the future. The future for our people. A dog spoke to me in the language of our fathers. This dog was very wise. This dog spoke to me like a man. This dog told me, the future of the Indian people is not gaming casinos or bingo parlors. The future of the Indian people is golf courses. Beautiful places set up in nature, where people pay good money to go torment themselves. Places where people drive around in little electric carts, eating sandwiches and drinking beer, playing an addictive game of little or no consequence to their real lives. In the vision, I saw busloads of tourists, really just wallets with arms and legs, pouring their hard-earned money into Indian enterprises where all we had to do was plant some grass seed and water it on a regular basis. The dog told me, plant the seeds and the golfers will follow. And now here we are. This moment has been foretold. I have seen it all in a vision."

Blaze and Hub belly up to the bar. "We'll take whatever he's been drinking." The bartender pours them some tea.

"It's a little local concoction. Strictly herbal. We call it Brain Wreck."

Blaze and Hub look at the steaming mixture, then at each other.

"What the hell! When in Rome." They both drain the Brain Wreck and wince at the taste.

"What is this going to do to us?" Hub asks.

"Just give it an hour or so, then just make sure you don't operate any heavy machinery. And believe me, out here, it is all heavy machinery."

With the pulsating drum beat of a good old fashioned Navajo pow-wow mirroring the drum beat pow-wow going on inside his head, Blaze Jones is trying to gather his thoughts, what few he has left, as Donna Dina approaches.

"This is some kind of shindig!" Donna says genuinely trying to be friendly.

"It is absolutely metaphysical. Almost an out-of-body experience."

"Are you okay?"

"I've never been better. I'm beginning to see things clearer by the minute."

"What do you mean?" Donna presses in.

"I just mean, I see all the pain. I see where the injuries are. But I'm also seeing where the healing part comes from." Blaze looks down at his beer. "I also see where all the crutches are." They look each other in the eyes. "I think I'm finally ready to be a better person. To stop the blame game. To stop being a lazy son of a gun and take some responsibility for my choices. I've been running all my life, but like some kind of fricking cartoon character, I've been stuck in the same place the whole time."

"I think I know what you mean. People look at me, like I'm just another dumb blonde with a pretty face. They don't see all the pain behind the mask. They don't see the shy little girl who is terrified of standing in front of a crowd. They don't see the person who could eat an entire bag of potato chips while watching *Sex and the City* reruns."

"Yeah, I love that show too. And I'm partial to crinkle cut because they hold the dip better. But nobody lives like that. It's all make- believe. They make it and we believe it."

"Hey, you've got to believe in something. Why not love?"

Blaze and Donna lock eyes. If two people could fall for each other over their love of bags of fried potatoes and *Sex and the City* reruns, then anything is possible.

---

Back at the bar, Chief Johnny Got Rocks is talking with E.Z. and Ben Ichi, swapping tales of acid flashbacks and vision quests.

"I really like your vision. Golf is the future. Golf is hope. Golf is love," Ben says meaning every word of it.

"I liked the part about it being addictive." E.Z. adds. "I sure know I'm hooked."

"We all have our vices and addictions. If golf is as bad as it gets, then I guess you're doing pretty good," the Chief breathes heavily.

"We have an ancient saying, it goes something like, a man is only as strong as his vices, and as weak as his virtue."

"You are very clever with your sayings. We've got a couple of good old sayings as well. Old Indian saying, man who runs in front of bus gets tired. Man who runs behind bus gets exhausted. But man driving bus feels pretty good, because he has a job where he sits down all day."

"I think I get it. We all need to be driving our own buses. We're in charge of our bus. We get to let on the people of our choosing. Some people we charge. Others get to ride for free. It is brilliant. You should meet my father. You would have lots to talk about." Ben Ichi is almost wistful thinking of his father back home.

"I'm more like the guy who gets run over by the bus," E. Z. says with a chuckle. "I'm the bloody mess left on the pavement after the bus has left the station. And somehow, it is always my father or brother who is doing the driving."

"We have another old Indian saying, if the son is ignorant, blame the father. But if the son is a success, credit the mother."

"And we also have another old saying, man who argues with wife all day, gets no piece at night."

"You know, this is the problem with being a white guy," E.Z. laments. "We just don't have any good old sayings."

---

The next morning arrives crisp and fresh, like a new beginning where the light illuminates the world in a different way. The golfers are all assembled at the edge of town. Chief Johnny Got Rocks stands in front of the small gathering.

"Before we bid you farewell, I would like you to meet my grandson and he has a brief demonstration which I think you will find most interesting. Please meet my grandson, Little Jimmy Straightshooter."

A small Indian boy, with big brown eyes and dark stiff hair steps forward shyly. His grandfather pushes him forward, then hands him what must be the smallest golf club ever made. It is a homemade club with an ancient leather grip. The chief tips over a bucket of range balls and points in the direction of a bushel basket that sits about a 100 yards away in an adjacent field.

Little Jimmy steps up and without hardly looking, nonchalantly chips a ball into the bushel basket. Then he does another and another and another. Everyone stands dumbstruck. This kid must be some kind of golf prodigy. Boris and Ludmilla look at each other, like they are witnessing the second coming. Then Chief Got Rocks pulls out a bandanna and blindfolds Little Jimmy. Just as easily, he strokes 10 balls right into the basket. The crowd breaks into spontaneous cheers at the sight of this golfing miracle. Chief Got Rocks just smiles knowingly. He has seen the future and the future is love.

# CHAPTER 9

## "THE FOUR WEARY HORSEMEN OF THE APOCALYPSE STARE INTO THE ABYSS, AND THE ABYSS STARES RIGHT BACK"

THE FEARSOME FOURSOME MAKES its way across the high desert of Arizona, one shot at a time, one stroke after another, one foot in front of the other. After 38 days, only two strokes separate the playing teams. They all look a little worse for wear, their clothing is bedraggled, and their hair and beards a little longer. They look like they've been pulled through a knot hole. They've got callouses on top of callouses. Blisters on top of blisters. Cracked lips on top of cracked lips. They're a mess and they are exhausted, like the men running behind the bus.

"So, what are you going to do with your money?" Hub asks.

"Oh, I don't know. I'll probably blow it on something stupid. Booze or babes or the ponies. Probably all three," Blaze answers. "How about you?"

"I don't know. Probably pay off some bills. How about you guys?"

"I'll probably move out and get an apartment," E.Z. says.

"I'll probably invest mine in the Asian stock market," Ben says without much enthusiasm. "You know, when it comes right down to it, what we've gone through for only a few thousand dollars isn't really fair."

"Yeah, you're right. Plus after we pay taxes, what do we really get out of this whole thing? A lot of sore muscles and chump change," Blaze says rubbing his shoulder.

"It's the four old guys who are making out like bandits. They've got plenty of money. They get all the notoriety for the club. They'll have their pictures in *Golf Digest*."

"Yeah, we'll have to go back to our old jobs. They'll still be rich."

"We'll be yesterday's news. A bunch of washed up old has-beens."

"Unless we come up with a plan and I mean fast."

"You know, I might have an idea," Blaze says. "But we would need to have a tie score and I would need to make a few phone calls."

"Hey, we're not going to just give it to you. We're up by two strokes," E.Z. protests. "Besides, Boris and Ludmilla would never let us cheat."

"If we need to be tied, you're going to have to catch us the old-fashioned way, fair and square. And you are running out of holes to do it. We've got about 20 more miles and if you are going to make your move, you better do it now," Ben says with emphasis.

And so, with only days to go, the match is set anew. A new resolve comes over the players. As so often happens in golf, when push comes to shove, when the options have run their course, miracles do happen. Champions do crumble. Underdogs can win. And life can be fair sometimes.

---

The final hole always presents special challenges. It is seldom designed to be the most difficult hole on the course. It is usually one of the easier holes, that way golfers are always happy to return. The last hole is meant to leave a nice taste in the golfer's mouth. But not on this course. The final hole has been designed for maximum challenge. As if 400 miles wasn't enough of a challenge. This hole defies the imagination. It must have been designed by a madman with a chip on his shoulder. It spans the width of Canyon de Chelly to Canyon del Muerto, with a couple of raging rapids thrown in for good measure. This hole gives the idea of a water hazard a whole new meaning. This hole actually makes golf a full contact sport. A hole where a golfer actually might die, not from embarrassment or a heart attack, but from the rigors of the hole itself. It gives the concept of up and down a totally different connotation.

This is the kind of hole that can make grown men cry like small children. This is the kind of monster hole that gives golfers nightmares. This is the kind of hole that can take a man, chew him up and spit him out like so many stale pretzels. This is the kind of hole that can try men's souls and then bury them alive. If there is a devil, then this must be his playground. And if there is a God, then even He would have a hard time getting a par on this beast.

Cookie sits in the Conestoga wagon looking over the North Rim. Peabody is by his side. Boris and Ludmilla are dressed for backpacking and rock climbing. The foursome take practice swings overlooking the abyss.

"I guess this is where I'll leave you. I'll take the wagon and meet you on the other side. Assuming you make it to the other side. I've packed some snacks. You should make it to the bottom of the canyon, spend the night and climb back up the other side. I'll be waiting by the green for you. This place is just no good for an old geezer and his broken down horses and rickety wagon."

"Hey, I wish we were going with you. At this point I think we're all tired and ready to go home. But we've got to finish this thing," Blaze says with a new found determination.

"Finish this up strong gentlemen and you'll soon be on a flight out of Flagstaff, back to Burning Bridges. Funny, a town named after the flag stick. But just be extremely careful, especially in Canyon del Muerto. Not even the Indians like going in there. Canyon de Chelly itself means 'inside the rock' and that pretty much describes it. And I don't need to tell you what Canyon del Muerto means." Cookie means what he says.

"What does it mean? I didn't ever take Spanish," E.Z. asks.

"It means Canyon of Death, dickwad," Blaze says.

"That's just great. Nearly 40 days out here and we have to finish in the Canyon of Death? Just great!"

"Let's stop bellyaching and tee off. The sooner we get started, the sooner we'll be enjoying a nice hot bath and clean white sheets." Hub tees his ball up and cranks a monstrous shot that screams into the abyss.

Ben Ichi is next. "Ancient Chinese saying, when man fears death, everything looks like a coffin, when man embraces life, everything looks like beautiful naked body. I don't really know what it means, but I do find the image to be very appealing." Ben creams another beauty which falls into the abyss.

Blaze steps into the tee box. "Although we walk into the Valley of Death, we will fear no evil. Not even a wicked slice." He hits an inside out drive which sends the ball into an ugly topspin that practically goes sideways.

"So much for fearing no evil," E.Z. says as he addresses his ball. "You know evil spelled backwards is live. And I say live and let live. Just as long as we win. Because you are not going to catch us with shots like that." E.Z. smashes a huge drive that is the very definition of perfection.

"This is the beginning of the end. May you rest in peace."

Donna Dina is back up in the helicopter, hovering over the scene.

"This is the beginning of the end. The last hole in the wilderness, before the golfers are whisked back to Burning Bridges. And this hole is a monster. Covering 11 miles, as the crow flies, but it is a whole lot of up and down. This has got to be the steepest golf hole in the world, with more than 5,000 vertical feet to navigate. And the golfer's support team won't be of much help as the terrain is too rough for the horses and wagon. Of course, the RAGU officials will be accompanying the golfers, keeping score. As it stands, just two strokes separate these teams. Can the team of Harbinger/Ichi hold off Hogle/Jones, or can they make a move to close the gap? It all comes down to this, and ladies and gentlemen, if history is any example, hold on to your seats because this is going to be a very bumpy ride. We'll be checking in by air, as the terrain has also proven to be too difficult for our crew. I'm Donna Dina reporting live over Chinle, Arizona."

The helicopter banks hard to the right, opening up a vast panorama with six tiny specks making their way down a thin ribbon of a trail. The immensity of the landscape practically swallows the golfers whole.

---

On the trail, the four golfers make their way down the dusty path. With each passing switchback and around every corner, the landscape grows ever more forbidding. It is like walking into some kind of fiery furnace, the rocks contorted into ever more grotesque shapes and impediments. If the hike down is difficult, the hike back up the other side can only be considered very nearly impossible. With each passing step, with each tug of gravity, the joints and tendons ache, the blood pumps, the lungs cry for air and the sweat runs profusely. The final hole is proving to be the most difficult of all. Fittingly, the bastards saved the worst of it for the very end.

"I'm starving. Let's take a break on this ledge and see what Cookie packed for lunch," Hub says rubbing the sweat from his brow.

"Sounds good to me. Would you look at that view!" Blaze says as he puts his golf bag down.

E.Z. breaks out the lunch as Boris and Ludmilla join them.

"Vhat's for lunch?" Ludmilla asks.

"Looks like ham and cheese sandwiches." E.Z. says cramming one into his mouth.

"Are there any pickles? You've got to have pickles with a ham and cheese," Hub asks.

"Sorry. No pickles. I don't think they pack well. They leak."

"How about some brewskies?" Blaze asks.

"I think those were in your bag."

"No wonder it was so heavy." Blaze retrieves a beer and opens it. "Too bad they're warm."

"Zat is how ve drink zem back home. Ze ice cube vas on endangered species list," Boris says as he cracks a beer.

"How did you guys meet?" Ben asks.

"Ve met at gymnasium. Ludmilla vas veightlifter. I vas vrestler. It vas love at first benchpress." Boris winks at Ludmilla and she winks right back.

"Boris vas irresistible, dressed in those little spandex outfits. A girl could see vhat she vas in for, that's for sure. He pinned me on ze first date."

"And how did you get into golf?"

"Vonce ve left KGB, ve started taking ze lessons and ve found golf vas perfect fit for us. It brought out our natural totalitarian tendencies. Ve love a game vith lots of ze rules."

"Well, you guys have sure been thorough at enforcing the rules. We can all agree on that. But you've been fair," E.Z. says, the one who has probably been the unfortunate recipient of most of their determinations.

"Vell, ve just call zem as ve zee zem. And ve both have ze excellent eyesight. Ze 20/20 in both of ze eyes," Ludmilla beams in that way that only buxom women can beam.

"Well, I hope we can find our balls down at the bottom of this canyon, because that shot of Blaze's was ugly and if it is lost, that will cost them another two strokes." E.Z. crams another sandwich into his mouth. "And at this point, two more strokes could be the final curtain."

"Don't get too far ahead of yourself, friend, because anything can and probably will happen. That we can be sure of. If I've learned anything in my life, it is that the only constant is change." Blaze drains his warm beer. That at least never changes. Blaze and beers are always a constant.

"You know, there is an ancient Chinese saying, goes something like, when going gets tough, time to start to walk sideways until easier path opens up," Ben says as he scarfs down a sandwich. "When one finds the snake, move backwards slowly. When one finds the coyote, move forward quickly. When one finds a raven, teach it to speak. When one finds an eagle, learn to listen."

"Is there some kind of manual you guys study to come up with this stuff?" Hub asks.

"It just comes with the territory," Ben just shrugs. "We can't help it if we are the fountain of wisdom passed down through the ages in odd little sayings."

"You know you are like a walking, talking fortune cookie," E.Z. says.

"Are there cookies?" Hub asks.

Ludmilla reaches into the backpack and pulls out a cellophane bag full of broken cookies.

"I guess that is just ze vay ze cookie crumbles."

---

Later, near the bottom of the canyon, each player looks for his ball amidst the geologic wonderland. Hub's ball is squeezed in a narrow ravine, which requires him to suck his stomach in and attempt to wedge himself between the sandstone walls. E.Z.'s ball has landed in a sand bar, hitting the sand so hard the ball has practically buried itself an inch deep in the wet granules. Blaze's ball ended up finding its way into a large sandstone ampitheater which acted like a slingshot, whipping his ball around the curved wall and depositing it happily at the bottom of the canyon, with a perfect lie on the edge of the plunging rapids. Thus is the luck of golf. Sometimes even the worst shot turns into gold.

Ben's ball is not so fortunate. His ball has perched itself on the edge of a very small, very dark opening in the sandstone. As he approaches his ball, he can hear a distinct sound that resembles a baby's rattle being rattled by a baby on amphetamines. It is a powerful sound coming from a powerful critter. And Ben knows exactly what it is. He has been living in dread of this moment his entire lifetime. All his father ever talked about were snakes. They were always the animal of choice for his proverbial lessons. Ben stands perfectly still, only the beads of sweat building on his forehead show any signs of movement. He stands there long enough that the beads turn into torrents. Then the torrents turn into rivers and the rivers into oceans, and you pretty much get the idea. And the rattling goes on until it becomes one with Ben's heartbeat.

Blaze carefully approaches Ben. "What's up little brother?"

"Rattler," Ben whispers. "Don't make any sudden movements."

"How long have you been standing there?"

"My whole life."

"What are you going to do?"

"I have to confront my fear." Ben swallows hard. "I must hit away."

"What are you thinking of hitting?"

"Sand wedge. Chip shot to the beach," Ben turns to Blaze. "Watch my back, man."

Ben moves carefully towards the ball. The rattling grows ever more incessant. Ben steps in front of the ball and without even bringing the club to any kind of address, he winds up to hit the ball and just as he does the rattling stops! It is unsettlingly silent, and just as Ben is bringing down the club head, with all its centrifugal force, the diamond back strikes! The fangs are fully exposed as the club hits the ball and at the same time hits the snake square up side of its head. The result is a looping shot and a loopy snake who has just had his brain rearranged.

"Oh, nice shot! Though the snake might not agree."

"Oh my God! I may have just saved my life with a sand wedge."

"I think you may have knocked some sense into the little guy."

The snake comes to and slithers off in a crooked path, like a cross-eyed drunk walking home from the bar.

"I have finally met the serpent and he is mine. I have touched my fear and now I own it. I will never fear the serpent again."

"May we all be so lucky," Blaze says as he drains his warm beer. "I've always had more of a fear of succeeding." He belches.

"You mean a fear of failing," Ben says.

"No, I've been proving all my life that I have no fear of failure. I'm afraid of success. The few times in my life I've ever been close to succeeding, I've always found a way to sabotage it."

"We all need to face the thing we are most afraid of. Then perhaps we can face the future with a clear mind and a clean slate. But in the meantime, I think I've pooped my pants," Ben says with a wry smile on his face and a pinched up nose.

Later, at the river, the players have built a campfire and made camp for the night. Boris and Ludmilla have pitched their tent nearby. Ben is drying his freshly washed underwear on a stick by the fire.

"The fangs on this thing were huge!" Ben says as he twirls the stick.

"I guess this is why they call it Canyon del Muerto," Hub remarks as he eats an apple.

"You know those rapids aren't exactly going to be a picnic tomorrow," E.Z. says with more than a little trepidation.

"I spotted a place we might just get across. We'll take our shots then have to hopscotch across some boulders to get to the other side," Blaze offers between shots of tequila. "It shouldn't be a problem. Though we might get a little wet."

A group of nearby coyotes howl into the night, creating an eerie sound down in the bottom of the canyon. The sound sends a chill down everyone's spine.

"Let's keep that fire burning real bright tonight. I've always been a little bit terrified of a pack of wild, well, wild anythings." Hub says staring into the darkness.

"Yeah, well I'm all for turning in. We'll need to get an early start tomorrow if we're going to reach the top. And it is going to be one motherhumper of a climb." E.Z. climbs into his sleeping bag.

"Sounds good fellas. Sleep tight and don't let the bedbugs bite."

The friends crawl into their sleeping bags, with the stars shining bright and the glow of the campfire illuminating the canyon walls with dancing flickers of light and shadow, like some kind of courtship ritual, between good and evil, between success and failure, between life and death.

---

Deep in the night, deep in slumber, the foursome each has a different dream. Dreaming in Canyon del Muerto can be dangerous to your health. There is a spirit that lurks there and it is decidedly not benevolent.

Ben's dream finds him sitting cross-legged and serene, meditating. As he opens his eyes he is face to face, eyeball to eyeball with the diamondback rattler. He notices that the snake's eyeballs are crossed and this makes Ben smile. From behind his back Ben reaches for an apple, which he offers to the cross-eyed snake, like the Garden of Eden story in reverse. Ben takes a bite of the apple and just smiles.

E.Z.'s dream is a bit more turbulent. He is floating down the rapids, like a champagne cork at a wedding, and then the rapids start to pick up speed. And E.Z. is not that great of a swimmer. His father and Gyll stand on the beach, and just point and laugh at him as he floats by. Giselle waves goodbye. And then he hears the falls before he sees them. And they are thunderous. And he is going over them, tumbling like a barrel falling off the back of a truck. And he is lost in the mist.

Hub's dream finds him alone in the forest. He is dressed only in a loin cloth and realizes he is being hunted by a group of wild boars. He can hear them running through the forest floor, snorting and grunting, and he begins to run. The path is rocky and the trees swat him in the face. The wild pack of boars is getting closer and closer and he is running faster and faster and then, just as they are about to get him in their horrible snouts and he is to be eaten by an angry gang of spiral hams and slabs of bacon, he goes over a cliff and falls into a deep pool of water, where Lady Godiva calls to him in song from behind the waterfall.

Blaze's dream is different than all the others. Kind of like Blaze himself. In his dream, he is camped, just as they are, by the side of a river in a deep canyon gorge. The stars are out in full force and Blaze is standing looking up at them. Suddenly a bright white light illuminates the ground and moves like a spotlight over Blaze. He is taking a leak. A long leak. And then a strange sound, like an electronic buzzing, is heard as Blaze finishes his business. And then he sees the spacecraft. It is a magnificent vessel, the size of Yankee Stadium, but spinning slowly. It is not only the size of Yankee Stadium, it is actually Yankee Stadium. But the House that Ruth built, not the new imposter. It has thousands of lights, all vibrating and flashing. And then a giant glittering escalator is extended from the bottom of the ship and two large figures emerge from inside the spaceship. They ride the escalator down but with all the lights it is hard to make them out. Blaze rubs his eyes, squinting to see. As the figures reach the bottom, there standing in front of Blaze are Donald Trump and George Steinbrenner.

The Donald speaks first. "We have come to you as figures you might be familiar with so as not to frighten you. If you were to see us in our real configurations, you would not be able to stand with us."

"Space does some really weird things to you," George says.

"The reason for our visit is plainly stated. Ever since your astronauts visited the moon, we have been trying to understand this game with the stick and the ball."

"You mean golf?" Blaze asks.

"Yes. And we have seen what you and your friends have been doing," The Donald says.

"All the way from outer space?"

"Outer space is closer than you think. Especially if your ride is one of these pimp mobiles." The Donald gestures towards the spacecraft, which honks back like a xylophone on steroids.

"What is the reason you play this game?" George asks.

"Well, that's a tough one. Different people play it for different reasons. Some play it as a distraction. Some play it as an obsession. Some people just play it for fun."

"We understand obsession, but what is this, fun?" George Steinbrenner asks quizzically.

"It is an intangible thing. It makes people happy."

"We have heard of this thing called happiness, but we really don't understand it." The Donald adjusts his hair.

"You know, it brings a smile to your face. Lifts your spirit. Makes the world a better place."

Donald Trump and George Steinbrenner just look at each other, dumbfounded by the notion.

"All this from playing golf?"

"Pretty much."

"We thank you for the knowledge. And we wish you many more shots at your game."

"Well, actually in golf, unlike most sports, you actually want to have fewer shots. The fewer shots, the lower the score. The lower the score, the better you have done."

"No one ever told us that part. We both thought that more is better. More is always better."

"Not in golf. Less is more."

"We will take this information back to our people. This has

been immensely helpful." The Donald hands Blaze a $1,000 chip from his casino in Atlantic City. "Don't blow it all in one place, kid."

And with that, Donald Trump and George Steinbrenner go back up the escalator and get back inside the spaceship. The spinning Yankee Stadium disappears into the night without making a sound. Just the sound of rushing wind.

In his dream, Blaze waves goodbye. "That was definitely weird."

---

The next morning everyone rises refreshed and energized and ready for the final day of golf. The foursome is taking practice swings on the edge of the river. In the middle of the roaring rapids is a set of large boulders, which form something of a bridge across to the other side. But one slip and you'll be washed away with your body stonewashed like a pair of Farrah Fawcett's old jeans.

"Man, I had some strange dreams last night."

"Oh yeah, me too. It must have something to do with this canyon. As pretty as it is, it kind of gives me the creeps," Hub says as he scarfs down some breakfast.

"You really think we can get across the water here?" E.Z. asks.

"You know how to swim, don't you?" Ben asks.

"Hey, I'm not Johnny Weissmuller or anything. But, sure I've spent my time in the deep end of the pool."

"Well, there is only one way to find out. You've got honors."

E.Z. tees his ball up. He eyes the other side. No matter how many times people have faced it before, water hazards are like magnets for golf balls. The sounds of the rapids are deafening. E.Z. seems more nervous than ever before. He steps away from the ball, trying to get his head on straight. He re-addresses the ball. He takes the club head back and as he is about to begin his downward stroke, a bead of water from the rapids hits him in the eye. His swing comes down hard at the ball and tops it badly, sending the ball topspinning towards the middle of the river. By some kind of miracle, the ball hits one of the boulders and barely manages to avoid the water, landing on the edge of the bank on the other side of the river. The ball sits in a couple of inches of bubbling brook. It wasn't pretty but it could have been worse.

"Hey, lucky break."

"That wasn't fair. I got something in my eye just as I was about to hit it!" E.Z. pleads his case to Boris and Ludmilla, who break out in wild and unrepentant laughter.

Ben is up next. He hits a beauty, straight as an arrow, right up the open canyon on the other side.

Next up is Hub. He tees up his ball and steps back. "This could be our opening." Hub addresses the ball, sets his shoulder and hands, cocks his chin into his sternum and winds up for a massive strike of the ball. The ball screams into the wild blue yonder, out distancing Ben's shot by 50 yards.

Finally, it is Blaze's turn. "You made that look easy, partner." He tees up his ball, eyes the horizon and lets rip with a masterful shot that bounces still 50 yards past Hub's enormous shot.

"That's my partner! You had better watch yourselves now gentlemen, because we're taking no prisoners on this hole." Hub slaps Blaze on the back.

---

Donna Dina and Dan Flavin and the helicopter come zooming over the ridge to see the crew hop-scotching across the boulders in the middle of the river. E.Z. is teetering on the last boulder and the sound of the helicopter is enough to send him over the edge. He tumbles in to about two feet of water. He flips the bird as the copter passes by.

"From the looks of it, E.Z. Harbinger has run into some trouble on this water hazard. This could be the opening Hogle and Jones have been waiting for. The question is whether they can take advantage of it. With only two strokes separating these gallant teams, every stroke counts as it all comes down to this. Not to get all mythological on you, but this is playing out like some sort of Greco-Roman play. Like the myth of Sisyphus, rolling the stone up the mountain only to have it roll back down, or Prometheus, the titan who gave fire to humans but who angered the gods and whose eternal punishment was to be chained to a rock where an eagle would eat his liver each day and then it would grow back at night."

Dan Flavin looks at Donna like she has lost her mind.

"All right, maybe its not exactly like that, but I minored in Greek mythology and I just find parallels all over the place."

E.Z.'s ball is sitting in the bubbling brook, on the edge of the rapids. To keep from incurring a penalty, he will have to play the ball out of the water. Since he is already wet, he climbs down into the stream bed, grinds his feet into the sand and gravel and scans the horizon for a sweet spot to land his shot. Knowing that the water will impede his club, all he can really hope for is to advance the ball more than taking a penalty and a drop would do. But like a physician, the first priority is to do no harm. Which can be tricky. If he swings at the ball and makes no contact, it will still cost him a stroke and the ball will not have advanced. Thus is the multitude of choices, the thousands of tiny calculations that make the game of golf what it is. And Boris and Ludmilla are right on top of it. They stand on the shore, with their arms folded and waiting.

"Ve can't vait here all ze day mister. Ve have to keep ze pace moving. Take ze drop or make ze play."

E.Z. looks up and down, back and forth, almost as though by sheer force of will, or cranial activity, like a bobble-headed doll, he can get the ball to go exactly where he wants it to go. And then he sets and begins the time honored, open-stanced, smooth but powerful swing that enters the water like a mallet, breaking the molecules into thousands of beads of water, each with a rainbow of colors refracted by the early morning sunlight. The club head dives towards the ball like a pelican after a fish and strikes it just behind the ball, deep in the sand and gravel. The ball explodes out of the water, riding a wave of dirt and lands with a thud about 10 feet on the shore. Like all golf, a great deal of effort for a marginal result. And a great deal of risk for a miniscule reward. And some extremely wet shoes and socks, that squeak with each sloshing step, as E.Z. must make his way to his ball, with the three worst words in golf ringing in his ears, YOU'RE STILL UP!

The three other golfers wait near their shots, but know that E.Z.'s miscue off the tee has cost his team a stroke. All they need to do is pick up one more between here and the hole. As the players look towards the canyon rim, they can make out the faint image of a Conestoga wagon on the edge, with a cantankerous old hoot waving his hat wildly in the air. And in the breeze, ever so faintly, like a flag in a military campaign, there shuttering in the wind, is the final goal, the flag stick, waving in all its glory.

---

Back at the Burning Bridges bar, the four old timers are sitting around a large table, with a lot of paperwork and bills, scattered before them. Monty has his reading glasses on and doesn't like what he sees.

"Four thousand dollars for filet mignon? Two hundred cases of beer? For Christ's sake, they've spent 500 dollars on Tabasco sauce!"

"These guys have been living pretty high on the hog. Hell, they eat better than I do!" Sal says as he eats the celery from his Bloody Mary.

"We'll have to have a little chat, once they get back to the club. We were suppose to be sponsoring a contest, not a gourmet vacation." Riley says without a hint of irony.

"The way these guys have been eating and drinking, I bet they've gained weight," Wiley says, probably the skinniest one of the bunch.

"Some of this is going to have to come out of their wages. Fourteen thousand dollars for ice? Two thousand dollars for jumbo shrimp? Three hundred dollars for cocktail sauce? These guys are taking advantage of us."

Something Monty knows a thing or two about.

---

Back in Canyon del Muerto, the players are all making their way with great difficulty. Sisyphus would have been proud. Playing a mountain course is difficult. Playing a canyon course is even worse. Playing a canyon that becomes a mountain is almost impossible. No matter where you look, it is all uphill.

The players are huffing and puffing their way up the hillside. They take a break on the trail.

"I think I understand now why they call this Canyon del Muerto. The hike out of it will kill you," Hub says wiping the sweat from his brow.

"Yeah, I ache in places I didn't even know I had," Blaze rubs his sore leg muscles.

"I am so ready for this to be over," E.Z. says. "I'm even looking forward to getting back to work."

"Are you sure you are feeling all right? I think the heat has finally gotten to you," Ben says to his partner.

"Hell, I'm even looking forward to seeing my brother Gyll and his lovely wife Giselle."

"Now, I know you are out of your mind with fever."

"No seriously. I've had a lot of time to think about things out here, and I figure, what the hell, let bygones be bygones. Life is short. So I got a mean, sadistic, know-it-all brother. It could have been worse. There could have been two of them."

"Well, I think that is mighty big of you E.Z. It takes a man with a large heart to forgive and forget," Hub says. "I should know."

"I'm not saying I'm forgetting. And I'm really not forgiving either. I'm just choosing not to dwell on it so much."

"Well, I think that is a step in the right direction." Hub slaps E.Z. on the back.

"Speaking of ze steps in ze right direction, gentlesmen, ve think ve know vhich direction ve need to be valking. Ze final hole is just over ze rise. Let's finish zis turkey!"

The golfers all get back on the trail, lugging their clubs, like their dreams and ambitions, their hurts and disappointments, like so many bent clubs in the bag. Each dent, each blemish, each mistake, each miscalculation is there on the equipment, and in their souls, for all the world to see. To be reminded, on a continual basis, how humbling life and golf can be. Hard scrabble beginnings and hard knock lives make for hard won victories. But that is the beautiful thing about golf, and maybe about life, when a miss hit shot puts a tear in the plastic hide of a golf ball, they still call it a smile.

---

The final approaches are all laid out underneath the final hole. None of the players can see over the rim, so they'll have to shoot blind to the green. On top of the canyon rim, Cookie and his team of horses and wagon are cooking up the final feast. Donna Dina, Dan Flavin and a bevy of international journalists await the final shots. The green is literally surrounded with photographers, with very large cameras strapped around their necks, and those big old honker lenses that can see a fly on a horse's ass at 300 yards.

Hub's approach to the final green is a tricky blind shot to the flag stick. His ball is resting nicely on a stack of pine needles, like an altar to his final chip shot in the wilderness. As he steps up to the ball, the sun comes out from a cloud and the whole scene is illuminated in an ethereal light. After thousands of shots in the past 40 days, Hub swings his club with a fluidness, with a oneness, making the weight of the club light as a feather. He hits a soft shot that floats like a butterfly up and over the rim. The ball lands with an almost silent touch, rolling perfectly towards the cup. It stops about two feet away and a deafening roar goes up from the gathered crowd.

Hub can't see what has happened but from the sounds of it, he couldn't be happier unless it went in. His pace hastens as he is anxious to see where his ball landed, always holding out that hope of hope, that somehow the ball might actually have even gone in. Even after 40 days and 40 nights, one can still dream.

Ben's shot is also difficult to gauge. His ball is on a steeper pitch, with a large rock impeding his backswing. He takes a couple of practice attempts, chokes down on his club and steps up with a very open stance. He takes the club back slowly and then comes down sharply on the ball causing it to pop practically straight up, but with just enough topspin to send it up and over the ledge. The ball rolls to within 10 feet of the cup and the crowd goes wild. Ben smiles that beautific smile that says he knows it was a great shot, especially from where he was. He waves to the cameras like a star.

E.Z.'s ball is continuing on its difficult path. His ball has ended up nestled up against a barrel cactus. He has a shot, but it won't be easy, no pun intended. Really nothing is easy for this guy. Never has been, never will be. But he's got one chance to get this one right. If he misses, he'll end up with cactus guts and spines all over himself, not to mention probably losing the whole match. E.Z. is sweating blood over this one, that is if people could actually sweat blood. He takes out his sand wedge, even though he isn't really in sand. He wants the weight of the club to have enough momentum that it powers through the ball and perhaps just nicks the cactus. He approaches the ball and makes some half attempts with his wrists, imagining how he wants to hit the ball. He lets fly with a near perfect shot. It soars with only a hint of cactus floating through the air. The ball lands on the putting surface, as does the cactus, landing just in front of the ball. As the ball rolls towards the cup, it hits the fresh cactus flesh and turns away from the hole. The ball ends up about 12 feet from the cup, certainly a makeable putt. The shutterbugs click off thousands of shots.

Finally, it is Blaze's turn. His ball is in the worst position of them all. His ball has found its way, like a drunken sailor, into a rotten log, coming to rest amidst the crumbling and decaying growth rings, like so many sunken ships. Many a sailor's hopes and dreams have been dashed by such shivering timbers. Blaze analyzes his situation and quickly deduces he's pretty much screwed. His only hope of reaching the green involves a nearly impossible bank shot, a circus shot if there ever was one, hitting out of the dead wood, banking off a large boulder, and with any luck clearing the ridge and bouncing on to the green and staying there. Anywhere. Just as long as it gets on the putting surface. The whole match comes down to this shot. Get it on the green and you give your team a chance. Miss it and that will pretty much dictate the outcome.

Blaze steps up to the ball. He suddenly feels a sense of calm that comes over him like a warm shower on a snowy day. And suddenly, the words from his dream come back to him. "Less is more. Less is more!"

Blaze steps up to the ball, improbably aiming sideways to the hole. "Less is more." He aims for the boulder and instead of hitting the ball hard, he strokes the ball very softly, just lifting the ball out of the wood and carrying it towards the rock. The ball hits the rock, bouncing hard at an angle, carrying itself just barely over the ridge and lands on the green like a homing pigeon on a rooftop after a very long flight. The ball rolls about 25 feet past the hole, but all-in-all, an impossible shot made to look easy.

People in bars all around the world are high-fiving each other. The gathered crowd of journalists roar their approval.

Donna Dina addresses the camera.

"And there you have it, ladies and gentlemen. All the players are on the final green. Only one shot separates the two teams at this point, but Blaze Jones has a very difficult putt. If he makes it, it would put the pressure on the team of Harbinger/Ichi. At this point it would appear that Hub Hogle's putt is very makeable, but in this crazy game, you never know. It all comes down to this final hole in the wilderness, before the players fly back to Burning Bridges for the stroll up the 18th in this incredible match."

The players make their way to the final green like conquering heros. All the journalists break into spontaneous applause as the players stride to the green. Despite their haggard appearance, their tattered clothing, their long hair and scruffy beards, each of the players walks a little taller, carries himself with a little more confidence and nobility. It is as though they have emerged from the wilderness as changed men, and not just on the outside, but deep down inside themselves. They know they have accomplished something no one else has ever done. They've played golf continually for 40 days. In the bloody wilderness! If there was any question before as to their collective sanity, that question has been answered. They are as crazy as they look. It isn't by accident that the word wild is buried in the word wilderness. And people who spend long periods of time in the wilderness have a measurable amount of wildness buried in them too.

Blaze walks to his ball 25 feet away from the cup. The green AstroTurf glistens in the afternoon sun. The players' shadows cast long silhouettes across the shimmering surface. Billowing clouds dot the horizon. This is as pretty as golf gets. If golf could be a religion, this setting would be why.

Blaze bends down and holds up his putter in an effort to read the slope of the green. The line looks to break left, then to the right as it gets to the hole. Hub confers with his partner Blaze.

"Just give it enough to give it a chance. If you're going to miss, go ahead and miss it long."

"Who says I'm going to miss?" Blaze spots Donna in the crowd and gives her a wink. "I've been waiting all my life for this putt." Blaze steps up to the ball and bends over it, cleaning the surface of any debris. He takes his position and carefully brings the putter up to the ball. He looks down the line again and then focuses all his attention on the ball. He pulls the club head back and, in that timeless moment, he strikes the ball and his fate is cast. The ball rolls, wobbly at first, bouncing on the rough surface, then settles down, like the little engine that could. The ball breaks to the left, has plenty of momentum, then breaks, as if on cue, to the right, as it runs to the hole. The ball falls into the cup like a rabbit to its hole. The crowd goes crazy! Even Blaze is amazed by how easy it looked. Hub runs up to him and hugs Blaze like he is a long-lost relative who just won the lottery.

The chorus of reporters break into song. "What a difference a putt makes, 25 little feet…"

Donna Dina whispers into her mike, "That putt could change everything. The pressure is now on. Its officially knee-shaking time."

E.Z. has got a 12 footer, which in terms of putting, separates the men from the boys. Make this, you are a hero. Miss it, you are just another weekend hacker. Strangely, players who can consistently putt from this distance consistently have lower golf scores, and also have better sex, more often and with better looking people. He steps up to the putt. He's a little too cocky, with the new audience to play to, so he resorts to bad habits.

"Are those cameras rolling? Because I don't want anybody to miss this." E.Z. lines up the putt. It is pretty much a straight shot, slightly downhill. He lines it up and hits it just right. The ball is rolling purposefully towards the hole, it hits the edge of the cup and rims out. The crowd moans. E.Z. is crestfallen. He steps up and taps out, grimacing as he picks the ball up out of the hole.

"And there you have it folks, we are tied! After all this, we are tied!" Donna shouts into the microphone.

Ben is up next. He eyes his 10 footer and steps up calmly to his ball.

His line is slightly uphill, with a slight break to the left. Like the Zen master that he is, he taps the ball with a delicate touch, sending it rolling merrily along. The ball breaks to the left and just as it gets to the hole, it runs out of momentum. It teeters on the very edge of the cup, and with barely a wisp of energy left, falls into the hole with a beautiful thud. The crowd practically explodes. E.Z. slaps Ben on the back and he sighs with relief.

Finally it is Hub's turn. His little three footer suddenly grows in length and importance. As he lines the putt up, he has some sort of tunnel vision effect, which causes everything but the ball and the hole to go kind of fuzzy. He steps back from the ball and blinks and rubs his eyes.

"Are you okay," Blaze asks.

"Yeah, I'm fine. But I'm a little nervous with all these people and cameras. Do I look puffy?"

"No more than usual. Go ahead and make the shot. You can do it. Just a little tap in."

"You know, I hate it when the pressure is on."

"No pressure here. Just a nice friendly game."

"Yeah, with a ton of money hanging in the balance," E.Z. adds trying his best to psyche Hub out.

"That's true but you know what? It's not our money. So who the hell cares."

Hub steps up to the ball. He caresses the leather handle of the putter as though it were a woman he was quite familiar with. He locks his little finger of one hand to the forefinger of the other hand, bends over the putt, glances one more time at the hole. His eyes lock on to it and draw a line in his imagination from the ball to the hole. He cocks his wrists and then pulls the club head back and with the slightest of prodding, coaxes the ball towards the hole. Everyone holds their breath as the ball slowly turns towards the hole. Anyone who has ever played the game knows full well how nerve racking a three footer can be. None ever more so than this particular three footer. The ball drops into the hole like it was sucked in by an industrial vacuum cleaner. The sound of the ball falling into the cup is practically deafening. The crowd jumps at the sound, bursting into applause and groaning that groaning sound that only golfing aficionados can groan.

"And there it is, incredible! Just incredible! After 40 days of continuous play, tens of thousands of strokes, we are tied! Ladies and gentlemen, it just doesn't get any better than this for a dramatic finish. We will be picking the game back up, on number 18, at the historic Burning Bridges Country Club. With one hole to go, we are tied! And to add one little twist, the organizers have made the final hole a best ball, which means all the players will hit away, but each team will play from the position of the most advanced ball. It should prove to be an interesting way to finish what has been a one-of-a-kind golf match. Hold on to your hats folks, because we are headed home."

# CHAPTER 10

## "SETTLING OLD SCORES"

THE PLAYERS ARE ABOUT to board a private plane on the tarmac in Flagstaff, Arizona. Blaze is on the phone in a pay telephone booth on the edge of the runway. He is speaking with his mother.

"Yeah, Mom, it's been great. But here's the thing. I want you to withdraw all the money you've got from the bank."

"What are you talking about?"

"Just listen to me. Bring it all with you tomorrow to the club."

"Are you in trouble again?'

"No Mom, it's nothing like that. This could be our ticket. You've got to just trust me. For once in your life, you've got to just trust me. I know what I'm doing. Really Mom, for the first time in my life, I actually know what I'm doing. Just don't be late."

"This is just crazy."

"Hey Mom, I love you. And I'll see you tomorrow. And remember, everything you've got."

Blaze hangs up the phone. He plugs a bunch of quarters back into the phone, pulls a little piece of paper out of his wallet and dials a number. A voice answers.

"Hello, you don't know me, but I've got to get a very important message to Ted. All of our futures may hinge on it."

The next day dawns a new beginning. Burning Bridges has never looked so good. The fairways have never looked greener. The greens have never looked fairer. It is as though man and nature have finally come into harmony with one another. Into balance. On a golf course. The birds are singing chirpier. The sun is shining brighter. Even the range balls are smiling. After 40 days playing golf in the wilderness, an honest-to-goodness golf course has never looked more inviting. A golf course is really a thing of beauty. Like the curves on a beautiful woman or a classic car, it is sculpted and refined, manicured and magnificent. And it looks so easy.

And today the club is a hive of activity. Like the finale of any big, prestigious golf tournament, the place is crawling with spectators, club members and the media. Jim Nantz and David Feherty are there to call the final hole. Of course, Riley, Wiley, Sal and Monty are basking in the limelight the match has brought to them and to the club, as they stand with Harvey Wallbanger and his staff. Bob Post is beaming with pride because the whole gosh darned thing has turned into an international sensation, as he stands next to Boris and the lovely Ludmilla, who has only grown more athletic and vivacious. Apparently 40 days and nights in the wilderness agreed with her. Teams of spouting sports reporters from around the globe are gathered around the 18th hole. It sounds more like the Tower of Babel than a normal golf match. If the Tower of Babel, that is, was a country club with a championship golf course.

Mixed among the many celebrities, including Donald Trump, George Steinbrenner, Howie Mandel, Regis Philbin and Alex Trebek, are a hodge podge of people the foursome has met along the way. Of course, Cookie and his horses and wagon are there, with Peabody by his side. Mayor Freddie Fender is also there, with many members of his family, including his singing niece. They are dressed in their traditional Mexican garb. A mariachi band plays in the background, lending a kind of carnival atmosphere to the surroundings.

Lady Godiva, mostly clothed, is there. So is Yongo, with his bongo, who tries to keep beat to the band. Bernie Calderwood, Leigh Sauerbratten and Sean Connery are chatting it up, swapping tales of desperadoes. Joe the Pro is there too, with his four square dancing daughters, Jo-Ann, Jo-Beth, Jo-Cell, Jo-Dawn and the three Johnny Cashes.

Chief Got Rocks is there with his grandson Jimmy Straightshooter. Ted Black Head and Billy Crazy Horse are there but without their ponies. Bud Weiser and Little Bo Peep are also there, looking all spruced up in their Sunday best. Moses Abbey is there taking pictures of the cowboys and Indians all standing around together.

Of course, Gyll and Giselle are there to root for E.Z. Ben Ichi's father is also there, dressed in sandals and robe. Even the Dalai Lama is there in one of his orange saris. He has a very nice smile and apparently is a big golf fanatic. He stands with the Winnebago family who lost their hamburgers in the desert. When he spots Cookie, the Dalai Lama gives him a big wave like they are old friends.

Blaze's mother pushes her way through the crowd, arriving barely on time and clutching her purse. Even the sporting goods salesman is there, dressed in a nice pastel golfing outfit. It would seem everybody who is anybody in the world of golf is there. Even the lady with the golden harp is there. And, yes, she is playing the harp. Dan Flavin is filming her. Donna Dina is doing her stand up in front of the harp. It looks on TV almost as though she has taken up residence in heaven. People in bars all around the world are watching, transfixed on the edge of their seats.

"And here we are, in this heavenly setting for what could only be described as a fitting ending for a golf match through hell. Beautiful Burning Bridges Country Club is the site for the conclusion of this epic match and everyone is gathered here on the 18th hole for what must be a bittersweet ending for these four valiant golfers. Golfers who've endured 40 days and nights in the wilderness, chasing the little white ball, through wind and rain, through sandstorms and tumbleweeds, through backyards and small towns, through canyons and over mountains, to attain the impossible, to achieve the improbable, to play golf through nature, the way the game used to be played. Whether you love the game of golf or hate it, whether you play the game of golf and still hate it, or whether you play the game of golf and still love it, you've got to salute these gritty players. They're a plucky bunch and we're a lucky bunch to have been able to bring their story to you. The golf course is full of famous players here to witness history, but none more famous than our incredible foursome, E.Z. Harbinger, Ben Ichi, Hub Hogle and the adorable, if I do say so myself, Blaze Jones."

The players emerge from the clubhouse like conquering heroes, like astronauts returning from a long mission. They are all cleaned up, showered, shaved and spit-shined. They look like members of the frigging Osmonds' family they are so squeaky clean. Bob Post nods his approval to Boris and Ludmilla, who give a quiet KGB nod in reply. In the world of country club golf, apparently, Republicans do rule. The crowd responds with polite applause, as though they were at a musical recital and the musicians have just taken the stage.

The players tune up their bodies with some practice swings. Standing on a firm, clean tee box, between enlarged blue golf ball markers, the players notice the difference from what they've become accustomed to. If the question is nature or nurture, at this point nurture is looking like a pretty good bet. This is a clean, near perfect surface, from which to hit the ball. Even with a miss hit, to call the rough rough would be a misnomer. After 400 miles of wilderness, nobody knows rough like these Rough Riders. And they've got a plan of attack.

That ridiculous Lalo Schifrin inspired music kicks in announcing that golf is starting on the television. Jim Nantz and David Feherty sit in an announcer's booth- really just scaffolding and plywood. They have a bird's eye view of the 18$^{th}$ green. Hoards of people surround the tee box, the fairways and the green, silent, shuffling and shifting, as though in attendance at a religious service. From the looks of it, you'd think the Pope played golf here.

"Welcome folks for what is sure to turn out to be a large asterisk in the annals of golf history, the conclusion of the one-of-a-kind golf match cooked up by a group of philanthropists and members here of this prestigious and historic Burning Bridges Country Club."

"That's right Jim. Ya know when this bird first took flight, a lot of people in some very high places questioned the sanity of the proposition. Some felt it was nothing more than a publicity stunt, some even thought it demeaned the purpose of the game. Some snooty golfing folk even thought it defamed the game. But after following this match for 40 days, I think it is safe to say the eagle has landed. And I, for one, am looking forward to this final hole."

"And who could have known, we'd be tied. After all those strokes. All those lost balls. All the blood and bandages. After 400 miles of golf in four states. What a finish we're set for here today."

Bob Post reaches for a microphone at the 18th tee box.

"I'm Bob Post, executive director of RAGU, here to welcome you to this special event. We've been blessed by wonderful weather, an adoring crowd, worldwide media coverage that you couldn't begin to pay for, and a special bunch of players who have survived a special kind of challenge. They are now members of a special club of their own making. An exclusive club to which there can be no new applications. A club of just these four players. And you know what's amazing, they've all arrived here in one piece. No one got killed or seriously injured. They are all still speaking to one another. And they've managed to provide all of us, and golfers all around the world, a marvelous ending to a fairy tale match. May I now introduce to you the players!"

A huge cheer goes up, as much an appreciation for Bob Post to stop speaking as it is for the players' introduction.

"First the team of E.Z. Harbinger and Ben Ichi." Everyone cheers, none more proudly than Gyll, Giselle and Ben's father.

"And now the team that made such a marvelous comeback, Hub Hogle and Blaze Jones!" The crowd reaches a decibel level near the sound of a jet airliner at take off.

The players are all embarrassed by the adulation. They were not aware they had risen to near rock-star status. But hey, what's not to like. Everybody deserves their 15 minutes. And that's about how long the standing ovation goes on.

Bob Post steps into the circle of players. "As you know gentlemen, as previously arranged, we'll be playing best ball on this final hole. E.Z. Harbinger has been selected to call the coin toss." Bob flips a shiny silver dollar into the air.

"We'll call heads."

The coin flips over and over and lands in the grass.

"Heads it is. The team of Harbinger and Ichi will hit first."

E.Z. steps into the tee box. He places his ball on the tee. Takes a couple of half-hearted swings, looks down the fairway like a pilot at the runway. He addresses the ball, sets his wrists and chin. Everything is silent. He takes the club head back and brings it down like hammer on a nail. The ball explodes off the tee, tiny blades of grass jump into the air. The ball sails into the air like a rocket ship entering the second stage. People stand in awe at the wonder of the shot. They've never seen anything like it. The ball bounces into the middle of the fairway. It should be pretty difficult to beat. The crowd screams their approval.

Ben is next up. He sets his ball on the tee, looks back to his father and smiles. He addresses the ball and with one smooth motion sends the ball just shy of E.Z.'s monster drive.

Hub congratulates Ben as he takes the box. He tees up. Wipes his sweaty palms on his pants. He spots Lady Godiva in the crowd and gives her a wave. She is enough of a muse to inspire him. He sets his ball, gazes down the fairway and steps up to it. He cranks a huge shot that slices right, but still lands on the edge of the fairway. Not a great shot, but playable.

It is up to Blaze now to get his team into contention. He sets the ball on the tee and it rolls off. He sets it again. He's showing signs of nerves as he takes a couple of uncomfortable practice swings. He spots his mom in the crowd. She waves to him and raises her purse. He spots The Donald and George and remembers his words to them from his dream, "Less is more." He spots Donna and she blows him a kiss for good luck. He mutters under his breath, as though giving himself a pep talk. "Don't try to kill it. Let the club do the work. Think success, not failure."

Blaze steps up to the ball. He looks down the fairway one last time. It is now or never. He takes the club head back very slowly. It reaches the apex of the swing and begins the trajectory back towards the ball. He hits it dead solid perfect. The sounds of the club making contact with the ball reverberate through the entire course. There is not a sweeter sound in the world to a golfer. His mother bites her lip as the crowd follows the ball. It lands about five feet behind E.Z.'s shot and then rolls just past it. The crowd can't believe their eyes. They jump out of their shoes, and move like a thousand footed centipede, en masse to the middle of the fairway.

"Wow! Incredible shots from these players who must be fatigued. But you couldn't tell that from the way they've started this longish par four, with the difficult approach and the undulating green."

The players carry their worn out golf bags, full of their beaten clubs. Judging from the bags and clubs you'd think they'd been playing golf in a war zone. And the players do look weary, like soldiers returning from battle, with limping limbs, busted blisters, and sunburns on top of sunburns.

E.Z.'s shot is his team's best play so he hits away with a 4-iron. He pounds another beauty and the ball lands about a hundred yards from the green. Ben is up next, dropping his ball near where E.Z. hit from. He also hits a 4-iron and it lands almost exactly where E.Z.'s ball landed.

Next up is Hub, who places his ball near Blaze's masterful shot. He takes out a 3-iron. He is trying to reach for it. He clips the ball low, sending it on a slight trajectory, but the ball gets a good bounce in the fairway and it rolls to just behind E.Z.'s and Ben's shots.

Finally, it is Blaze's turn. He pulls out a 5-iron and hits a smooth shot that lands together with the other balls. The players all shake hands, like this was part of a plan. They walk to their balls where they drop their bags and signal to the RAGU officials.

"Wait a minute, what's going on here? They seem to be summoning the officials, for some kind of ruling." Jim Nantz stands to see.

Bob Post, Boris and Ludmilla all join the golfers in the middle of the fairway.

"We need to speak with our sponsors," Blaze announces.

Bob Post gets on the walkie talkie. "Ah, we've got some kind of problem here. The players want to speak with the sponsors."

Suddenly from out of the crowd comes two gold-plated golf carts with Riley, Wiley, Sal and Monty. They ride up to the group.

"What's the problem?" Sal wants to know.

"Well, gentlemen. As much as we've appreciated the opportunity you presented us with, we've concluded that what with all the hardship we've endured, we need to find a way to get a little bigger piece of the pie," Blaze says for the group.

"What, all the filet mignon wasn't enough for you? You should see the bills we've got from this damned thing," Riley says.

"I told you guys this was going to cost us all a lot of money," Monty reminds everyone.

"Hey this whole thing has brought all of you a lot of notoriety," Wiley points out to the foursome.

"Yeah, well try paying your light bill with notoriety. It doesn't work," Hub says.

"Hey, we're willing to do this in a fair way," Blaze says. "Here's what we're proposing. We're willing to bet you, straight up. Your best player against our best player."

"But that's not fair. None of us are in your guy's league. We're a bunch of old men."

"You can pick anybody you like."

"Anybody?"

"Anybody who is here and ready to finish this hole."

"But you guys don't have a pot to piss in. How are you going to come up with any money?" Sal makes a point.

"Well, we're willing to bet all the money you owe us," Blaze says. "Plus," he waves his mom over to the group. "This is my mom."

"Pleased to make your acquaintance, Mrs. Jones," Riley says taking her by the hand. "Haven't we met before?"

"You can call me Dot. And yes, it was a long time ago."

"So what brings you to the party?"

"Well, I've got a purse full of 100 dollar bills, that says these guys can beat your butts."

"How much did you come up with mom?"

"I've got $62,000 in my purse. As you can see, it is a large purse."

"So we can pick anybody and if we win, we get to keep the money in the purse and not have to pay you guys?" Monty asks.

"Yep."

"But what about our original bet? The whole reason for this catastrophe?" Wiley asks.

"It still holds, exactly the same. That bet was between you guys," Blaze encourages. "And that bet ends in a tie."

The four old timers gather in a circle and talk among themselves. After a moment they emerge. "We'll take Gyll, the club pro." They signal Gyll to come out of the crowd.

Gyll hustles out and approaches the group. "What's up?"

"We've got a little change of plan. You're going to finish the hole for our team."

"Hey, sounds good to me. Let a real pro take over, fellas."

"So, who are you going to pick?"

"We're going to pick someone you've never heard of." Blaze signals to Chief Johnny Got Rocks, who shepherds his grandson Jimmy Straightshooter on to the course. ""We're picking Jimmy Straightshooter!"

"Is this some kind of a joke? He's just a little kid." Gyll protests.

"What's the matter Gyll, are you chicken?" E.Z. asks.

"This will be like taking candy from a baby."

---

Upstairs in the announcer's booth, Feherty and Nantz are informed of the changes.

"Apparently, we've got a little change in plans for the finale. The golfers have challenged the sponsors of the match to a side bet that involves each side picking their best player, really any player they want, to make the final shots at 18."

"That's right Jim, it is a mad crazy way to finish a mad crazy golfing match. Nothing has been conventional about it from the get-go, why end it now?"

"Apparently, the sponsors have picked Gyll Harbinger, the Burning Bridges club pro for their side and the players have picked an unlikely player in the pint size person of Jimmy Straightshooter, an unknown kid they met on the Indian reservation. I've heard of some crazy finishes, but this one takes the frigging cake. Can I say frigging on television?"

"Well, you just did. Twice."

"This is utter insanity. I think the players may be suffering from heatstroke. Or they've been hitting the sauce a little early today."

"No matter, the rules have been set and let's get down on the fairway for the final shots."

Gyll is taking E.Z.'s ball, so he is to hit first. He's a smarmy dude, all spit and polyester. He knows the course like the back of his hand. The back of his hand that E.Z. is quite familiar with.

"Just a little up and down Gyll. Like a walk in the park," Sal encourages.

Gyll steps up to the ball. He's got a 9-iron out and he has made this approach thousands of times. He sets his club, adjusts his feet and hits a high-arcing shot headed right for the pin. Everyone holds their breath, as anything is possible from a hundred yards out. The ball lands on the green, just inches from the cup. It spins immediately to a stop. It is practically a gimme.

"Like I said, like taking candy from a baby." Gyll waves to the crowd.

Chief Got Rocks rubs little Jimmy's shoulders. "You can do it. Just like at home. Just like we've practiced. This is your destiny. Reach out and grab it by the balls."

Little Jimmy swallows hard. This really isn't at all like home. He pulls out his tiny, ancient golf club. Gyll snickers in the background and E.Z. shoots him a look, which shuts him up. He just shakes his head.

Little Jimmy steps up to Blaze's ball. It isn't a great lie, in fact, it is in a little bit of a sinkhole. He eyes the flag which flutters in the breeze. He focuses all his attention on the ball. He takes his club back and with the smoothest stroke you've ever seen, picks the ball up out of the sinkhole with barely a sound. The ball floats high in the air, and almost seems to stay there, it hangs for so long. It lands hard on the green, about 10 feet in front of the hole and starts to run towards the stick. It hits the stick and stops immediately trapped between the stick and the cup. The little guy holed out from a hundred yards! Gyll and the sponsors can't believe their eyes. The crowd goes absolutely nuts. The players all raise Little Jimmy on their shoulders. Chief Johnny Got Rocks starts to tear up.

"This was just how it was in my dream."

"Oh my! Oh my! I've never seen anything like this! It was like watching a butterfly land on a flower. What is this kid's name?

Sign him up now, because this kid has got some kind of future. He's just a kid and he's just holed out in the biggest event in his life! If I hadn't seen it with me own eyes, I wouldn't have believed it. It was frigging amazing!"

Blaze is hugging his mom. Lady Godiva runs out on the course and practically bowls Hub over. Donna Dina runs out and throws her arms around Blaze and his mom.

"Mom, I want to introduce you to someone I've met."

E.Z. consoles his brother who is in shock.

"Taking candy from a baby is harder to do than it looks." E.Z. says as he spots the woman from the pro shop, with the bucket of balls. She winks at him and gives him the thumbs up sign and it makes his whole day.

Ben's father joins the group. He bows deeply to his son.

"You have brought great honor to our family."

"Dad, I wanted you to meet Chief Got Rocks here. You guys have a lot to talk about."

They eye each other warily, like sparring partners, or long-lost relatives.

"It is a pleasure to meet you, like an old sunset from a favorite porch."

"Equally, it is a pleasure to meet you, like the morning sun warming an old cat."

Dan Flavin runs over and gives Ben Ichi a big bear hug. "You are the wisest man I've even known. I've fallen in love with you and I want us spend the rest of our lives together." Ben is taken back by the proposal.

"How did you know I had a weakness for bald men with goatees?" Ben smiles and then they kiss. On the lips. For a long time.

"I told you guys this was going to cost us a lot of money," Monty laments.

"Oh hell. Why don't you stop bellyaching and start writing checks," Sal answers his partner.

Riley approaches Blaze's mom. "So, Dot, I do remember you. What have you been up to all these years?"

"Just raising our son," she replies. Riley stops in his tracks. Blaze leans in like he just swallowed a chicken bone.

"What did you say mom?"

"Honey, there is a good chance this old codger is your father." Riley is speechless. Blaze looks at him and if you look really hard, they do look alike. "And if he isn't, then there's a better chance it is his brother." Dot turns her gaze on Wiley. He looks sheepishly at the group.

"Good to see you again, Dot. It's been a long time."

Blaze is dumbfounded by the news. Donna takes his hand and squeezes it. He tears up. "This is way more twisted than I could have ever imagined."

Riley and Wiley step forward and offer their hands. "Welcome home, son." Blaze hesitates, as if this is all too much to handle, and then lunges at both of them, hugging them like tree trunks, which turns into the best hug of any of their lives. They are finally a family. A family of golfers. This is what golf and life are all about. Hugging tree trunks and loving it.

Finally, Cookie rides up in his wagon. Three-legged Peabody is by his side. Peabody barks at Bob Post's little Cockapoodle, who barks right back, like there could be a future there. "Well folks, I guess this is where it all ends. I'll be pushing on from here. You all are a pretty funny bunch. I don't mind admitting, I enjoyed spending a little time with you." Cookie wipes a tear away.

"You can't leave Cookie. Who'll take care of us?" Hub asks with his arm around Lady Godiva.

"Well, it turns out, I've met somebody here too, and I think we're going to be shacking up around these parts." From out of the back of the wagon, the lady with the golden harp pokes her head out and smiles.

"Funny how life works out isn't it? All from a silly little game of golf. Who knew golf could change your life?"

"I did," Chief Got Rocks answers. "It was all in my dream."

He looks at Little Jimmy who just smiles the biggest smile you've ever seen. It is the kind of smile that could change the course of history.

It is a smile that should give all the world hope. A smile that says I'm a winner. A smile that says I'm part of a special club. A smile that says I'm a golfer and good, bad or ugly I plan to take it as far as I can. It is a smile that lives in every athlete's heart. It is the smile that keeps life meaningful and beautiful. It is the smile of hope. And golfers are deep down full of hope, the hope that tomorrow's round will be just a little better than today's and today's round will be just a little bit better than yesterday's. And that hope springs eternal. It is the hope of the ages.

Little Jimmy also happens to be missing two front baby teeth, which are resting at home, under his pillow, waiting for a visit from the tooth fairy. And everybody believes in the tooth fairy, right? And the Easter bunny and Santa Claus and the hereafter, where there's always an open tee time. Especially for golfers and the people who love them. Turns out golf is love and love is all that really matters.

# THE END

LaVergne, TN USA
01 March 2011
218478LV00002B/123/P